SHOT IN THE DARK

Also by Annie Ross

Moving Image

SHOT IN THE DARK

Annie Ross

HEADLINE

First published in 1996 by
HEADLINE BOOK PUBLISHING

10 9 8 7 6 5 4 3 2 1

British Library Cataloguing in Publication Data

Ross, Annie
Shot in the Dark
I. Title
823.914 [F]

ISBN 0–7472–1454–9

Typeset by Palimpsest Book Production Limited,
Polmont, Stirlingshire
Printed and bound in Great Britain by
Mackays of Chatham PLC, Chatham, Kent

HEADLINE BOOK PUBLISHING
A division of Hodder Headline PLC
338 Euston Road
London NW1 3BH

For my sisters
Mary, Zoë and Hilke

ACKNOWLEDGMENTS

I would like to thank my agent, Clare Roberts, for all her help and Marion Donaldson at Headline for her perceptive editing of this manuscript. Tony Buchanan, Rodney Archer and Carol Bristow provided valuable information about police procedure, but are not responsible for any errors! Sister Bernadette was endlessly patient in answering my questions about convent life, while Andy Barton supplied data on surveillance equipment. Last, but not least, I would like to thank my family for their long-suffering support.

Prologue

It was the look in her eyes that did it. He had wanted to see fear there, and shame – then she would never again think herself better than anyone else. It had brought it all back when he spotted her in the street several weeks ago – all the hate. So he started following her, circling closer and closer, tightening the net. She hadn't guessed a thing, she was so stupid. He'd chosen his moment. Then he'd pounced. The Lord of the Jungle.

It was when he shoved her to the ground that she pulled his mask off – not deliberately, but as she fell, an awkward old-lady fall, clutching to stop herself from hitting the ground too hard and hurting herself.

While it was all happening, she looked at him strangely – different from the others. There was something in her eyes – as if she *understood* him, as if she *forgave* him, the patronising cow. But then she'd always been like that.

Only now he was in charge. She had to do what he wanted now. She could feel his power, how strong he was.

The others had kept quiet – he made sure they had too much to lose if they didn't. They knew about his secret weapon, his little time bomb. All they had to do was utter one word and he would show them to the world for what they were. It kept them in their place.

And then somewhere in the depths of those eyes he saw the light of recognition – not of him as he was now, towering over her, but as he was then. She

1

spoke his name, as if she couldn't believe it was him doing this.

He wouldn't be able to shut her up, he could see that.

He pulled the belt tighter round her neck and yanked as hard as he could. Just to show her. It was such a rush. Life or death in his hands. Simple.

Then he was running along the street in broad daylight, almost knocking over some old woman. His feet thudded on the pavement, blood drummed in his ears, bursting through his veins.

It was his first killing. It upped the ante – meant the police would know and would be looking for him. So he couldn't do it every time. But he had the taste for it now.

Chapter One

'They're back in the building!' Viv, the production assistant, replaced the receiver and gave a sigh of relief.

I leaned forward, picked up the telephone in front of me and dialled the number for our Outside Broadcast Unit. Frank Johnson, the reporter, answered at once.

'Yes?' I could hear the echo-ey roar of people and a tannoy system in the background.

'It's Bel. How's things?'

'So far so good. The plane touched down about ten minutes ago. The players are going to sign autographs for a bit then there'll be a presser. Did you get that tape of interviews with the fans I sent back?'

'Yeh. That's been cut. We'll probably go to that first then come to you live later on. I still haven't a clue what's happening. For God's sake have someone watching the monitor. I may have to come to you in a hurry.'

'Fine.'

I rang off abruptly and glanced at the clock. Five minutes to 'on-air'. I leaned back and ran my hands through my hair. I was out of practice. I've worked at Regional Television for about eight or nine years – six of those as a television director— but it was ages since I'd worked on anything live. I'd forgotten how frantic it could be, directing the evening news.

'Someone's bringing the rest of the tapes down now.' Viv had just got off the phone. 'At least that's something.' She heaved a sigh. We were running close to the wire. All the tapes should have been down in V.T. half an hour ago, but there was such chaos in the newsroom and editing suite upstairs that everything was late.

I glanced at the running order in front of me, which showed the line-up of stories for the programme. On a normal day, the format for the six o'clock show is pretty well set in the morning conference when reporters and crews are assigned and it's decided what news stories to cover. The only change to that plan would be a late-breaking story – anything like a murder or a fatal accident would demand coverage, however late it happened. We had had three of those today.

The first had occurred less than two hours ago, at about four o'clock, when news had come in of a major drug bust. The runner had been dispatched to the car park to stop the early camera crew from going off shift. They had only just left with Ron Polly, one of our veteran reporters, when we got a tip-off that the body of a child had been spotted floating in the river. Then barely an hour ago we heard of a nun who had been found dead at a local centre for drug addicts. My friend Mags had dropped what she was doing and raced off to try and get something for tonight's programme.

Now, according to Viv, Ron and the other reporter were back in the building with their stories. I could well imagine the panic in the cutting room where our new picture editor would be frantically working against the clock to get the tapes edited in time.

With only a few minutes to 'on-air' all we knew about what would be on the news was that we *didn't* know.

There were heavy footsteps coming down the hallway outside. I swung round as the door leading from the corridor burst open and the portly figure of Trevor, our recently appointed news editor, stood framed by the light behind him. I had a quick impression of short clipped hair above a sports jacket and slacks before he stepped forward

4

and the door swung shut, returning us to the twilight world of the studio gallery. Here there was only the pulsing blue glow from the bank of monitors before me and a few spotlights directed onto the counter at which I sat with Gary, the vision mixer on my right and Viv on my left.

Trevor dropped a sheet of paper in front of each of us and sank heavily into a revolving chair at the far end of the counter where he had access to a phone and his own talkback.

'Headlines live,' he gasped, out of breath. 'Tapes are on their way down.' I felt a stab of apprehension. Normally the news headlines for the top of the programme are pre-recorded because they have to be timed to the second and we rarely get it right first time. Doing them live would put extra pressure on all of us for a programme that looked like being chaotic enough.

I glanced at the sheet of paper. It itemised the film clips to be used to illustrate the headlines. They were on three different tapes. I looked up sharply.

'This won't work.' A wary look came over Trevor's face. 'We've only got two Beta machines in V.T., Trevor, plus the one-inch machine for the titles, so we can only use two tapes at a time. The third clip has to be edited onto the first tape.' He looked at me blankly so I added, 'We go BETA one, then BETA two, then back to BETA one again. It all has to be edited onto two tapes and timed exactly.' Trevor was staring at me, transfixed. I felt a surge of panic. The rumours I'd heard on the grapevine came back to me.

'Put him in a tight corner and he just freezes. He won't do a bloody thing to help you,' was how Colin, the director I'd replaced, had phrased it. That thought galvanised me into action.

'Albert in V.T.,' I spoke urgently into the microphone in front of me. There was an answering beep to indicate that he had heard. 'You should have new headlines tapes.'

There was a crackle. Albert had moved over to the microphone in V.T. 'There's three of them. What—'

'I know,' I interrupted, looking up at the clock. Three minutes to on-air. 'Can you edit three onto one leaving an eight-second gap then run it manually?'

'Christ!' The intercom went dead. Beside me, Viv was already on the phone asking for someone to go and help out Albert.

'Look, this is an emergency!' she snapped before banging the receiver back down. I looked at the clock again. It was going to be a near thing. In the corner, Trevor still sat, frozen, saying nothing.

I scanned the monitors before me. All three cameras were up and running and the two presenters were in their places. Geraldine, one of our more experienced reporters, was calmly using the camera lens as a mirror to flick a strand of hair out of her eyes. John was new to presenting. He looked pumped-up on adrenalin and his lips moved as he silently rehearsed his script.

I took a deep breath.

'Geraldine and John.' My voice sounded a lot calmer than I felt. They both reacted by looking straight at the camera, knowing that was their link to me. Obviously their earpieces were already hooked up and they could hear the output from the gallery.

'We're doing the headlines live.' I saw a look of panic on John's face. 'We're not sure if the pictures will be ready. You may have to do it on camera.' Geraldine nodded calmly. John looked uncertain.

I glanced at the clock, then felt adrenalin surge through my body. 'Standby, everyone!'

'Thirty seconds to on-air.' Viv's voice was steady and authoritative next to me. Her eyes were on the clock on the wall. In front of her were two stopwatches.

'Standby to roll Titles,' I said quietly, watching the

monitor for the one-inch machine. There was an answering beep. Either Albert had given up on the headlines or someone was down there helping him.

'Ten . . . nine.' Viv had started the countdown.

'V.T. eighteen . . . roll!' I gave the cue as she reached five and watched as the clock which is recorded at the head of every tape counted down to zero and the Titles went out on air. We had twenty seconds to get ourselves sorted out.

'Albert,' I spoke urgently. 'Any luck with the headlines tapes?' At that moment there was a whirring of images on the monitors for the Beta machines and then the clocks for both headlines tapes appeared.

'Great.'

'Fifteen seconds.'

'Geraldine and John, we've got the tapes but talk to camera just in case.'

'Nine . . . eight . . .'

'BETA one . . . roll! Cue Geraldine.'

As she began to read the first headline, taking care to look up at the camera, the pictures from the first tape appeared on screen.

'BETA two . . . roll! Cue John.'

We were onto the second headline. My gaze moved from the on-air screen in front of me to the monitor for BETA one on the left. Albert was fastforwarding the tape. It stopped suddenly on a still frame.

'Roll BETA one!' I called out. Then as Gary mixed smoothly from the pictures of tape two back to those of tape one, I added, 'And cue Geraldine.' She started to speak and there was an audible sigh of relief in the gallery. We'd got through that little lot by the skin of our teeth.

But Gary was already mixing out of the last pictures of the headlines and coming to John on camera two. There was a slight tremor around his eyes – not surprising given the mayhem he had been hearing through his earpiece. He started to read the link off the autocue to introduce the first item – the tape Frank had sent back from the airport.

I leaned forward to the microphone. 'Albert, the footsie tape goes up on BETA two next.' There was a brief pause, then Albert's voice crackled back over the intercom.

'I don't have it. It still hasn't come down.' I felt suddenly nauseous. In the panic over the headlines, I hadn't done the usual last-minute check to make sure we had all the tapes. On my left, I could hear Viv already on the phone trying to find out what had happened to them.

I swung round to Trevor. The content of the programme was his responsibility.

'What do you want us to go to, Trevor?' He shrugged helplessly. I turned back to the microphone.

'Do you have anything at all, Albert?' Talkback crackled.

'I don't have a bloody thing.' Albert sounded at the end of his tether.

I glanced at the on-air monitor. John looked shaky even as he was reading the script. I leaned forward and tried to speak calmly.

'John, we don't have the tape.' He was petrified, I could tell. In his own self-defence, he had probably stopped listening to the din coming over his earpiece and mentally shut it out. All he cared about, the only thing he could rely on in a world in chaos was the script on autocue in front of him. And he was going to read that, come hell or high water. Any second now, he would come to the end of the link, cue us into the football tape which we didn't have, we'd stay on him, he wouldn't know what to do and he'd come unhinged, I could tell.

In desperation, I scanned all the monitors in front of me, coming to rest on the one showing the output from the Outside Broadcast Unit. It was all we had. I heard John say, 'This report from Frank Johnson.'

'Take the O.B.,' I yelled. Gary's fingers responded automatically and the pictures from the O.B. came up on the on-air monitor, showing the football team trooping into place before a screaming crowd of fans. I held my breath. We'd given them no warning. Then came Frank's measured tones.

'And the team have just appeared at this press conference at the city airport.' I breathed out.

On either side of me, Viv and Gary relaxed. Frank was a professional. He would keep talking about nothing if necessary, for as long as we needed him. I could cheerfully have gone home right then.

'Okay,' I said into the intercom. 'Albert, any tapes yet?'

'The canal story's come in.'

I turned to Viv. 'Have we got the script?' I muttered, off-mike.

She nodded. 'Just arrived.' She picked up a sheet of paper lying on top of my script and waved it at me.

'Okay.' I was back to the intercom. 'Script change, everyone. Canal story next. Page –' I glanced down at the sheet of paper in my hands, 'eight of the script. Albert, that tape on BETA two.' There was an answering beep from Albert, back on duty at the machines. The autocue monitor showed the operator scrolling through the script until she stopped at the page for the canal story.

Ten seconds later, the clock for the tape appeared in the monitor for BETA two. Apart from counting off the seconds to the start of the pictures, the clock carries the label which has been given to identify that particular tape. The main picture editor was a twenty-eight-year-old called Julian. He was renowned for his witty tags, which were much appreciated by all of us on a run-of-the-mill day. But I noticed with relief that on this occasion, he had chosen the innocuous title, 'Canal'.

Somehow we stumbled on, even though all of us were pretty rattled. There was no particular order to the programme. We simply went on to whatever item we had ready next. Occasionally I'd turn to see if Trevor was still with us but he sat frozen without saying a word. At one point he lit up a cigarette.

'Put that damn thing out!' snarled Gary as smoke drifted past him. Trevor meekly obeyed.

With ten minutes still to go, we had used all the available tapes and I was wondering what we could do next when a call came through from Mags. She was in Reception.

'I've sent the tape up to Julian and asked him to edit together some G.V.s,' she gasped, referring to the general shots of the scene which are the staple of news stories. 'I've no idea if he can get it done in time. It could fall off the end of the programme. I can come in and do a report live, though.'

I swivelled round in my chair and leaned forward over the desk to catch Trevor's eye. Even in the dim light, I could sense his fear.

'Mags is back. We might get the pictures in time but it's unlikely. She can do a report live from her notes. Do you want that?' I asked him. He looked at me owlishly, opened his mouth as if to reply then shut it again.

'You have to say *now*!' I insisted, automatically glancing round at the monitors. Viv read my mind.

'Two minutes to go on this,' she said, nodding towards the screen where our last tape was playing.

I turned back to Trevor. 'Yes or no?'

Trevor nodded, bug-eyed.

'Yes. Get in here as fast as you can,' I spoke into the receiver before hanging up. 'Marci,' I was on talkback again, speaking to the floor manager, 'Mags is coming in to do a live piece to camera. Put her in position C. Jack on camera three, can you pick that up?' I shifted my gaze to the monitor for camera three and saw the picture move up and down, as Jack nodded the camera head in reply.

I watched Mags slide into the seat, using the camera lens as a mirror to swiftly smooth down the dark hair which swung in a gleaming pageboy style around her face. She didn't need to bother. Somehow she was always immaculately groomed. But her small even features looked tense and her large green eyes were clouded with anxiety. I could see one of the sound assistants plugging in her earpiece. She said a couple of words for a sound check.

'Can we come to you now?' I asked.

'Fine.' She wriggled in her seat, sat up straight and took a deep breath, glancing at the notebook on the desk in front of her. Viv was giving a ten-second countdown out of our last tape.

The phone rang. I heard Viv pick it up as the tape ended and I called out, 'Cut to three. Cue Mags.'

Viv was speaking to me. 'It's Julian. There's a thirty-second piece on its way down. Do you want it?'

I made one last plea to Trevor. 'Trevor, it's Mags' tape. Should we use it?' I could see him trying to rally, to get back in the game.

'Yes!' he said decisively, but it had a hollow ring to it. I glanced up at the monitors. A new clock had appeared, paused on a five-second pre-roll. Julian was back to his old tricks. It was labelled 'Nun deader'.

'BETA one roll,' I ordered. Instantly the clock started, the hand moving from five to four to . . .

'Don't take it,' Trevor yelled.

'Stop tape!' I shouted. The clock froze. But Gary's fingers had a life of their own. They were already reaching for the button. As Mags continued with her account of the tragedy, she was replaced on screen by the image of the clock, paused at one second to go, with the label 'Nun deader' for all to see.

Before I could say anything, Gary had reacted, the clock was gone and Mags was back on camera.

'Christ!' I heard him mutter. 'Oh, Christ!'

Behind me, the door to the gallery opened and then swung shut. Trevor had left us.

Mags had come to the end of her report. Geraldine ad-libbed a few pleasantries to fill in the last seconds before both presenters said, 'Good night.' We cut to the wide shot on camera three, gradually pulling back to show the whole studio as the lights dimmed. I kept my eyes on the on-air monitor, and as our studio shot was replaced with the opening titles of a network gameshow I leaned towards the mike.

'They're off us,' I said, with relief audible in my voice. 'Thank you very much everyone for hanging in there – and sorry for the cock-ups in the gallery.' I switched off my mike.

Gary did the same for his. He looked at me. 'That was a fucking shambles!'

I put my finger to my lips and turned to watch as Viv threw the switch on Trevor's talkback. Now we could speak without being overheard.

'Who is that numbskull?' Gary banged his fist on the counter. Viv was gathering stray pages of script up off the floor. She looked at Gary with a puzzled expression followed by dawning realisation.

'Of course, you've been on holiday, haven't you? You won't have worked with him before. It's like this every night!'

Gary leaned back in his chair and closed his eyes, letting his arms fall limply by his side. He had just returned from six weeks in New Zealand. Like me, this was his first encounter with Trevor.

'Where did the arsehole come from?' he asked, through gritted teeth.

'*Daily Chronicle*,' I replied briefly. 'He's never done telly before, but he's an old drinking buddy of the powers that be.' I was feeling slightly nauseous now that the adrenalin was draining from my system.

'He got the job over Mags Lawson,' Viv added.

Gary jerked his head round to us. 'What? They appointed that idiot when they could have had someone who knew what they were doing?'

'Our reaction precisely,' said Viv with heavy emphasis, stuffing scripts into the bin. 'I mean,' she gestured with a handful of pages, 'even if they didn't want Mags, they could have hired anyone in that newsroom and they'd do a better job.' She shook her head in bewilderment. 'It can't go on. Tonight was bad enough. It's only a matter of time before we have a complete disaster.'

The telephone rang. I picked it up. 'Studio C.'

'Who's that?' Martin Kember's voice vibrated with barely contained anger.

'It's me, Bel,' I answered calmly. I knew Martin of old. He used to be the news editor. We had worked together for years until he had been promoted to Head of Factual Programmes in the general shift upwards following the demise of our former Director of Programmes.

'I'd like to see you and Gary in my office at once.' He hung up. I replaced the receiver and turned with a wry smile to Gary. 'That was Martin. Guess what?'

Gary sighed. 'A post mortem. In his office.'

I nodded and hauled myself to my feet. My legs felt weak and I hardly had the strength to pull the weighted door open. The corridor outside looked bleak with its cement walls painted a pale green and the grey linoleum tiles streaked with black where heavy equipment had been hauled along. We walked towards the fire door at the end in silence. As we passed the Green Room, Mags emerged.

'Are you on your way up to Martin's office?' she asked

tersely. I grimaced and she fell in beside me. 'What the hell happened?'

I heaved a sigh. 'It's a long story.' In glum silence, we proceeded to the lift and went up to the third floor. Julian was loitering in the corridor. He always reminded me of an ostrich, towering above the rest of us, with his beaky nose, and his soft floppy hair cut short at the temple so that it stood up in a tuft. He was clearly very nervous, his movements jerky.

He joined us in silence as we moved soundlessly on thick blue-green carpet. I could see that the door to Martin's office was ajar. As we approached, the murmur of voices floated out into the corridor. I could clearly make out Trevor saying, '. . . she should be fucking fired.'

I paused outside, my hand raised to knock. I could see Martin's face through the opening, his gaze on someone – presumably Trevor – on the other side of the room. Martin had changed quite a bit in the past year. His close-cropped dark hair was threaded with silver and the brown eyes were clearer in the lean face since he had stopped drinking. He was wearing a smart, dark-grey pin-stripe suit and a pale-blue shirt. The hard drinking newsman had turned into an executive. He was shaking his head.

'It was your responsi—' Martin stopped as he caught sight of us standing in the doorway. He straightened up. 'Come in.'

In silence we filed into the long, narrow room. It was in the corner of the building with large windows on the two outer walls. A desk stood at one end, but Martin was seated at the long conference table which ran down the middle of the room. Opposite him sat Trevor. The four of us pulled out chairs at the end of the table, midway between the two men.

'Right.' Martin picked up the fountain pen lying in

front of him and began to fiddle with it. 'I'd like to find out why we had that shambles this evening. Trevor, you start.'

Trevor coughed and shifted heavily in his seat. 'It's very simple really,' he began. 'I told Mags I wanted that story for tonight but she got back too late. A good journo would have been back a lot faster than that. As it was, the tape came down at the last minute. I said I didn't want to use it because I had no idea what it showed but it went out anyway.' He pursed his lips and sat back, folding his arms.

Martin stared at him. He turned abruptly to me. 'Bel?'

I glanced sideways at Trevor. 'That isn't quite how I remember it. Mags got back in record time.' I turned to her. 'You didn't leave till five, did you?' She nodded, her gaze hostile as she looked at Trevor. I continued, trying to keep my voice neutral, 'I got a call to say the tape was coming down. Trevor said take it. I rolled tape. He said stop. I said stop. Albert froze the clock with one second to go, but we didn't give Gary enough warning and he punched it up.'

'It was a reflex. There was nothing I could do,' Gary chipped in apologetically. 'I just got off it as fast as I could when I realised what had happened.'

Martin was tapping the pen on the table. He was in a quandary, I could see. On the one hand, he had to support the man he had recently appointed news editor. On the other hand, Martin knew what it was like in the gallery during a hectic programme and, for all his faults, he would never have passed the buck when he was in Trevor's position. If something like this had gone wrong, he would have accepted responsibility.

He looked up abruptly. 'The bottom line is,' he began, surveying us all, 'I don't ever want this to happen again. Mags – I realise you were working

15

from your notes. I thought you did a good job under the circumstances.'

There was a snort of derision from Trevor. Martin stared at him until Trevor, noticing the silence, looked up and caught his steely eye. There was a long pause.

'Julian,' Martin continued, turning to the younger man, 'from now on, no tape leaves your room with a title that couldn't be seen by the general public.' Julian looked crestfallen and jiggled one foot restlessly.

Martin's gaze travelled from one to the other of us. 'In future, everyone just needs to take a little more care. Thank you.' We all rose to our feet. 'Trevor.' There was a sharp note in Martin's voice. 'I'd like a word, if you don't mind.'

The rest of us began shuffling towards the door. I was waiting my turn to leave behind Julian when I sneaked a look at Trevor. He was staring intently at Mags. For a few fleeting seconds, he wore an expression of pure hate.

Chapter Two

It was evening when I emerged from the building, the sky still radiant with a rosy sunset but chilly for May, with a stiff breeze blowing through the darkening streets. Nevertheless, I took the top down on my old rattletrap of a sports car. Being buffeted by the wind as I drove home was soothing and seemed to clear my mind.

It was already twilight by the time I parked the TR6 in the lane alongside my house. As often happened, I couldn't be bothered putting it away in the garage.

I entered the garden through an old wooden gate and headed for the back door. I live in a Victorian farmhouse on the outskirts of town which my husband Jamie and I bought together – no frills, just a plain rectangular stone building with a grey slate roof. After his death a couple of years ago, I had decided to stay on alone.

There was a light visible in the kitchen as I approached, which meant that Lucinda was home. We've known each other since primary school and she had been sharing the house with me for over a year since her marriage broke up. I opened the back door.

'Get stuffed!' There was the crash of the phone being slammed back in its cradle. I dropped my bag onto the kitchen table. Lucinda stood at the far end of the room, near the telephone. Her forehead rested against the wall. Until about a year ago, she had been a police detective. I'd been used to seeing her in neat, conservative suits, her straight dark hair tied back at the nape of her neck.

Then she had decided to return to college to study law as a mature student – although, as she said herself, 'mature' was hardly the right word. Nowadays, her hair hung loose in a thick curtain, and she rarely dressed in anything except jeans with long sweaters or T-shirts and heavy boots. She was using one of these heavy boots now to aim a kick at a weighty tome lying on the floor.

'Had a nice day?' I inquired brightly.

'Oh, hello.' Lucinda looked round and grinned sheepishly, then jerked her head in the direction of the phone. 'That was Alan. I could kill him.'

'Alan as in your soon-to-be-ex-husband-Alan?' I queried as I filled the kettle with water.

Lucinda threw herself down onto a chair at the table, where several more large volumes and a notebook were spread out. She was finding it hard having to discipline herself to study again.

'The very same.' Lucinda ran her hands through her hair. She looked really fired up. Her naturally pale skin was tinged with pink and her large dark eyes sparked as she spoke. 'After being wildly enthusiastic about our separation for the past twelve months,' she continued, her voice heavy with sarcasm, 'he has suddenly decided that it's actually quite nice having someone around to wash his socks and cook his frigging mince and potatoes after all. He's called me three times today already, whingeing about can't we just have a talk, and if he calls here again, I swear I'll do something we'll both regret.'

I opened the cupboard and took out two mugs, filled them with tea and stuck one in front of my friend.

'Oh, I wouldn't get so worked up about it. He'll get used to the idea,' I said absent-mindedly. Lucinda and Alan had at least one fight a week, just for old times' sake.

Lucinda shook her head. 'I wouldn't be so sure. You don't know Alan. It's one of the things that always drove me crazy about him. Once he starts on something like this, he's completely obsessive. The thing is, he's convinced himself I've been having a little fling with one of the guys in my class. I didn't get a chance to tell you about this, but last week I went to the pictures with a crowd of other students, and –' her voice went up an octave in disbelief '– when we came out, Alan was standing in a doorway across the street!' She rolled her eyes. 'It was as if he was spying on me. Gave me the creeps!'

I looked at her sharply. 'And are you?'

Lucinda was flustered. 'Am I what?' Then, seeing my raised eyebrows, she dropped the attempt at being blasé. 'Going out with someone? No.' She shook her head and looked down at her cup. Then she shot a glance up at me and added mischievously, 'But I've been thinking about it.'

We giggled. One of the things about knowing someone since you were small is that there is a part of both of you that never grows up. There are days when Lucinda and I can go into fits of hysterical laughter about nothing really, as if we were still little girls. This was one of them.

'I felt there was something going on apart from overwork,' I commented, sobering up. 'So who is it?'

Lucinda squirmed uncomfortably. 'It's one of the people in my class. He's a bit older, like me. He used to be a social worker, someone said. He's got a really nice face, sort of friendly and grown-up.' There was a pause.

'And . . .' I prompted.

'And nothing.' She shrugged. 'He's so quiet, I've hardly been able to get him to talk to me. I think he's interested but he's just too shy.'

'Can't you give him a little nudge?' I suggested.

'Oh Bel!' Lucinda buried her face in her hands. When

19

she looked up again, she seemed flustered and uncertain. This was very different from her usual exuberant self-confidence. It was years since I'd seen her so vulnerable.

'It's been such a long time,' she was saying. 'I feel like something extinct next to all these kids with their rampant hormones. It's easy for them, but I started going out with Alan when I was sixteen and there's been no one else since! I don't even know how to flirt any more.'

'You could try,' I countered.

Lucinda made a face. 'Anyway, I've never been known for my subtlety, have I?' She stared at her mug moodily, then suddenly brightened up. 'I could always arrest him and take him into custody, I suppose. Now that would be more my style.' We howled with laughter.

The doorbell rang. Lucinda choked on a mouthful of tea, jumping to her feet and gathering together her books. She headed into the hall, whispering frantically over her shoulder as she ran.

'If that's Alan, tell him I'm out. Tell him I've cut my wrists. Just get rid of him.'

I opened my mouth to object but Lucinda had disappeared round the bend in the stairway. I felt extremely exasperated. I had agreed to Lucinda moving in partly to help her out when her marriage broke up and she went back to college, but also to make things easier for me by having someone in the house while I'm away filming. I had not bargained for this melodrama and having to fend off her lovesick husband when I'd just got home from a hard day at work and was starving.

So I couldn't have looked very welcoming as I yanked the front door open. The slender figure standing on the step pulled back a little, when she saw me. But my expression quickly changed when I realised that it was Caroline, the single mum who usually comes in to clean for us twice a week. She stood uncertainly on the doorstep, her hair permed into a reddish frizz around her small features, nervously clutching her old grey jacket close to her body. I hadn't seen her for about a month because she'd been ill, and I was struck by how thin and haggard she looked.

I stood aside. 'Caroline – come on in.'

She walked past me, then stood awkwardly in the hall, as if waiting for instructions. This was not the woman I knew, who had always been full of confidence. It was as if something had sapped her very core.

'Just go on in,' I urged. 'I was about to make myself some supper. Would you like a cup of tea?'

Caroline followed me into the kitchen and sat down on the edge of a wooden chair. She looked nervous. 'No, thanks. I've left George on his own. I just popped out for a minute.' I knew Caroline lived in a council flat about a ten-minute walk away. She cleared her throat and looked down at her hands. They were still reddened from her cleaning work, although she had been off sick for almost four weeks now.

'How are you feeling?' I slid into a chair across the table from her.

That was her cue. She took a deep breath and raised her head to face me. There was a look of bravery in her expression.

'That's what I came about.' She swallowed then tried again. 'The doctor wants me to go into hospital for some tests. She said it could take about a week. They're calling me an emergency so I've been put to the top of the queue and I'm supposed to go in the day after tomorrow.' She paused, eyeing me as if to see how I'd take that piece of news.

'Well, at least they're doing something.' I tried to sound encouraging, but it had already occurred to me that she must be in trouble if she had succeeded in jumping the queue in the post-Thatcher NHS.

Caroline was nodding in response to my words. 'Yes, I've been telling myself that. But the problem is . . .' She suddenly stopped and tears sprang into her eyes. But before I could offer sympathy, she wiped them away. 'The problem is,' she continued doggedly, 'the problem's George.' She looked me straight in the eye at this with a mixture of resignation, fear and pleading. I knew that George is Caroline's nine-year-old son. I had heard umpteen stories of his misdemeanours, but I had only met him once, when he was seven. Then he had been an angelic, tousle-haired little boy who had been too shy to utter a single word to me.

'What's wrong with him?' I prompted when it seemed that Caroline wasn't going to continue without some encouragement.

'Nothing's wrong. It's just that there's nowhere for him to go. There's my mum, but she's alone now since my dad died and George wouldn't be able to keep on at his school here, he'd have to go to the village one at Brierley for a bit and he hates that. And Mum's got angina. George is at that age where he just drives her batty and goodness knows what would happen if I left them alone together for even a week.' She stopped again and looked down at her hands, her face working as if she was rehearsing what to say next.

'Won't the social services find somewhere?' I asked, frowning in sympathy.

Caroline looked up abruptly. 'Oh yes. There's no problem with that. It's just that,' she paused, before continuing in a quieter, less emphatic voice, 'I can't bear the thought of him going to strangers. You read these terrible stories in the newspaper . . . and anyway, George got nearly hysterical when I suggested it. He said he'd run away and live in the woods.' She smiled wryly. 'And I believe him. He's mad about animals as it is. I wouldn't put it past him to try living with the blinking squirrels in the treetops or something daft like that.' She sighed. 'The other thing is . . . I'm scared to let them have George. What if they decided to keep him? What if they decided he was better off with some childless couple who wanted a son and who had lots of money? I'm broke most of the time. There's just our council flat. We don't have any nice furniture or anything. I can't afford these fancy trainers he goes on about.'

I shook my head. 'They wouldn't keep him. They wouldn't have a leg to stand on if they tried to take your son away.'

The tears were back in Caroline's eyes. 'I know that. But just supposing. Once they have George, they've got him, haven't they? I won't know where he is necessarily. If some social worker gets a bee in their bonnet about keeping him, how do I get him back? What power do I have? I can't afford a solicitor or anything. You read about people losing their kids and then they say years later, 'Oh sorry, it was a mistake', but it's too late then, isn't it?'

I gazed at her helplessly. 'What about your friends? Can't any of them take George? It's only for a week. Surely someone can manage that.'

Caroline shook her head slowly. 'No. They'd all like to. A couple of people have offered to look after him when he gets out of school. But all my friends are as hard up as me. They're all in places that are too small for their families. No one's got room to take in another kid overnight.'

Caroline stopped, and her eyelids fluttered, closing momentarily. It was as if she was steeling herself for something. Without taking her eyes off her fingers twisting round and round each other on the table before her, she said in a voice that was unnaturally level, 'I don't suppose he could stay here, could he? It would just be for the bed. He could come last thing at night and be gone first thing in the morning. He can go to his friend Billy's the rest of the time. Barbara, Billy's mum, said it would be fine if he did that. He just needs somewhere to sleep.' As she finished, she turned her gaze towards me, her eyes bright with tears.

I was dumbfounded. I have such a chaotic lifestyle that the idea that *I* might look after George had never entered my head. But now the subject had been broached, there was no way I could refuse. I had three bedrooms upstairs, plus the big attic room which my husband Jamie had used as a studio. I could hardly claim I didn't have space for one little boy.

'Of course. I'm sorry I didn't think to offer. He can be here as much as he likes, as long as one of us is at home. I'm sure Lucinda won't mind.'

The tears Caroline had been fighting since she arrived flooded from her eyes. She tried to speak, then realising that was impossible, she simply nodded.

'Thanks,' she managed finally. 'Thank you.' She stood up. 'I must get back. George is on his own.' She paused at the door. 'Could I bring him round tomorrow night? Would that be all right?'

I thought for a moment. 'That should be fine. If not, I can give you a call.' Caroline nodded again and left, still muttering incoherent thanks. When she'd gone, I stopped to consider what I'd just agreed to. I wasn't quite sure how I'd break this to Lucinda. I knew she wasn't terribly keen on big boys at the moment, especially ones called Alan. But it was anybody's guess how she'd feel about little ones.

I had picked the evening newspaper up off the mat as I was showing Caroline out. Now I glanced idly at the front page.

What with all the kerfuffle in the gallery, I hadn't actually listened to any of the news today. There was a big piece on the little boy whose body had been found in the river. He was nine and had been playing with friends after school, sailing home-made boats. His had been ahead of all the others. In his excitement, he had slipped and fallen in. An ordinary tragedy which had left an entire family bereft.

The drug bust had involved a shipment from Amsterdam which had been tracked across the North Sea and had arrived in the local harbour today. Five men and a woman who worked at the docks had been arrested.

The last of our big stories was barely mentioned – presumably because it had happened so late. A few lines in the Stop Press simply announced that a sixty-five-year-old nun had been found dead in the office at 'Cloud Nine', a drop-in centre for drug addicts run by a local charity. The police were treating the death as suspicious.

Ah well. I tossed the paper aside. I would doubtless hear more about it tomorrow. I'd had enough of the news for one day.

Chapter Three

I drove to work next morning with the top down on my car, in absurdly high spirits. The air felt like cold wine and all the trees and shrubs were a delicate green. To my relief, Lucinda had taken the news that George was going to join us surprisingly well when she appeared downstairs in the morning.

'A little boy!' she echoed incredulously. 'You've acquired one just since last night? A real one, not a wind-up one we can keep in the cupboard?'

'A real one,' I replied emphatically. No use beating about the bush. 'His name's George.'

'I can't leave you alone for a minute, can I?' Lucinda rolled her eyes. 'Well, it's going to be fun watching you play at being Mummy.' She rushed off to catch her bus and I heaved a sigh of relief.

So the sound of shouting which greeted me as I walked into the newsroom was a horrible shock to my system. I'd heard stories that Mags and Trevor had been having regular showdowns since he'd started work at RTV a month ago, but this was the first time I'd witnessed one myself.

Mags was standing by her desk, slim and immaculate as always, dressed in a pale lemon suit. She was rigid with fury, her complexion flushed and her green eyes flashing. Trevor faced her. All I could see of him was the back of his head above a loud mustard-coloured checked jacket and sharply pressed grey slacks. He was yelling at the top of his voice, gesturing wildly with both arms. Frank Johnson and Ron Polly hovered in the background by their desks, shifting uncomfortably from foot to foot, aimlessly flicking through their mail.

'You think you're such an ace reporter – well, I don't give a fuck for your reporting! If you can't even get to a simple presser on time, then you're no use to me.' Trevor half-turned to leave, then swung back with a last retort. 'I know cub reporters who wouldn't make the mess that you've made.'

There was a glint of anger in Mags' eyes as she tried to interject, calling after Trevor's retreating back: 'My car wouldn't start. The garage said they'd fixed it, but they hadn't. What was I supposed to do – *fly* myself down to the Carlton? Anyway,' she slammed her notebook down onto her desk, 'they must have fifty press conferences a week for that bloody football team. Who gives a damn who's coming or going down there? The whole lot of them could transfer to Florida for all I care.'

Trevor had almost reached the glass booth in the corner of the room which served as his office. Now he stopped in his tracks and, with exaggerated slowness, turned around. His red, pouchy face was suffused with anger. Although he was only in his mid-forties, years of hard drinking had made him look older, coarsening his skin and leaving his eyes permanently bloodshot. Stabbing the air with one finger, he began walking ominously back the way he had come.

'That "bloody football team" as you put it in so ladylike a way, means a damn sight more to this town than you do. You think you're so high and mighty! No working-class culture for you, oh no! You're far too grand for football, that's really what this is about, isn't it? You could have made it to that presser if you'd really thought it was important, couldn't you? It was just that—'

'Trevor!' The voice was sharp and authoritative. Martin stood in the doorway, the muscles of his face clenched. There was total silence for several seconds.

'Mags, I'd like to see you in my office if you don't mind.' Martin turned on his heel and walked out. Trevor shot Mags a look of triumph.

'Run along, dearie. Your master's voice.'

Mags gazed at him with fury. 'Bastard!' She spat the words in his direction before sweeping out of the door.

Trevor took a step menacingly after her. 'That'll go in your personnel file!' he yelled.

Mags was gone a long time – at least an hour. Martin was usually someone who was short and to the point in his dealings with staff, so such a lengthy meeting was heavy going by his standards. Just after noon, there was a knock on my office door which was partly open and Mags flung herself into the room and sat down. She still looked angry. Beneath the make-up applied to accentuate her delicate features, her face was flushed. I got up and closed the door.

'Well, what did he say?'

In a singsong voice, Mags replied, 'The party line is that I'm jealous of Trevor because he got the job I wanted and I've to stop making life difficult for him. He's new to RTV so he needs our support while he finds his feet. Martin knows I'm an excellent reporter so it's just a question of my sorting out my attitude.' She grimaced and added in her normal voice, 'He must think I'm some kind of baby! He could at least give me credit for being a bit more professional than that.' She took a deep breath. 'Anyway, he suggests that I leave News for a while and work in documentaries. He thought perhaps you and I could come up with a project we could do together.' She closed her eyes for a moment, before asking in a calmer tone, 'Any ideas?'

I shook my head. 'Not off the top of my head, no, but

I'm sure we can think of something.' I sank into the chair on the other side of my desk. 'That's probably a pretty good suggestion, you know. It'll at least get you out of Trevor's way for a while.'

Mags gazed restlessly around the room. 'I know. It's eminently sensible.'

I glanced at the clock. 'Look, I've got to get down to the gallery and see what's planned for the lunchtime programme. Why don't we go out of the building for something to eat after I'm done?'

Mags nodded. 'Good idea.' As I headed off in the direction of the studio, she called after me, 'It'll be nice to escape from the zoo for a while!'

She was waiting for me in Reception when I emerged from the gallery an hour later. 'Come on,' she said, linking arms with me. 'Don't bother going up for your bag. This can be my treat.'

She led the way out of the RTV building and down the road to a small Italian restaurant, where we were shown to a corner booth festooned with plastic vine leaves. Both of us automatically looked around the room, checking that none of our colleagues were also eating there. It was too late for the lunchtime crowd, however, and the place was empty apart from us.

As soon as we were seated Mags ordered a couple of glasses of wine, which was unusual for her. Normally neither of us drank during the day because there was no room for slip-ups in either of our jobs.

'What the hell!' Mags chinked glasses with me and took a sip. 'Let's live and be merry. I refuse to let that bastard get me down.'

'He's not worth the trouble,' I agreed.

Mags smiled wryly. 'If it was only one arsehole it wouldn't be so bad. But Barry's giving me a lot of trouble about the kids at the moment. He's come up with a new one. Suddenly, I'm an unfit mother. This,' she gestured with her wine glass, 'from the man who used to get peeved if I paid more attention to the children than I did to him.' She moved aside as a plate of spaghetti was put down in front of her, and then took a long slug of her wine.

'How does he work that one out?' I bit into a mouthful of lasagne. I had never understood why Mags had married Barry O'Brien in the first place. He was a property developer, shrewd in business and extremely wealthy, but he and Mags had absolutely nothing in common.

'Oh, he's decided that since I work such long hours, supporting his kids because he pays hardly any maintenance,' Mags voice was ironic, 'the children would be better off with him and his Swedish tart Serafina who is home all day and would *love* to love them – I don't think!'

I shrugged. 'Well, so what? No judge is going to give him the kids on the strength of that, is he?'

Mags held up her glass, twirling it so that the wine winked in the light. She hadn't even started on her food. 'Probably not. But he can tie me up in court for ages, and cause me sleepless nights and cost me an awful lot of money I can't afford in solicitor's fees.' Her eyes travelled from her glass to me. 'In other words, he can make my life hell.'

There was a few moments' silence. Then Mags' natural resilience took over again. She was the sort of person who always bounced back, no matter what. Pushing her untouched spaghetti to one side, she leaned forward on the table.

'Enough of that. Let's talk about this documentary we've got to do. We must have some ideas and the sooner I get started the better.'

I made a face. 'Well, there's a tip-off that one of the city councillors took a kickback on that new shopping centre . . .'

'Boring,' Mags interrupted. 'Next?'

'There is no next. That's it. We seem to have hit the silly season early,' I said, referring to that period in late summer when everything closes down for the holidays and we are reduced to manufacturing news out of nothing. That's when we do stories about hens that cluck *Yankee Doodle Dandy* etc.

Mags and I sat in thoughtful silence for a few minutes.

'Well, we have to come up with something because I am sure as hell not going back to News,' Mags said flatly. She thumped her glass onto the table, so that some of the wine slopped out. 'What about the nun who was found dead? Couldn't we do something on that – perhaps follow the police investigation?'

I frowned, trying to recall the details. 'You'll have to fill me in on that one. I didn't pay much attention to your report last night.'

Mags grimaced. 'I'm not surprised.' She leaned forward, fired with enthusiasm. 'A sixty-five-year-old nun, Sister Catherine – one of these Mother Teresa types – was found naked and bound . . . oh yes!' she said, seeing my shocked expression. 'I didn't mention that on the news last night, but it's true. It's not official yet, but one of the uniform coppers tipped me off. She was raped and strangled.'

I shrank back from that image. 'Do the police have any leads?'

Mags wrinkled her nose. 'Not as far as I know. It's rather an odd case. She was alone in the office at the drop-in centre. The place had been ransacked.' She caught hold of one of my arms and shook it. 'Come on – what do you say? It'd make a great documentary!'

'Mmm.' I was dubious. 'You know as well as I do that there's never much you can do on this sort of case till it comes to court. The police don't let out information unless it's to help them catch someone, and then when they do get the guy it's all *sub judice* and we're not allowed to say anything.'

'Yes, but—' Mags was desperate. She switched to a wheedling tone. 'Henderson likes you,' she said, referring to the local Chief of Police. 'Ever since you tracked down that bunch of murderers last year you've been his blue-eyed girl.' I was quiet. That had been a harrowing experience. I had come close to being killed myself.

'Why don't you give him a call?' Mags wasn't going to let this rest. She was like a terrier when she got hold of a good story.

I nodded. 'Okay. It's worth a try. Perhaps we can do some kind of deal where they let us film their investigation in progress on condition that we don't broadcast until after the trial. You never know.'

Mags hustled me out of the restaurant and back to my office. Since I'd helped out on one of his most difficult cases the previous year, Henderson always took my calls, provided he wasn't tied up with anyone else. So it was no surprise when he came on the line almost at once.

'Bel! This is a nice surprise. How are you?' His bluff, friendly tones were encouraging.

'I'm fine. Busy as always,' I replied. Then, because I knew how pushed for time he would be, I got straight to the point. 'I'm calling with a proposition.'

'Oh, yes?' Henderson's tone had changed. Now he was the professional, suspicious of dealing with the media. 'What's that then?'

'You know this murder involving the nun? Well, Mags and I – you remember Mags Lawson, one of our reporters?' Henderson grunted in assent. 'Well, we were wondering if we could document your investigation as a way of giving the public some insight into police work . . .' I got no further.

'Normally I'd say a flat-out no, but it just so happens you may have come at the right time. We've been talking

about something like this. Why don't you come down and
see me?' Henderson suggested. 'Better make it sharp,
though, I'm free in half an hour if you can get yourself
here smartish.'

'Great. See you then.' I hung up and shook Mags
excitedly. 'We've to be at Headquarters in half an hour.
I never seriously thought they might agree to this!'

Mags did a little dance round the room. 'Bye bye,
Trevor!'

I sobered up. 'We'd better go and run this by Martin.
But I can't imagine he won't be thrilled.'

My prediction was correct. Martin was incredulous that
after years of badgering the police to let us film a murder
investigation and being knocked back, we now had our
foot in the door after just one phone call.

'It's not certain, of course,' I injected a note of caution
which I didn't take seriously myself.

Martin grinned. I could imagine this was the perfect
solution to a lot of problems, not least the Mags–Trevor
situation. 'I'll talk to Katy in Resources about getting you
a crew. We may have to pull in some freelancers because
if they give the go ahead, you don't want to miss any
more than you can help.'

'Can I come off News?' I pleaded.

Martin nodded. 'I'll see what I can do. Colin's back
from his hols next week but we may be able to sort
something out before then.' He looked from one to
the other of us, grinning. 'This is more the spirit I'm
used to!'

Police Headquarters was an ugly seventies tower block
in the centre of town. Henderson's office was in a corner
on the fifth floor so that it had a panoramic view of
the city. That was its only saving grace. Although the
cream walls looked as if they might have been recently
painted, the effect was undermined by chipped fake
wood-panelling and battered veneer furniture clouded

by the dingy atmosphere that comes from years of cigarette smoke.

Henderson got up to greet us with a broad smile when we were shown in. He had aged quite a lot since the last time I had seen him. The curling iron-grey hair was now streaked with silver, but there was still a twinkle of mischief in the blue eyes.

He was brisk and to the point. 'The thing is, we're a bit anxious about our image at the moment. Feeling a little vulnerable, you might say. That unfortunate incident over at Kempton about that man getting beaten up in custody and winning his lawsuit hasn't helped, let me tell you. And in these days of citizens' charters and cutbacks in public spending and so on, we thought it might be a good idea if we let people see what we actually do for the money.

'Now, I've had a quick word with my bosses and the ninnies in our PR Department and told them I know you pretty well and that I think you can be trusted.' He paused and gave me a look that conveyed the silent message – *or else!* 'So we will agree in principle to you following our investigation – on condition that,' he counted off on his fingers, 'you only film what we say you can, you do not broadcast anything at all until after the trial or unless we give specific permission, and that we have final approval of the finished programme.' He leaned back in his chair.

'Great. I'm sure we can meet all your conditions,' I paused, 'except for one. No broadcasting company will ever agree to let you have final cut. But,' I hurried on as Henderson made to object, 'I'm sure you could see it before it goes out, and they would take anything you say very seriously. And you could always sue,' I added with a feeble attempt at humour.

Henderson shook his head, but he was smiling. 'I told them upstairs they wouldn't get that, but they thought we should try. We'll want all this on paper, of course. Who should we deal with for that?' Quickly I supplied him with Martin's name and telephone number.

'Right.' Henderson snapped his notebook shut and looked up at us. 'Now about my make-up. Can I have the lady that does Robert Redford?'

'No problem,' I grinned. 'When can we start?'

'Now.' Henderson reached for his phone and dialled a couple of numbers. 'Tell Sykes I'm bringing the young ladies down in a few minutes,' he barked into the receiver, then hung up without any of the usual civilities. He leaned forward on the desk and gazed at his hands clasped in front of him. When he spoke, he appeared to be choosing his words carefully.

'I should perhaps fill you in on Sykes.' He glanced up sharply. 'Just between us, of course.' He waited for our nods of agreement before continuing. 'Very smart chap – definitely the new type of copper, fast track and all that. Studied criminology at university so he can quote statistics and forensic psychology at the drop of a hat. Not quite my cup of tea, I have to say. Bit autocratic. Tends to rub his team up the wrong way, which is not a good idea because this whole place runs on their good will. They get exploited right, left and centre nowadays, particularly on the inquiry team because now we can only pay so much overtime and after that they end up working for nothing.'

As he spoke, my eye strayed to a framed photograph on top of a cadenza near the window. A young woman in a graduation gown and mortarboard smiled happily to the camera. I knew Henderson had a daughter whom he'd brought up on his own after the death of his wife and whom he adored.

He had pulled an elegant pen from an ornamental holder on his desk and was tapping it absent-mindedly against its plinth.

'So,' he was looking at both of us, 'if he gives you any

trouble – and I don't really think he will – you just let me know.' He got to his feet heavily and jerked his head in the direction of the door to the hall. 'Let's go.'

We crowded into a tiny lift which took us down a couple of floors. The door to an office with the nameplate of *Detective Chief Inspector J.A. Sykes* was standing open and Henderson pushed his way in without knocking. A tall thin man with close-cropped curly hair stood up behind a desk. He had a thin angular face with a small moustache and cold grey eyes. The smart grey suit and dark striped tie would have allowed him to pass for a merchant banker or a successful solicitor.

DCI Sykes, Henderson was explaining, headed up the investigation. Perhaps it was something to do with the briefing we had just had, but I didn't find myself warming to him.

While Henderson did the introductions and filled him in on the outcome of our discussions, Sykes' pale grey eyes travelled slowly over my body from my feet upwards. Something in his expression told me that a tallish, rangy-looking woman dressed in jeans and a cowboy shirt with short dark-blonde hair wasn't quite his type. I was waiting for him when he finally reached my face. I inclined my head a little and raised my eyebrows, but there was no glimmer of embarrassment as he stared me out.

The uncomfortable spell was broken by Henderson putting his arm around my shoulder so that I had to give him my attention, and saying, 'Now you take good care of these ladies. And pay special attention to whatever this one says. She's got a better track record for catching villains than we have.' Then he was gone as abruptly as he had entered.

Sykes gave us a sour smile and motioned to a couple of green naugahyde-upholstered chairs. 'Letting the media in is not my idea of a smart thing to do, but there you go,' he commented, sitting back down behind his desk. 'I suppose we'll give you whatever co-operation we can, but let me just say this.' He wagged a long spindly finger at us. 'This is *my* investigation, and whatever they say upstairs, I run it the way I think fit. If you get in the way, you'll be out that door so fast your feet won't even hit the ground. Okay?' He smiled his thin, mirthless smile again.

I beamed at him, just to show I wasn't impressed. 'Wonderful! When can we start?'

Sykes ignored me. He reached for his phone. 'I'll have someone fill you in on the details so far. I've still got the crime scene closed off till Forensics are done. You could have a look at the Centre, but you won't be able to get anywhere near the room where the murder took place. I'd rather you stayed out of the Incident Room as much as possible for the moment. They're all running around in there like blue-arsed flies. It'll probably calm down a bit by the end of the week. I'd like you to take a day to suss things out then let me know each evening what you want to film the next day and I'll think about it.' He gave us an arrogant look and paused before continuing.

'We usually have a meeting every evening about six to compare notes and decide what we're doing next.' Without waiting for a response from us, he dialled a couple of numbers, spoke briefly into the receiver, hung up and got to his feet. He held out his hand. 'Thank you very much, ladies. I wish you all the best. Now I've got work to do.' We were treated to the thin smile again as we shuffled out of the door.

A fresh-faced young policeman was waiting outside in the corridor for us.

'PC Burke,' he introduced himself. He seemed quite excited by our plans for filming and eager to help. 'If you need any extras, just let me know,' he said, demonstrating his talent with a little tapdance. Unfortunately, the thick rubber soles of his regulation black shoes stuck on the linoleum and after a couple of ambitious twirls, he fell full-length on the floor. I darted forward to catch him.

'Oops!' He staggered to his feet, unabashed. 'Not quite Fred Astaire,' he added, dusting himself off. 'But I've got a lovely personality.' He led us down the hall and into a large, untidy room.

'This is the Incident Room,' he explained. 'Every serious crime is assigned a room like this, usually at Headquarters because it helps to have access to Holmes, the Home Office computer.'

I looked around. It reminded me of a newsroom. There was the same detritus of scraps of paper with scribbled notes and information, mixed in with newspaper cuttings and overflowing ashtrays. Although the crime was recent, the room already looked grubby and there were a couple of plates of congealed leftover food on a tray by the door. There were windows all along one side of the room, but every other available wall seemed to be filled up with bulletin boards of one kind or another. Under the heading *Inquiry Team* on one of them was a long list of names, headed by that of DCI Sykes. I noted with interest that his deputy was someone called DI Bateman. Unless there was more than one Bateman in the building, that must be Lucinda's husband Alan.

Other boards had scribbled notes under titles like *Lines of Inquiry* or *Victim*. People came and went with an air of frantic intensity. A couple of middle-aged men were on the telephone carrying on weary conversations and taking notes from time to time. At one end of a long table, four people faced each other at computer terminals, typing away furiously from forms and notebooks at their side.

'The thing about murder investigations that surprises most people and that you never see on the telly is the amount of paperwork involved,' Burke explained helpfully. 'See those people over there,' he indicated the four sitting at the terminals, 'their whole job is just to log in all the information that the inquiry team bring back every day. Then it's sifted by whoever's in charge – that's DCI Sykes or DI Bateman in this case – and they decide what to follow up on.'

He stepped back smartly to get out of the way of a harassed-looking woman rushing past. 'At this stage it's madness because we follow up on everything. They're doing door-to-doors at the murder scene and also where the victim lived. They'll be talking to everyone she worked with or knew, trying to find witnesses, or working backwards from possible motives to identify suspects. Hopefully, by the end of the week, we'll begin to get some solid leads out of all this, then we'll narrow the investigation and things'll calm down a bit.'

He led us over to one of the wall boards. 'That's her,' Burke pointed with a stubby finger. I leaned forward to examine a black and white photograph of an elderly woman. It was part of a larger picture and had been blown up so that it was rather grainy. Sister Catherine had one of those open, trusting, friendly faces. Large, kindly eyes shone from behind round spectacles and she had a soft, gently lined face. She wore an ordinary light-coloured blouse and a cardigan. She might have been someone's adored granny, were it not for the plain white band and dark headdress on her hair. It was unthinkable that anyone could have had a motive for raping and killing her.

Burke was reading from a file. 'Sixty-five. Joined the convent when she was nineteen. Still lived there. Taught at Saint Xavier's for thirty-five years then when she retired five years ago, she started at the Centre doing the office work and keeping the books. Loved by one and all. No enemies. Now.' He turned over another sheet. 'Here's the scene.' He handed me a series of photographs. The first was the exterior of the church, shot through some trees, showing a flight of stone stairs at the back of the building with a door at the top.

'That's the entrance to the office. Only way in. Usually kept locked from the inside.' I looked up at him and he answered my unspoken question. 'The door wasn't forced, so she must have let her killer in. Either that or she forgot to turn the key – who knows?'

He passed over six or seven more pictures, showing the interior of the office and the body of Sister Catherine, bound and gagged on the floor. I could just make out the ends of the belt wrapped around her neck. The expression of the face and eyes was grotesque. Her hands were tied as if in prayer, her body arranged in an exaggeratedly sexual position, like a centrefold model, her legs splayed wide apart. Only she wasn't a model. She was an elderly woman, her muscles slack and her skin wrinkled. It made the indignity of her death all the more poignant.

'Usually,' said Burke with self-conscious importance, clearly beginning to hit his stride, 'there is some sort of link between the murderer or rapist and his victim. Finding that link is our best chance of tracking down the criminal – unless, of course,' he gave a laugh that suggested chance would be a fine thing, 'someone saw him commit the crime and can identify him. We're working on one theory that the motive for the crime was robbery. It was a break-in by someone she knew – that was why she let him in. She refused to hand over the loot; he threatened her with his knife and the rape was an afterthought.'

I stared at the photographs of the scene of the crime.

'How much was stolen?' Mags asked.

Burke considered. 'About twenty quid, give or take a few bob. There's a filing cabinet,' he sifted through the photographs and pointed to the cabinet in one of them, 'that had been ransacked, but we're not sure what was taken.'

'That's not enough to kill someone for, surely?'

'It is if you're a junkie.'

'So,' I chipped in, 'that's the theory you're working on – that it was one of the clients from the Centre, or perhaps a former client who was back on drugs?'

Burke nodded. 'That office is really out of the way. No one else had any reason to be there or to know the setup, except for tradesmen and the cleaners, of course, and we're checking them.' He began stuffing the pieces of paper he had removed back into the file. 'Look, I'm really sorry, but I've got to go soon. I'm supposed to be taking statements from the neighbours.'

I glanced at my watch. 'We need to get back to work, too.' I gazed at the crime photos one last time, before handing them over. The police theory didn't make sense. Someone had laid out the body very carefully, almost ritualistically. And tying Sister Catherine's hands in prayer was a twisted and deliberate act. I was sure the rape was no afterthought. It had been planned and carried out according to some bizarre pattern. The question was why, and by whom?

Chapter Four

We emerged into the dappled sunshine of late afternoon. I glanced at my watch. 'If we get a move on, we could probably take a run by the drop-in centre before I have to be back for the news,' I suggested.

Mags nodded a little uncertainly. 'That's fine. I might have to leave sharpish though because I've got to take the kids for a doctor's appointment at five.' She rolled her eyes in mock exasperation. 'It's never-ending. Doctor's appointments, dentist's appointments, opticians, tapdancing, Cubs, theatre group, swimming, skating. On and on.'

The Cloud Nine Drop-in Centre was only a short walk from the police station. It had been set up by a local charity in a disused church on a quiet backwater running parallel to the High Street. It still looked like a church, the only difference being the garish handmade signboard tacked above the front entrance. This showed a brilliant blue sky, with a crudely painted rainbow spanning fluffy clouds from which the name of the Centre burst forth in a shower of golden stars.

On the right-hand side of the building stood a parade of small shops. But a narrow street, Friar's Lane, ran down the left side. As we strolled along it, I marvelled at how quiet it was here although we were only a stone's throw from the city centre.

The area at the rear of the building had been turned into a car park, bordered by large old trees. Through the overhanging foliage, we could just make out a stone staircase which mounted the exterior at the back of the building. It was closed off by bands of yellow tape, and a uniformed policeman stood guard at the foot.

At the top of the stairs on the first floor was an old-fashioned door with frosted panes of glass set into the top half. One would normally never notice it, tucked away out of sight at the back of the building, unless one happened to glance to the right in passing. I was beginning to understand why the police were focusing their inquiries on people connected to the Centre.

'Shall we go in and see if there's anyone we can talk to?' I suggested.

Mags looked reluctant. 'Actually, I think I'd better go. The kids will be waiting for me. I'll catch a taxi from the rank on the High Street. Why don't we get together for a meeting first thing tomorrow and discuss how we're going to do this?'

We arranged a time and then she hurried off. I wandered up the front steps into the lobby of the building. It was dark and cool inside. Each wall had been crudely painted a different colour – red, orange and purple – in an attempt to subvert the hallowed atmosphere of this former church. On the red wall ahead of me hung a homemade bulletin board, headed *Staff* in swirly black lettering. Down one side was a list of names with photographs next to them and on the other side was a place to indicate whether they were in or out.

At the top of the list was the name Andrew Marmot, the Director of the Centre. He apparently was in the building at that moment. Beneath him was the name of his deputy, Tammy Soames, who was on holiday, and below that, 'Sister Kate'. I looked at the photo next to her name. All the others were passport size, but hers was full-length, a snapshot taken in the street showing a dumpy woman in a long pleated skirt and cardigan. The picture had been trimmed at the sides to fit the space allotted to it.

'Can I help?' I spun round in response to the mellifluous voice which came from behind me. A slim dark-haired man in his late thirties, dressed in jeans and a T-shirt, stood in a doorway on the far side of the hall. As I approached, I noticed that his sallow skin was deeply pockmarked, but his sharp features were softened by large, liquid-brown eyes.

I held out my hand. 'Hello, my name is Bel Carson. I'm a television director with RTV and I'm working on a documentary about the work of our local police.' That was fudging the issue a little, but I thought I'd approach the topic gently.

'Andrew Marmot.' He shook my hand briefly then gestured for me to go past him into the office beyond. 'Please come on in.'

It was a small, rather gloomy room painted a dull blue in contrast to the defiant primary colours in the lobby. A plain wooden desk stood in the window looking out onto the street at the front of the building. A few photographs were arranged above an empty black iron fireplace, but apart from a couple of orange moulded-plastic chairs, there was nothing else in the room. Andrew Marmot followed me in and closed the door.

'What can I do for you?' he asked, motioning me to one of the chairs and taking the other himself. There was something very self-conscious and affected about his movements.

'We're thinking of filming a documentary about the investigation into Sister Catherine's death,' I began. 'I just wanted to have a look at the scene and gather some background information.'

He gazed at me in silence for a moment, clearly sizing me up. 'What do you want to know?' The question was not exactly hostile, but it wasn't terribly eager either.

'Can you tell me who discovered the body?' I asked.

'I did.' He folded his arms and watched my response.

'Can you tell me how that came about?'

He sighed. 'I've told the police all this already. Kate was in the—'

'Kate?' I interrupted.

'That's how she was known to her friends. Kate.' Unexpectedly, tears formed in his eyes. 'She was a lovely person. The best.' He swallowed hard. 'She was working in the office. She kept the books for us, did it for nothing. I left her there about ten o'clock to come down here and help in the coffee bar. I locked the door behind me, as always. She could open it from inside. It was about noon before I went back up there, to get my sandwiches. The door was still locked. I thought she'd already left – she only worked halfdays, anyway – because I couldn't see her through the glass. Then when I got in . . .' He stopped and looked at me. There was a tremor in his face.

As if to distract himself, he turned round awkwardly in his chair and reached behind him to remove a framed photograph from the mantelpiece. He held it out so I could see. 'That's the photograph the police used. We didn't have any others. She was a tireless fundraiser.'

Sister Kate was in the foreground, smiling in a dazed way at the camera. She held one end of a cheque which was several feet long and at least two feet wide. The sum of ten thousand pounds was printed clearly on it and the other end was held by a well-to-do man in a business suit. Several men similarly attired crowded around in the background.

When I glanced up at Andrew, he was gazing at the photograph, a sad, faraway look on his face.

'Why would anyone want to harm her?' I asked.

He shook his head dully. 'I've no idea. The police think it might have been a burglary which went wrong. Personally, I find that idea a bit unbelievable. Everyone knows we don't keep drugs around here. We work on a shoestring – there's never any money to speak of. And only people here really know about that office. It's completely self-contained because it used to be the caretaker's bedsit when this was used as a church.'

'Do you think . . .' I paused, wondering if he might take offence at what I was about to ask.

'Yes?' He looked at me warily.

'Do you think it could have been one of your clients? I believe the police are working on that theory.'

He sighed. 'Yes, I know they are. The thing is, as I've already told them, drug addicts, even recovering drug addicts, don't really function like normal people. If you're a junkie, then getting your next hit is the most important thing in your life. It destroys your morals, you stop caring if you eat or sleep, you lose interest in your loved ones, you get fired from your job if you have one – it just takes over, pushing out everything else in your life – *including sex*. Believe me, most junkies couldn't care less. They're probably too wrecked even to think about it, and when they're in a recovery programme, it takes everything they've got, every last little bit of physical and mental energy to fight the addiction and stay clean.' He paused and laughed dryly. 'I'd be very, very surprised if it was any of our lot, to be honest.'

Carefully he replaced the photograph on the mantelpiece. He touched the face delicately with one finger. Tears had begun to roll down his face again and he leaned across to his desk and pulled a couple of tissues out of a box of paper hankies.

'Sorry,' he apologised, when he had blown his nose. 'Kate was the nearest thing to family I've ever had. I came here ten years ago as a client. She used to help out with the meals in the evenings. That was while she was still teaching full-time.' He paused, staring into the distance.

'I was a wreck – filthy, covered in sores, disgusting. She led me out of that.'

There was silence again. Somewhere in the depths of the building a clock chimed five. As that registered, I jumped to my feet.

'Oh my God. I have to be going. I'm directing the news in an hour's time.' I paused at the door, turning to offer my hand. 'Thanks for being so patient, Mr Marmot. I realise this must be very difficult for you.' He waved my apology aside. Glancing back as I reached the front door, I saw him leaning in the entrance to his office, watching me sadly.

As I drove back to the studios, I reflected on our meeting. The whole thing had made me feel uncomfortable although I couldn't say exactly why. Perhaps it was because I wasn't used to seeing men I hardly knew weeping in front of me.

The news programme went very smoothly that evening, which was fortunate because my mind wasn't on the job. My head was still reeling with facts and unanswered questions as I set off for home.

So I was caught offguard when I heard voices as I opened the back door and realised Lucinda had a visitor. I didn't feel like polite conversation so I simply nodded and smiled to the rather overweight woman sitting at the kitchen table.

'Bel, this is June Evans, Alan's cousin.' Lucinda rushed forward to make the introductions. She turned away from June towards me, so that I could catch the heavy emphasis of her expression as she added, 'Alan asked her to come round to plead his case.'

'Oh, Lucinda! You make me sound like some sort of do-gooder!' June had a soft, little-girl voice. I looked at her more carefully. She was probably about the same age as Lucinda and me, in her mid-thirties, I'd have guessed. Her short brown hair was layered and curled softly about

48

her face. She wore glasses and had a round face and her clothes were rather frumpy. But there was a sincerity in her myopic expression which could not be missed.

'You know, Harry and I fight,' she continued earnestly. 'Sometimes we have terrible rows. But we always make it up. Someone, I think it was the wife of an American President or something, said that you should never let the sun go down on your wrath and I believe—'

'June.' Lucinda cut her short. 'That's it. No discussion. No negotiation. Nothing. I'm getting a divorce from Alan.'

June looked crestfallen but Lucinda turned away, unbending. I was taken aback by this behaviour, because for all her brashness, Lucinda is usually quite gentle and sensitive in her dealings with those close to her.

'Would anyone like a cup of tea?' I asked tentatively. June nodded, apparently not daring to speak. Noisily, to cover the painful silence, I filled the kettle and switched it on, then opened the cupboard. It was bare. I stared at the empty space like some sort of mental defective.

'Lucinda, do you know if there are any clean mugs or cups anywhere?' I queried delicately.

Lucinda shrugged, unrepentant. 'I used the last one this afternoon.'

'Oh well,' I said cheerily, ever the little homemaker, 'I'll just wash some up.' Since there was still silence, I chattered away nervously to June, who seemed gradually to be recovering her composure. 'Our cleaning lady, Caroline, has been off ill for the last four weeks and I come and go at such odd hours and Lucinda's been frantic studying for her exams so the housework has just been let go. It's all a bit of a mess.' I dried the three mugs I had just washed.

'I could come in a couple of times a week, if you like, just to tide you over,' June offered in a tiny, tentative voice, peeking sideways at Lucinda.

I stared at her. This was such an unexpected solution to all our problems. It had already occurred to me that it was one thing for Lucinda and me to muddle along like this, but if I was supposed to be responsible for a child, things would have to improve. Before I said anything, I glanced instinctively at Lucinda, mindful that she might consider such an arrangement akin to having an enemy agent in the house.

To my surprise she was smiling as she said, 'Oh June, that would be great! What do you think, Bel?' I nodded, too amazed to speak. Lucinda turned back to June. 'Even a couple of weeks would be a help,' she said with enthusiasm. 'My exams should be over by the end of the month and I can cope after that.'

June smiled happily, looking pleased. 'Oh, don't worry, it's no trouble. It'll keep me busy. It gets a bit lonely sometimes during the day – especially if Harry's working away from home.' Her eye strayed to the clock on the wall. 'Actually, I think I'd better go. I'd no idea it was so late. Harry said he'd be home around eight and he likes me there when he gets in.'

She rose heavily to her feet and smiled at me. 'I'll start tomorrow if you like.'

'Great!' I watched as Lucinda showed her to the door.

'You were a bit snappy with her, weren't you?' I commented on her return.

Lucinda groaned. 'Yes, I know. You're right.' She sank into a chair. 'I feel guilty about that now. It's just that I can't deal with any mention of Alan. Do you know,' her voice rose indignantly, 'I finally managed to have a coffee alone with that guy I'm keen on – his name's Ian, by the way. We were just getting along nicely and things were warming up and I actually think he would have asked me out but then, would you believe, there's this rapping on the glass. We were sitting at a window table in that café opposite the university, and when I looked round, there was Alan! Next thing I know he comes in, introduces himself as my husband and sits down!' Her voice was so high it was squeaky. 'I couldn't believe it. Then Ian said he had to go, and left before I had a chance to explain. I could kill Alan.'

'No reason to take it out on June,' I persisted. 'She seems such a nice woman.'

'She is,' agreed Lucinda, remorsefully. 'Alan should have married someone like her instead of me.'

'Nah!' I said, opening the fridge door to inspect the contents. 'Alan loves you *because* you're bloody-minded.'

'She was the only one to welcome me into the family,' Lucinda continued. 'Maybe because she was a bit of an outcast herself. She never had any boyfriends, so they made fun of her a lot. Until she met Harry.'

The fridge was empty. 'Is there anything at all in this house I could eat for supper?' I asked hopefully.

'Nope,' replied Lucinda emphatically. Then, as an afterthought she opened a cupboard. 'Crisps,' she suggested and tossed a large packet of her favourite food onto the table.

I rolled my eyes. 'Looks like it's pizza again.' I reached for the wall phone and called in our usual order.

'It's great about June being willing to help out,' I remarked as I sat down again at the table.

'What? Oh yeh.' Lucinda nodded. 'I'm not surprised she's bored though. June's a smart cookie, really. She used to be head bookkeeper at Lorimer's. Harry persuaded her to give it up.'

'Why?' My willpower dissolved and I reached for the packet of crisps. 'Have they got kids?'

Lucinda winced. 'For God's sake, don't ask her about that. June had a miscarriage last year. They're desperate

51

to have a baby. Harry was brought up in an orphanage so I think he's really keen to have a family of his own. He wants June to be at home, to be Mummy and keep the hearth warm and look after the kiddies – only no kiddies.'

The doorbell rang. 'That was fast.' I stood up and walked down the hall to the front door, but when I opened it, I was confronted not by mushroom and anchovy pizza, but by Caroline and a small fair-haired boy.

'Hello,' she said uncertainly. She placed a hand on top of the blond head. 'This is George.' George didn't look up, so I couldn't see his face. He was small, wearing a grey sweatshirt advertising some American football team, black jeans and black basketball boots with the tops unlaced. There was a plastic bag hanging from one wrist and both arms cradled a wooden box which had slats halfway along one side.

'Come in.' I stood aside to let them pass, closing the door behind them. 'Lucinda, George is here!' I yelled as I ushered them towards the kitchen.

'Go on.' Caroline was nudging George ahead of her. At each push, he would be jolted another step along the hall, before stalling until his mother shoved him again. With great reluctance, he stepped into the kitchen, dragging his feet. He shot me a covert glance, but looked back down at his shoes again the instant he caught my eye. I had a glimpse of a small round face with a pink and white complexion. The blue eyes behind wire-rimmed glasses held together by sticky tape at the bridge were full of suspicion.

'Say hello,' Caroline prompted him anxiously.

George bit his lower lip and stubbed his toe into the floor tiles.

'I'm terribly sorry. He's not usually so awful,' Caroline apologised.

'Yes, I am!' George's face shot up and he stared at me defiantly.

I started to laugh. It was all coming back to me. I could remember behaving like this when I was first taken to the children's home after my mother's death.

'Well, that's a relief,' I said. 'I was worried I was going to get some boring little idiot.' George eyed me up, as if trying to assess whether or not I was serious.

'What's this?' I asked, pointing to the box he still cradled in his arms.

'It's Chipper,' George replied, scowling at me.

'It's his white mouse.' Caroline was wringing her hands with anxiety. 'Barbara said he could leave it at Billy's but he insisted . . .' she tailed off, looking at me beseechingly.

'Chipper stays with me,' George stated belligerently. I looked down into the small face. He was still scowling, but there was anxiety in the eyes behind the round glasses.

'That's fine,' I said.

Something softened in George's expression. 'He can stay in my room,' he offered.

'Okay. Come on and I'll show you where it is.' I picked up the holdall his mother had dropped on the floor and led the way upstairs. Caroline trailed behind us.

'What does Chipper eat?' I asked conversationally.

'Crisps. And cheese,' answered George. He moved his arm so that the plastic bag rustled. 'I've brought the cheese.'

I opened the door to the bedroom on the landing next to mine. It was quite small, with a window looking out to the back. George stood in the doorway, surveying it. Then he turned and walked out onto the landing again.

'What's upstairs?' he asked, beginning to mount the next flight leading to the attic.

'Upstairs?' I was taken by surprise. 'Oh, nothing. That's where my husband Jamie used to do his painting.'

George paused and looked down at me through the bannisters.

'Where is he now?'

'Jamie?' I was nonplussed. Most people tiptoed delicately around the subject of my husband. 'He's dead,' I said.

'What from?' George had reached the top of the stairs and was leaning over the railings.

I swallowed. 'Cancer.'

'Hmm.' He gazed at me for a moment without changing his expression, then abruptly turned away and disappeared. I decided I'd better follow. Caroline had sunk onto the bed in the room behind me and looked too tired to move. When I reached the top of the stairs, George was already inspecting Jamie's studio.

It was a large room which covered almost the entire area of the house. The ceiling towards the front was sloping, with three large skylights set into it at intervals. On the other side, windows had been built out overlooking the back garden so that the ceiling was level.

I walked slowly across the wooden floor. I rarely came up here. The cream walls were covered with Jamie's big bold brightly-coloured paintings. His easel and a box containing tubes and tins of paint lay abandoned near one window, next to a folding stool. At the far end, against the gable, was a divan. Everything had been left pretty much as it had been when my husband had died two years before.

'I think I'll stay here,' said George decisively.

I stared at him for a moment, shocked. I looked around the room. Suddenly I realised that it didn't really matter any more. I could hold onto my memories without this.

'Okay,' I agreed and was rewarded with a brilliant smile.

Chapter Five

The next morning was a bit of a shock to my system. I generally have enough trouble getting myself out of bed and off to work on time without having to worry about anyone else. George wasn't keen on getting up either so we were a lethal combination. I ended up flying out of the house with wet hair, wearing a tracksuit I'd pulled on hurriedly and dragging George after me. We skidded to a stop outside his school twenty minutes late.

'This is all your fault,' he admonished me indignantly. 'You'd better come in and explain.' I hadn't planned on appearing in public that morning until I'd at least had a chance to dry my hair, but I was so intimidated that I followed him in meekly and apologised to his teacher.

So I was really late by the time I finally left for work after rushing back home and pulling on an ankle-length linen skirt and a soft cotton sweater. Racing down the path towards the lane, I heard someone call my name. June was clambering out of a small red van. I suddenly recalled Lucinda saying that her husband ran a carpet and upholstery cleaning business. As I turned back to meet her, a middle-aged man emerged from the driver's side.

'This is Harry.' She introduced him proudly as I reached them. 'He had a job nearby first thing this morning so he came back to give me a lift here.' She beamed at him fondly as he came around the car, holding out his hand to me.

He was average height, certainly smaller than June,

and a little bit tubby. His brown hair was thinning, but he had swept it back in an Elvis-type quiff. There was something rather childish and vulnerable about that, as if he were drawing attention to his weak spot by the care he took to disguise it.

His shoes were polished to a high shine and he had on a dark-blue suit which gave him a businesslike air in spite of the fact that it was obviously well-worn. A large gold signet ring completed the impression of a dapper and genial middle-aged man.

'Pleased to meet you.' He smiled as he shook hands. 'June's told me a lot about you girls. Sounds as though you've got yourselves in a bit of a muddle.' I felt indignant. He made us sound like flighty teenagers, which wasn't how *I* perceived us to be. But Harry continued with the professional breeziness of a born salesman.

'I'll come along some time and give your carpets a going-over, if you like. I do cars as well – I've got contracts with a couple of garages downtown. I do their valet service for them. You can set it up with my Junie Moon here.' He glanced at his watch, brisk and efficient. 'Well, must be going.' He had started to turn away when his attention was caught by my TR6, which was standing in the lane.

'That's a nice old banger you've got there,' he remarked with interest. He walked across and leaned on the fence to inspect it. 'Bet there's a bit of oomph in that.'

June sighed. 'Harry's mad about cars.' She'd caught up with him and now she put her arm through his as if to restrain him. 'Especially the fast kind, isn't that right?' She gave him a playful nudge. 'You've always hankered after a sports car, haven't you? Just a little boy at heart.' She spoke with coy indulgence.

Harry laughed self-consciously. 'One of these days,

perhaps.' He looked at me, his eyes shining with enthusiasm. 'I sometimes get to borrow one of the high-powered models to take it for a spin. I had a Cosworth out the other week.' He shook his head in wonderment at the memory. 'That is some car, let me tell you.' Then he seemed to snap out of the reverie. 'Well, I must be getting back to work. Bye, Junie Moon.' He kissed his wife and with a cheery wave of the hand he trotted across the lawn, got back into his van and drove off.

Personally, I'd have been mortified if anyone had called me a name like that in public, but June looked radiantly happy and completely unself-conscious as she turned to me.

'Is there a key I could have?'

Quickly, I scrabbled under a flowerpot near the back door – the sort of hiding place any self-respecting burglar would head straight for – and handed her a set of keys. Then I left her to it and raced off to RTV for my meeting with Mags.

She was waiting for me, bright-eyed and full of enthusiasm – happier than I'd seen her for weeks. Obviously being out of the newsroom was doing the trick. Briefly, I filled her in on my conversation with Andrew Marmot. She frowned as I described his tearfulness.

'D'you think he's involved in the murder?'

I made a face. 'I don't think so. There was just something about him that seemed funny to me, that's all. In any case, surely he'd have been top of the police list of suspects. Whatever else we may say about old Sykes, I bet nothing much gets past him.'

Mags nodded in grudging agreement and we moved on to discussing what we would do that day. In the end, we decided to take Sykes' advice and get caught up on the background.

'Let's start at the place where she lived,' I suggested. A couple of phone calls later we were on our way.

59

The Convent of the Order of St Angela turned out to
be a substantial stone house set in a large garden, in a
residential area to the west of the city, not far from my
home. We were shown into a reception room on the right
of the main entrance, to wait for the Mother Superior. We
wandered around, examining our surroundings, talking
in whispers. Everything was spotless, but comfortable.
There were big chintz-covered armchairs and a green
and gold patterned carpet on the floor. Reproductions of
landscapes and still-lifes hung on the wall, and crocheted
mats adorned several of the smaller tables. But there was
none of the personal detritus one finds in a home – no
magazines or books lying around half-read, no bowl of
fruit on the table or knitting stashed down the side of
a chair.

'A bit institutional,' commented Mags in a whisper and
I nodded as the door opened and a small sprightly woman
of about seventy entered the room. She had soft white
hair gathered into a loose bun at the nape of her neck
and a calm, sweet face which was belied by her quick
impatient movements and bright blue eyes. She wore a
pleated skirt of some dark material and a bottle-green
high-necked blouse and navy cardigan. Like Sister Kate,
she could have been any older woman one might see in
the street.

This, we learned, was the Mother Superior, Sister
Pauline. When she heard why we were there, she was
cautious in her response, but agreed tentatively to answer
our questions.

To our surprise, it turned out that Sister Kate had been
one of the youngest members of the convent. Most of
the nuns had taken it very badly because of this, Sister
Pauline told us. They looked on Kate as the youngster in
the group and had all expected she would outlive them.
Her death had upset them greatly.

'Some of the very elderly ones haven't been told all the

details,' the Mother Superior confided in a low voice as she led us upstairs to view Sister Kate's room. This turned out to be tiny, barely furnished with a single bed, a small chest of drawers and narrow closet. It was scrupulously neat and anonymous and offered no clues to the character of Sister Kate, never mind why she was killed. Sister Pauline showed us back downstairs to her office.

'She was a teacher at the church school for a long time, wasn't she?' I asked when we were seated. 'Did any of the pupils have grudges? Children do sometimes.'

'No.' Sister Pauline shook her head slowly. 'She loved children and they loved her. They sensed her gentleness. They used to go to her with their problems or to confess when they'd done something wrong because they knew she would plead their case for them. She had no enemies.'

Mags spoke up. 'The office door should have been locked but there was no sign of forced entry. The police think she may have known her attacker.'

Sister Pauline sighed. 'She was the kind of person who would never bar the door against anyone. The police say she didn't put up any fight; there's no skin under her fingernails or something – I don't know how they work these things out.' She tossed a hand dismissively. 'But she wouldn't. She would have tried to talk to him, she would have prayed for his salvation, she would have done anything except lift a finger to do him the slightest harm.'

We sat in silence for a moment, digesting this information. I was overwhelmed once more by the senselessness of this crime. Then I broached the delicate subject of permission to film in the convent and to interview the Mother Superior herself. She seemed reluctant at first, and it was only when we assured her that our treatment would not be in any way salacious that she agreed to cooperate. I promised that one of us would phone soon to set up a time. As we were leaving I paused on the threshold.

'Did Sister Kate have friends outside the convent?'

Sister Pauline smiled and nodded. 'Kate did have one special friend – a Mrs Bellamy. She and Kate started working at the school around the same time. They were a bit younger than the rest of us and they got along really well. Mrs Bellamy lives at 35 Ronan Street. I'm sure she'd be happy to talk to you.'

As she saw us out, I noticed that the hand holding the door open was trembling and I felt a wave of sympathy wash over me. This was no superhuman icon, only an old woman who had lost someone very dear to her in a vicious and horrific manner.

The door to number 35 Ronan Street was opened on the first knock. Louise Bellamy had the sort of shape a child might draw for a woman – a series of intersecting circles. Her thick, bushy grey hair had been cut into a neat arc framing a round pink face. Her upper torso formed a soft curve fitting into the wider circle of her hips draped in a full skirt. Tiny feet in lace-up shoes peeked out from underneath the hem.

I introduced both of us, proffering my RTV staff card as proof, and asked if we might talk to her about a programme we were working on. She peered intently at the I.D. card for a moment, then nodded decisively, handing it back to me.

'This way.' Hobbling ahead of us at great speed, she led us into a chilly front sitting room which looked as if it were rarely used. She lowered herself into an over-stuffed armchair while we perched on the sofa. She blinked at us from behind her pink-rimmed glasses.

Quickly, I explained why we were there.

'Can you think of anyone who might have committed this crime?' I was beginning to get tired of asking that question everywhere we went.

Mrs Bellamy pursed her lips. 'The police asked me that. I told them there was only one boy I could think of, years ago, that was punished by Sister Kate and who took it badly. She caught him trying to molest one of the younger girls and reported him to the headmistress. It could just have been normal teenage experimentation, I suppose – we were a lot more narrow-minded in those days than they are now. But he was furious with her. I think he was expelled.'

'Can you remember his name?' Mags was sitting on the edge of her seat.

Mrs Bellamy shook her head. 'It was years ago. Twenty, maybe thirty years perhaps. I can't remember much about him. Although . . .' She paused, struck by some thought. 'There just might . . .' She pushed herself up out of her seat and walked heavily across the room to a bureau. From one of the drawers she pulled out an old photograph album covered in leather which had cracked and grown furry with time. She came over to us, turning pages.

'Here we are. I'd forgotten about this. The police were after any recent pictures but this one is so old I didn't bother showing it to them.' She tilted the book towards us, pointing to a black and white snapshot. 'That was taken when we had an epidemic of mumps at the school and I was rushed off my feet nursing the children who were in the Home. I don't know if anyone's explained to you, but there was a residential part of Saint Xavier's as well as day pupils. I was Matron for the orphans who lived there and Kate came and helped every moment she could.'

I leaned forward to stare at the picture, taken in what looked like a small hospital ward. A group of six boys aged from about eight to twelve were ranged on top of a bed with two young women standing alongside them. I recognised a much slimmer and younger version of Mrs Bellamy and the now familiar fresh-faced image of Sister Kate. She had hardly changed over the years.

Mrs Bellamy had taken the book back to scrutinise the photograph more closely. She ran a finger along the row of boys. 'There – that's him. But don't ask me his name because I couldn't tell you.' She handed the book back, keeping one finger on the photograph. I peered at the boy she was pointing out and my heart sank. It was a tiny image. Perhaps if one knew the child well, one could identify him from this picture. But I could not imagine anyone being able to use this as a means to track down an adult man who must now be in his thirties or forties.

I glanced at the other photographs on the page. Sister Kate appeared in all of them. There was a full-length Polaroid snapshot which was rather blurry and a copy of the photograph of Sister Kate receiving the cheque. Gently I handed the album back to Mrs Bellamy.

'I hope they catch whoever did this.'

We didn't linger, although I got the impression that Mrs Bellamy would have liked us to stay. It occurred to me that she must be rather lonely since her retirement.

I had to rush back for the lunchtime news after that, but we agreed that Mags would spend the afternoon researching Sister Kate's background – where she was born, who her parents were, that sort of thing – as well as checking the local newspaper files for any stories about her.

As soon as I escaped from the gallery, I contacted Sykes and got his grudging consent to follow some of his officers around the next day. He suggested we start in the Incident Room, then accompany two of the inquiry team who were interviewing clients at the Centre. He threw in the added carrot that the crime scene had been released and we could have a look at that.

Then I tackled Martin. I knew he was having to juggle budgets, but he agreed to hire a freelance crew for the next day and promised that if I would just cover the evening news for one more night he would find a replacement.

It was after four by the time I returned to the newsroom. Trevor was striding about importantly, issuing orders, a cigarette hanging from the side of his mouth in spite of our recently agreed no smoking policy.

'Bel!' he shouted across the room as soon as he caught sight of me. 'Big story just broke! Councillor Stevenson has been arrested on fraud charges. More arrests expected within the hour, according to my sources.' He paused to let this triumph sink in. 'I'm about to change the running order, just to warn you.'

Inwardly I groaned. This sounded depressingly familiar. All around me, there was an air of frantic chaos. Trevor strode up and down the centre of the newsroom, like some animal trainer, whipping his team to greater effort. Everything he said was yelled at the top of his voice, which only added to the general atmosphere of stress.

Eventually, I escaped downstairs to the gallery to begin preparations for the evening news. Trevor sailed in with one minute to go, tossing the last pages of the script in our direction. We launched into the programme. Trevor seemed excited. He kept intervening, giving directions over the talkback and chopping and changing the running order and the length of time we stayed on each item. It was only with great difficulty that we were able to keep up with his demands. Finally we reached the last story and I gave the cue to roll tape.

'We're out of time.' There was a note of panic in Viv's voice. I looked at her in alarm. One of the production assistant's tasks is to keep a running tally of how long we've been on-air and how much time we've got left. Viv was one of the best at the job.

'I've been totting up the figures, Trevor,' she said hurriedly. 'We've been jumping about so much I didn't get a chance before. We have to come out of this in thirty seconds.'

'Rubbish. We'll miss the most important bit,' Trevor spat back. He gestured grandly towards the on-air monitor. 'Carry on!'

'We can't.' I was aghast. 'It's a network show after this, Trevor. We have to end on the dot.'

'Stuff it!' Trevor looked furious. 'I'll decide what's important around here and this story—' I opened my mouth to interrupt. At that moment our news programme was replaced in mid-sentence by the opening titles of the gameshow which blared out through the gallery.

From the corner of my eye, I saw Gary buckle over and lay his head on top of the vision mixing board. Viv looked devastated. I turned to Trevor. Stabbing a finger in my direction he stood up and ground out through gritted teeth, 'You did that! You bitch! You did that!'

I shook my head. 'You don't understand, Trevor. The transmission controller is under instructions to go to the network show at specified times. He has no choice. It's up to us to make sure we finish our programme in time, otherwise we get cut off like just now.' The phone rang. I picked it up and before the person on the other end could get a word in I said, 'It's all right. We're on our way up.'

There was a pause, then Martin's voice, 'Too bloody right you are! All of you, I want to see all of you, including Viv.' I replaced the receiver slowly and turned to pass on the message. Trevor had already left the room.

Viv was gathering together stray pages of script. 'This can't go on,' she muttered.

'Oh, I wouldn't bank on it,' I said sourly, stuffing a sheaf of paper into the bin. We trooped up to Martin's office in silence. Trevor wasn't there. One by one, we gave as neutral an account of what had happened as we could. Martin made no comment, but I knew he would draw his own conclusions.

The first floor was deserted as I returned to my office. I felt unsettled. None of us liked being involved in a duff programme, no matter whose fault it was. As I was passing the newsroom, I heard the indistinct tones of an angry voice. Filled with curiosity, I stuck my head round the door. The main room was empty, but the door to Trevor's office was open and he was pacing up and down, clutching the telephone receiver to his ear, his back towards me.

'You should have seen the look on the bitch's face, Tigger, when she said,' his voice went into a falsetto, '"oh no, you can't do that!" I told her I can do—' he turned and spotted me standing in the doorway of the outer office. His expression changed.

'What d'ye want?' he barked.

I waved in a deprecating manner, like it was nothing really and withdrew hurriedly. But I found that little episode disturbing. Everyone knew that Tigger was a columnist for the local newspaper. As well as a daily opinion piece, he also wrote a weekly gossip column under the heading *Behind the Lines*. This had successfully destroyed the careers of sundry local people, by a process of innuendo and veiled accounts of incidents better left forgotten. I was pretty sure Trevor had been referring to me in his conversation with Tigger and it bothered me. The last thing I needed was to have my professional reputation attacked in print.

I didn't have time to dwell on it, however. George was in great spirits when I picked him up. He had just acquired a treasure trove of back issues of the *Beano* and the *Dandy* from Billy and he insisted on reading me all the best bits on the way home. They were the oldest, corniest jokes in the world with punchlines even I remembered from my childhood, but George's delight in them was infectious and we were both howling with laughter as I turned into my street.

Someone was standing at the front door, but we had sailed past and into the lane leading to my garage before I could register more than that the figure was male. The back door wasn't locked, which should have meant that Lucinda was home, but the doorbell was being rung insistently and there was no rush of footsteps overhead to indicate she had heard it. I walked through the house and opened the front door. The man leaning on the bell jumped in surprise. Evidently, he no longer expected anyone to answer.

'Alan!' I was almost as taken aback as he was.

'Bel!' He pulled himself together quickly. 'I wanted to talk to Lucinda. I know she's in there.'

'She can't be.' I looked puzzled. 'Surely she'd have answered the door if she'd been here. Perhaps she's popped out to the shops for a few minutes.' There was a pause. Alan stood there resolutely. It was clear he had no intention of leaving without seeing Lucinda. 'Would you like to come in for a drink or something?' I asked weakly.

He followed me into the kitchen with alacrity. George had settled down at the kitchen table, busying himself with crayons and a drawing he produced from his satchel.

Just then there was the sound of someone coming downstairs and Lucinda entered. Alan looked triumphant.

'I knew you were here all along. I just knew it.'

'Well, maybe it should have dawned on you that I didn't want to see you then,' returned Lucinda acidly.

A pleading look came into Alan's face. 'I just wanted to talk.'

'There's nothing to say.'

'Well, I've got things to say.'

'Forget it, Alan. It's over. Nothing will persuade me

to go back to you so give it a rest, for your own sake as well as mine.' Alan made as if to say something in reply but Lucinda cut him off before he got a word out. 'Stop hounding me!' she shouted. 'I've got enough to worry about without having you pestering the life out of me.' She turned and left the room, slamming the door. We could hear her feet pounding up the stairs.

There was an awkward silence. I was completely non plussed. I knew that Lucinda was worried about her exams, but clearly she must be feeling the pressure far more than I'd realised. Alan looked devastated. George was watching him in shocked horror. Then, with the instinct of a child used to taking responsibility for the adults around him, he thrust the picture he had been drawing in front of Alan.

'Look at this,' he commanded.

With difficulty, Alan brought his attention to bear on the sheet of paper in front of him. 'What's that?' he asked with a faint show of interest.

'A badger.' George couldn't keep the note of pride out of his voice. Alan swallowed hard, obviously trying to get a grip on himself.

'Oh yes, so it is,' he murmured feebly. Then with an attempt at conversation: 'There used to be a badger's sett just out back here in the wood behind Bel's house.'

George's eyes opened wide. He half got up out of his chair as if he couldn't wait to go and look. 'Where?' he asked excitedly.

Alan smiled in spite of himself. 'I could show you sometime. You have to know exactly where to look or you'd never find it. Although I don't know if they're still there any more.'

George stood up and pulled at his jacket. 'Can we go now?'

'Now?' Alan was incredulous. 'It's far too late. It

69

must be nearly your bedtime and I must be getting along.'

George made a face and began to wail. 'Oh please! Please!' pulling at Alan's sleeve as he tried to leave.

'Look, I'll come back another time,' he said placatingly, trying to loosen George's grip.

'When?' George let go and fixed him with an intense look.

'Oh, sometime when I'm not so busy,' said Alan vaguely. He reached the door and stopped as if something had just struck him. Turning to me he asked, 'Lucinda doesn't have classes on Saturday, does she?'

I shrugged. 'Not as far as I know.'

He smiled and turned to George. 'How about Saturday morning then?'

'Great!' I had never seen George look like this. He was an entirely different child, bright-eyed and smiling.

'Done!' Alan opened the door to leave, then paused one last time. 'Er, don't mention this to Lucinda,' he said, giving me a cunning look. Inwardly I groaned as I closed the door after him. I really didn't want to get in the middle of this.

Chapter Six

I met the crew and Mags at Police Headquarters next day and we set up in a corner of the Incident Room. For the next few hours, we tried to capture a sense of the frantic activity going on as well as the unremitting clerical work and sifting of information which was so vital to the progress of the inquiry.

The investigation had obviously calmed down a lot in the last couple of days, however. By mid-morning, most of the inquiry team were out on assignments and the only people around were the office administrator and the four people still glued to their computer terminals.

The results of the post mortem had come back the previous day, and PC Burke quickly drew them to our attention. Sister Kate had died some time between eleven and noon on the day her body was found. She had been raped then strangled with her own belt. Tests on the semen had revealed little except that her attacker had an extremely low sperm count – so low as to make him effectively sterile. The nun's hands had initially been clamped behind her back by something hard. The pathologist had suggested handcuffs, but whatever it was had been removed before the body was discovered.

As the Mother Superior had said, no skin had been found under the victim's fingernails, suggesting that Sister Kate had not put up a fight. The only other possible evidence which the forensic team had uncovered were a few strands of hair caught in her watch strap and some fibres from the carpet. The latter were dark blue and of a cotton and nylon mix that might have come from the sort of fabric used for overalls, apparently. That, as Sykes pointed out tiredly when I mentioned it to him, could mean it had been left by anyone from the plumber to the window cleaner. It was anybody's guess. They were trying to trace everyone who had been in the office over the past few weeks. As a final blow, the forensic report concluded that there were no fingerprints or footprints which could not be accounted for by the other people who also used the office regularly.

There seemed little point in hanging around the Incident Room so we decided to head down to the drop-in centre and follow a couple of young detectives around, to get a feel for the routine legwork which is the staple of most investigations. As we were leaving, I stood aside to let someone enter the Incident Room. To my surprise, I recognised Alan and I suddenly recalled seeing his name on the board.

'How's Lucinda?' he asked abruptly, tapping a sheaf of papers restlessly against the doorframe.

I shrugged. 'She's fine.'

He batted me lightly on the shoulder. 'Tell her I haven't given up. I always get my girl.' And with a conspiratorial wink, he hurried off towards the computer terminals.

We arrived at the drop-in centre to find that the two officers had commandeered Andrew's small office and were conducting interviews. Although most of the staff had already given statements, it was thought that some of the clients had stayed away because of the publicity and might show up today.

They began questioning a group of young people one at a time. Some of them were listless, others could barely keep still and seemed on the verge of falling apart. None of them had any useful information to give. They had seen nothing, they didn't know anyone who might have wanted to steal money from Sister Kate or hurt her and they personally hadn't been anywhere near the scene of the crime whenever it happened. To their credit, the two young detectives kept at it, trying to establish the whereabouts of each of them at the time of the murder, long after I had become bored.

I released the crew to go for a late lunch across the road. Mags rushed off to do some shopping, so I wandered out of the building and round the back to the staircase leading to the murder scene. A young policeman still stood guard, but the yellow tape had been cut, one end flapping aimlessly from the metal bannister.

I was allowed to pass after identifying myself and mounted the stairs. The glass-panelled door stood partially open. There was very little space inside. From the threshhold I could see that a white dust covered everything – something to do with their search for fingerprints, as I recalled. Opposite the door was an old fireplace and in front of that a large battered wood desk. On the wall to the left was a window and to the right of the desk, a filing cabinet. I knew from the photographs that that was where Sister Kate's body had been found lying.

As I entered the room, I became aware of a young woman standing there, half-hidden behind the open door. She was holding a couple of files as she turned to gaze at me, her face expressionless.

'Can I help you?' she asked politely. 'Are you something to do with the police? You shouldn't be here if you're not, you know.'

She was very young, perhaps about nineteen, with straight brown hair cut in an old-fashioned boy's short back and sides. Her brown eyes were full of suspicion. Quickly, I filled her in on why I was there.

She held out her hand. 'My name's Tammy Soames. I'm Andrew's assistant.' She seemed remarkably calm and detached as she looked around the room, surveying the damage. 'I was away when this happened. I just got back. I've been tidying up. Andrew couldn't face it.'

My curiosity was aroused. 'Was anything taken from the cabinet?'

She grimaced. 'I've no idea. Everything in there belongs to Andrew. He always keeps it locked and carries the keys with him so I don't even know what was there. It was probably just paperwork. But there are some files missing, I think.' She pulled out one of the drawers and rifled through it. I leaned forward to look.

'See,' she said, pointing. 'This lot are all labelled alphabetically. But a couple of them are gone. B,' she flipped through some more before adding, 'D and M.' She slammed the drawer shut and turned to me with a resigned expression. 'But it's Andrew's stuff and he insists nothing was taken, so who am I to argue?'

I eyed her speculatively. 'The police think whoever did it got the keys from the desk,' I said.

She looked at me oddly. 'Who told them that?'

'Andrew.'

She considered for a moment, then shrugged dismissively. 'Perhaps he just thought it would complicate matters if he said he had the only keys.'

I could hear a car horn sounding from down below and voices yelling my name. The crew and Mags were back from their break and were waiting to leave for Police Headquarters.

We arrived at the Incident Room just in time for the daily briefing. About thirty people crowded in, many perched on desks because there weren't enough chairs. Sykes himself led the meeting, covering all the lines of inquiry one by one and allowing everyone to report back on the results of their investigations.

One team of detectives had finished questioning all the people who worked in the vicinity of the drop-in centre but had come up with nothing, apart from a vague description of some man who might have been seen running along a nearby street around the time of the murder, wearing dark clothing and carrying a balaclava. None of Sister Kate's friends or contacts had been able to provide any clue as to who might have killed her.

As the meeting progressed, it became clear that no motive for the crime had been revealed and there was no evidence pointing to a suspect. You could tell from the faces of those involved that they were baffled. As there were no solid leads to follow up on, it was decided that only a skeleton team would continue working over the weekend and that they would start afresh on Monday with a brainstorming session.

Before the detectives had a chance to disappear, we did some impromptu interviews with a few of them, to record just what it felt like to be at this stage of an investigation with very little to show for all their hard work.

'It's so bloody frustrating,' one detective told us, his voice thick with anger. 'The victim didn't deserve this and we want to catch the bastard who did it. Some of us were taught by Sister Kate, you know – Alan was, and Gerry was as well. I don't think anyone will rest easy till he's caught.'

It was a relief to go and pick up George. It was amazing how quickly I had adjusted to the routine of looking after him. To my own surprise, I had even begun to look forward to our evenings together. Instead of brooding on whatever problems the day had thrown up, I now found myself being sucked into the latest hare-brained scheme occupying him. All the way home, I was entertained by his account of the football match he had played in that afternoon, followed by his and Billy's attempts to teach Chipper to speak.

When we arrived home, he bounded into the house

ahead of me and disappeared up to his room to see
Chipper. Halfway through my preparations for supper,
the telephone rang. It was Mags and she was furious.
'That bastard!'

'What's happened?' I asked, cradling the phone between
the side of my head and my shoulder as I drained a pan
of green beans.

'Have you seen tonight's paper?'

I put the pan down abruptly, filled with foreboding.
'No, why? It's Tigger's column, isn't it? I heard Trevor
on the phone to him about us the other night.'

'Got it in one.' Mags' voice was bitter. 'What a low
scummy way to treat your colleagues! He doesn't have
the nerve to say it to our faces so he gets one of his
cronies to do a bit of character assassination.'

'What does he say?'

'Oh, just an account of what happened the other night
on the programme, blaming unspecified radical feminists
who've got it in for men. You'd better read it yourself.
I'm too angry to see straight.' There was the sound of a
child screaming in the background. 'I'd better go,' she
said hurriedly and hung up.

I replaced the receiver and walked through to the front
hall. Usually the evening paper lay on the carpet beneath
the letter box until such time as I got around to picking
it up. But tonight, there was nothing. Irritated, I tried
phoning the newsagents, but I knew even as I did so
that they would be closed for the night by now, so I
wasn't surprised when no one answered.

Lucinda was still at the library. On an impulse, I walked
to the foot of the stairs and called for George. I could hear
him scrambling across the upper floor and then a door
opening.

There was a pause followed by the sound of him
rumbling down the stairs. He appeared hanging over the
bannisters above me.

'I don't suppose you've seen the evening paper, have you?' I asked.

He nodded, then added in a burst of defensiveness, 'I needed it for Chipper. He needs paper for his nest and he likes newspaper because he can tear it up.' George looked at me with a mixture of defiance and fear.

I groaned.

'Can I see what's left?'

'It's upstairs.' George disappeared up to his room and I followed. Chipper was scurrying about his cage. My evening paper was in shreds. It would have been hard to find a whole word of print, never mind an entire column. With an effort, I pushed down my irritation.

'George,' I said. He looked up at me, near to tears. 'Will you promise me never ever to touch my paper again?' He nodded and a stray tear trickled down his cheek. I felt evil.

'I tell you what, why don't we go and get some ice cream?' I suggested. George cheered up instantly. We drove down to the beach and bought giant cones from the kiosk there.

'I'm probably completely undermining all your mother's careful training,' I said, between mouthfuls of ice cream. 'I'm sure all the books on bringing up children say you're not supposed to bribe them with stuff like this.'

There was silence for a while, broken only by the sound of George slurping away at his cone. He looked worried. Finally he turned to me and said, 'I think that's just for babies. Ice cream's fine if you're older.'

'Phew, that's a relief,' I said as I bit off the end of my cone and pistachio nut and coffee dribbled all down my T-shirt.

On Saturday morning, George banged on my bedroom door at 8.30 am demanding breakfast. God only knew how Mags managed with three little children. Salvation was at hand, however. At ten o'clock sharp, Alan arrived to go badger-hunting. He kept looking around as he waited in the kitchen, alert for any signs of life from upstairs.

'Lucinda around?' he finally asked, affecting an air of nonchalance I knew he did not feel.

'I think she's upstairs studying,' I said tactfully.

'She's not coming down until we've gone,' George added, eager to fill in all the gory details. 'She said she never wants to see you ever again.'

Alan snorted. 'Well, she won't get rid of me that easily.' He put one hand behind George's head and gently nudged him towards the door. 'Let's go.' I watched them disappear down the path. George was leaping about, full of excitement.

Since we were completely out of even the most basic necessities of life, I took the opportunity to go to the supermarket. I had tried that once already in George's company and ended up with a trolley full of things he wanted and none of the things we needed. Lucinda met me at the door as I returned and helped me carry in all the bags.

'Great! My favourites!' She pulled out a giant bag of crisps.

'Sorry.' I snatched them away. 'Those are for George.' Lucinda was about to protest when the back door opened and George and Alan came in, kicking the mud off their boots on the step.

'Any luck?' Somehow I could tell the answer from their glum expressions.

'Nothing conclusive, but we haven't given up yet,' said Alan. He paused as he caught sight of Lucinda. She scowled in return.

'We found some evidence of badgers being there,' said George importantly.

'Well . . .' Alan was less sure.

'What?' said Lucinda with heavy sarcasm. 'You mean

that with all those years of training as an ace detective, you couldn't find one poor little furry animal?'

Alan shot her a look of hatred.

'Well, we found some fur on a bush which we're sure is from a badger and Alan followed its tracks through the wood . . .' began George.

Lucinda snorted. George paused for a moment, to look at her in bewilderment, before continuing: 'The problem is that they probably only come out at night . . .'

'It's all right, George.' Alan put a hand on his fellow sleuth's shoulder in a gesture of solidarity. George looked at him in puzzlement, but Alan's attention was on Lucinda. Their eyes locked for a long moment. Then Alan said, without removing his gaze, 'I think we need to step up our surveillance operation, George.' Lucinda rolled her eyes and turned away.

'I could sit in a tree tonight and watch for them,' offered George.

'No, you couldn't,' I said bluntly.

'Yes, I can.' George's face was going red and he looked suddenly furious. 'If Mum was here, she'd let me.'

'No, she wouldn't.' Somewhere in a distant part of my mind I was quite shocked at how totalitarian I was becoming.

George looked as if he was going to carry this argument on to the bitter end, but just then Alan broke in. 'You know what I think, George? I think we should set up a surveillance camera overnight.' There was a howl of derision from Lucinda, but Alan merely took a deep breath and continued resolutely.

'I know this chap who runs a security firm and he owes me a favour. I'm sure they have some old cameras kicking around that they don't use any more. Harry could lend us some cables or maybe rig us up a power supply. He's good at that.'

'I'm off. I can't take any more of this.' The kitchen

door slammed and Lucinda was gone. She opened it again almost immediately and stuck her head back in. 'And if you think this is the way to win my heart, by using this poor little boy as a pawn, then you can think again.' The door slammed shut once more. Crockery rattled in the cupboards.

There was silence. George looked at Alan. For a split second I thought of stepping in and bringing the whole episode to a halt. But my resolve melted as I watched George's face. There was clearly a lot at stake for him in this project. At least it was taking his mind off his mother's situation.

'I tell you what,' said Alan. 'Why don't we go and get a burger then we can drive over to see the chap that's got the camera. Maybe we can get it all set up for tonight.'

'Whoopee!!' yelled George and raced for the door.

Almost two hours passed before they arrived back, accompanied by Harry. They were all carrying something. George and Alan had cardboard boxes in their arms and Harry was lugging a car battery which he dumped unceremoniously on the kitchen table. 'Phew!' He grinned at me.

'Look at this!' George was so excited he could hardly keep still. He had dragged a small object out of his box and now held it up for me to see. I realised with surprise that it was a camera.

Over the years television cameras have shrunk in size from monster machines which it took two or more grown men to trundle about, to hardware which can be toted for hours at a time on someone's shoulder. But the piece of equipment which George was holding was even smaller and apparently very light, because he was swinging it in one hand.

'It only weighs a pound!' he exclaimed excitedly as if he had read the unspoken question in my mind.

'The quality's not too hot, of course,' Alan broke in, 'but it'll do for our purposes.'

I continued to stare at the camera in amazement. 'How did you get this? It must be worth a fortune.'

A look of triumph flooded Alan's face. 'Got it for nothing. The owner of the company's an old friend of mine. He owed me one. Actually,' he shrugged self-deprecatingly, 'it's four or five years old and was about to be scrapped. They've got much newer and better models on the market now. Although,' he was quick to add, 'it can take pictures by starlight, it records for twenty-four hours on one tape and runs off a couple of car batteries.' As if on cue, the back door swung open again and Harry staggered in with a second battery, a rolled-up extension cable hung over one arm.

'Right,' he said cheerfully, 'let's see if this all works.'

I left them to it and wandered through to the sitting room to listen to a new CD I had just bought and to read the paper. Half an hour later, I heard the back door open. Leaning forward in my armchair so that I could peer out of the French windows, I saw the three of them trooping across the back garden and disappearing into the wood through a gate at the end.

I moved to the sofa and stretched out, listening to the music. But my mind was drawn back irresistibly to Sister Kate's death. I thought about what Tammy had told me and wondered if she had passed on the information about the filing-cabinet keys to the police also. I doubted it.

Supposing, I mused, Andrew *had* killed Sister Kate. His fingerprints and footprints in the room – indeed, all forensic evidence linked to him would not seem out of place. He used that office, after all, and he had found the body. Could he have opened the drawers and spilled out the contents to make it look like a burglary? Or could it just have been that, having discovered the body, he had removed items he didn't want the police to find, scattering files and leaving drawers askew in the process?

I heard the living-room door open behind me and something red whirled into the room. I raised myself up on one elbow and blinked. Lucinda was spinning around wearing a low-cut cotton dress with a long, full skirt. She looked like a gypsy dancer, with the deep red of the fabric accentuating the lustre of her thick dark hair.

'What d'you think?' She came to a stop before me, an expression of anxiety on her face.

'It's beautiful!' I replied. 'What's it for?'

Lucinda looked suddenly bashful. She couldn't meet my eye as she said, with forced casualness, 'I've finally got a date with Ian.' She laughed self-deprecatingly. 'We were the last ones to leave the library last night. I'd just about screwed up the nerve to suggest we go for a drink when he suddenly asked me out for dinner tonight.' She grinned at me, blushing happily.

'Christ, it's taken you long enough,' I said in mock reproof. 'Why don't you borrow my gold hoop earrings?'

Lucinda gave another swirl of her skirt. 'Thanks.' She stood still for a moment. 'You know, I'm really sorry about that outburst a little while ago. I shouldn't let you or George get caught in the middle. It's just that I don't want Alan hanging around here at any time, but especially not today. Goodness knows what would happen if he saw Ian when he comes to pick me up! I'm nervous enough about all this as it is.'

'Don't worry.' I tried to sound soothing. 'He'll be long gone before then. I'll make sure of it.'

Suddenly, we heard the back door slam and George calling for me at the top of his voice. Lucinda shot out of the room and disappeared upstairs as I walked through to the kitchen. George stood in the middle of the room covered in mud and with a hole torn in the knee of his jeans. He was beaming. 'Can we have something to drink?' he asked. 'We got the camera turned on and I have to collect the tape in the morning.'

'I'll come over tomorrow night to set it up again.' Alan looked at me as he said this. 'Tell Lucinda I was asking for her.' He ruffled George's hair. 'Well, I must be going.'

'Me too.' Harry was washing his hands at the sink. He dried them hurriedly and followed Alan to the back door. 'Nice kid that,' he said in a low voice as I let him out.

As soon as they had driven off, I gave Lucinda the all clear. I knew that Ian was coming to pick her up around seven, so I made sure that George was out of the way showing Billy the new camera setup. I couldn't resist loitering by the sitting-room window myself, however. Lucinda was so nervy she couldn't sit down.

'Oh God, why am I putting myself through this?' she moaned. Then, after pacing up and down for a couple of minutes, 'This dress is all wrong,' she announced and headed upstairs again.

'No, no, no.' I caught hold of her and dragged her back into the sitting room. 'You look fine. I can't believe this. I've never seen you in such a state before.'

'I've never seen myself in such a state before either,' wailed Lucinda. Then she caught my eye and laughed in spite of herself.

The doorbell rang. Through the window I could see a dark-haired man standing on the doorstep. He had an open, friendly sort of face and an air of calm about him. I glanced back at Lucinda. She looked as if she'd been electrocuted. But she grabbed her bag, gave me a quick kiss and prepared to leave.

'Don't I get to meet him?' I queried.

'Not this time.' She blew me another kiss and slipped out. Then she stuck her head back round the sitting-room door again. 'And no waiting up for me, okay?' she added pointedly, before disappearing again.

There wasn't much chance of that, as it turned out.

That evening I went to see a film at the local cinema with George and Billy and an old friend of mine called Charlie, who works as a male nurse. By the time it was over and we had said our goodbyes, I was so exhausted that I went straight to bed as soon as we got home. So I didn't see Lucinda until she appeared sometime after noon the following day. She had a blissful look on her face.

'Well, how was your evening?' I demanded.

'Okay,' she said, smiling dreamily. 'It was fine.' She wafted upstairs again, leaving me in an agony of curiosity.

After supper, I took George to visit his mother in hospital. We found her in a side ward containing four beds, the other three occupied by women apparently recovering from surgery. Caroline looked wan and exhausted. While George was fetching water for the flowers he'd brought her, she whispered to me that the results of her tests were not good. The doctors wanted her to stay in for a bit longer for some exploratory surgery. I watched her as she told me this. Both of us knew what that meant. They didn't undertake such things lightly; clearly they suspected something was seriously wrong. George was fine with me, I told her. It was fun having him around.

Shortly after we arrived home, Alan turned up to review their first tape. Billy appeared too, but Lucinda was conspicuously absent. Alan said nothing, although he seemed restless. The tape offered little to distract him. The black and white images were grainy and indistinct. We could make out several squirrels racing past and various small animals which none of us could identify except that whatever they were they weren't badgers.

Afterwards the two boys and Alan trooped outside carrying torches to set up the camera for that evening. When they returned, Alan seemed anxious to be gone. It came as no surprise that he announced as he was leaving that he wouldn't be able to come back the following night, that George might have to carry on the surveillance operation on his own for a bit, perhaps with Billy's help, because Alan was going to have to work overtime on this murder case. Then he left.

If Alan had given up, however, George had only just begun. He was full of hopes and dreams of what they might discover as I tucked him up in bed.

'I think I'll try another place,' he murmured thoughtfully. 'I've found another hole on the other side of the wood. Billy can help me move the camera.' He curled up under the duvet.

At least, I thought, he didn't seem to be worrying about his mum.

Chapter Seven

Over the next few days, I was pretty busy with my own filming. Mags and I worked well together. She is a born reporter and is in her element when, as now, there is a good story to work on. Her personal problems seemed to have receded also. Barry had backed down on the custody issue, she informed me briefly. It was a relief to have her back to her old cheerful, energetic self.

We set about recording interviews with all the key people involved in the investigation, including the woman who claimed to have seen a man carrying a balaclava running away from the scene of the crime, as well as Andrew Marmot, Sister Pauline and DCI Sykes.

In addition, we had spent days trailing various police officers around as they made inquiries, and we had filmed background material at the drug centre, the convent and the school. Mags had contacted Sister Kate's relatives in New Zealand and arranged for her niece to send copies of family photographs.

But the investigation was fast reaching a dead end and, like the police officers involved, we were running out of things to do next. I could envision us setting the project aside until something new turned up. Already we had begun preliminary research into a possible documentary on the kickback scandal, and Mags had been asked to work in the newsroom any time one of the other journalists was off.

At home, George, Lucinda and I had settled into a

routine. Lucinda still spent most of her time studying, but she seemed to be more relaxed. I got the chance to meet her new boyfriend one evening when she asked him to join us for dinner.

'It's like inviting him home to meet Ma and Pa,' she groaned after George had given her the third degree about Ian. But he turned out to be as likable as she had said and the two of them were clearly very comfortable in each other's company.

Lucinda and George had also discovered a shared passion for eating crisps and watching soap operas.

'Have you seen that mouse?' Lucinda asked incredulously one evening as I was making a vain attempt to cook some supper.

'What mouse?' I asked in tones of rising panic.

'George's,' she replied calmly. 'He's through in the sitting room. Go on, have a look. But keep quiet.' With her following close behind I walked softly along the hall and peered through the open sitting-room door.

George was ensconced in the largest armchair, his feet not touching the floor, with Chipper sitting on his lap. Both of them were intently watching television and eating crisps which George doled out from a large packet at his side. Lucinda and I tiptoed back to the kitchen and shut the door behind us, choking with laughter.

George was also becoming obsessed with his surveillance operation, however. I got the feeling that the more worried he was about his mother, the more he concentrated on his recording. The first thing he did each evening when he got home was to go and check on the camera and change the tape. Billy often accompanied him and the two of them would sit down to review it either in my house or Billy's.

Since each tape covered an entire night, they were finding it hard to keep up and were having to share out the viewing between them. Nevertheless, they were falling behind, George confided. I ignored his broad hints that I should help out. I spent enough of my life looking at screens as it was.

One morning, George told me very seriously that he thought they were on the brink of a breakthrough. They'd moved the camera to another spot and were convinced that there had been a fleeting shot of a badger on one of their tapes. He and Billy were full of plans to extend their operations.

Then something happened to bring all that to an end.

George and I had been to the supermarket one evening where we'd bought enough crisps to last Lucinda, Chipper and him for months. Billy was waiting for us when we got home and as soon as I stopped the car, George jumped out and they raced off towards the wood. Fifteen minutes later, the back door burst open and George came running in, in tears, carrying the camera in both arms.

'Look!' he said, holding it out, as if offering me a baby to carry.

I looked at it, nonplussed. I couldn't see anything unusual. 'What? Is something wrong?'

'Yes!' He sounded wild with frustration. 'Something's eaten the electric wire. It's not working any more.' He took a few steps closer, still holding it out to me. 'Can you fix it for me?'

I was aghast. 'Good God, no! I don't know the first thing about cameras.'

'Well, someone at your work, then?'

I shook my head. 'They probably wouldn't know much about this kind. Anyway,' I picked up the frayed end of the cable, 'it's the power supply that's the problem, isn't it? You'd be better off giving Alan a call, or Harry.'

'That's a good idea.' George dumped the camera unceremoniously on the kitchen table and reached for the phone.

'What's Alan's number?'

'No idea. Ask Lucinda. She's upstairs, I think.'

He raced off and a couple of minutes later came back with a piece of paper with two phone numbers written on it.

'Lucinda said to try the police station for Alan first because that's where he probably is because that's one of the reasons she's divorcing him because he's always there,' he blurted out, punching away at the number pad with one finger. He jumped up and down with impatience.

A few moments later he got through to Alan. I could tell from this end of the conversation that Alan wasn't keen or was too busy; at any rate, he couldn't come to help today or tomorrow. George replaced the receiver, looking worried. He consulted his piece of paper and dialled another number. This time, I heard him speak to June. There were a lot of yeses then he hung up. He turned to me happily. 'Harry's going to come right over.'

'That's good,' I said. 'What's happened to Billy?'

'Oh, he's taken the tape home to look at it there because his mother goes mental if he isn't in by eight,' George replied dismissively.

Moments later, Harry breezed in, all jovial bonhomie and anxious to get cracking on the problem. His enthusiasm dried up when he was presented with the damage.

'Oh dearie, dearie me,' he said, shaking his head. 'This doesn't look good. How did this happen? I thought we had all the cable nicely tucked away.'

George looked uncomfortable. 'I think it might have been moved,' he murmured.

'Moved?' Harry spoke sharply. 'Moved where? You boys should've known that could be very dangerous.'

'We had it on the other side of the wood.' George sounded on the brink of tears.

Harry looked very worried. 'And when did this happen?'

'Last night.' George was standing on tiptoe to look over Harry's shoulder at the camera. 'Is it broken?'

Harry shook his head gloomily. 'Looks like it. The problem is that it might have damaged the innards of the camera.' He sighed. 'I think I'd better take it home with me and see if I can sort it. What about the tape? I should probably take that as well.'

George looked alarmed. 'No, you can't do that. We haven't looked at it yet. We're sure there'll be badgers on it,' he wailed.

Harry smiled at him sympathetically. 'Doubt it, m'boy. I'm pretty certain it'll be ruined.'

George's face began to crease and I realised with horror that he was about to start crying.

'It's probably okay,' I butted in. 'I've had equipment pack up on me before and the tapes have always been fine. Honestly,' I added reassuringly as George turned to gaze at me.

'Oh well.' Harry shrugged. 'That's all right then. Cheer up, soldier.' He chucked George under the chin, fortunately missing the scowl he got in response when he turned to pick up the camera.

'I'd best be off then.'

George watched him leave.

'I wonder if Alan could get me another camera?' he murmured.

But that turned out to be a vain hope because Alan had either lost interest and didn't feel like pursuing the matter, or he wasn't able to get hold of another camera. At any rate, he couldn't help.

George was heartbroken, but fortunately he was due to spend the following weekend at a camp organised through his Cub troop. The preparations for that soon distracted him as he packed and repacked his bag and gave me endless, convoluted instructions over the care of Chipper.

'He likes to watch the Sunday programme of *Eastenders*,' he told me.

'Fine,' I said. It was nice to think that my colleagues in the television industry were busting a gut for an audience of white mice, but who was I to argue?

Barbara didn't have a car so I'd arranged to pick up both George and Billy as soon as I got off work – squashing both of them onto the front seat and hoping we didn't run into any police officers. They were to camp in a large barn on an estate just out of town.

George was agitating all the way there, insisting they would be the last to arrive and would miss all the best bits because I couldn't pick them up until after seven and everyone else would have been there at six. We almost didn't make it because I was so distracted by their bickering and arguments over directions that I almost hit a van parked near the entrance to the estate.

As it turned out, George was almost right. Everyone else was already there except for one other little boy who had arrived a few minutes ahead of us and whose mother was just leaving. George was anxious to get rid of me.

'Stop fussing!' he growled in a stage whisper when I started to check that he had everything he needed. 'I can manage on my own. I'm not a baby!'

So after a quick word with the Akela, a hearty woman named Beryl, I left. It was dark by this time and my route lay down a narrow muddy track that dipped under low overhanging trees. My mind was on other things. The newsroom had been awash with rumours all day about the Trevor situation and whether or not he would be fired.

Suddenly I arrived at a crossroads. I skidded to a halt, perplexed. None of this looked familiar. I knew I was still on the estate, but we had been in such a rush on the way out, and George had created such a diversion, that I hadn't paid much attention to where I was going.

Looking round me, I realised I was completely lost. I knew that there were forty acres of woodland on this estate. I could be here all night, going round in circles.

I peered in all directions. Straight ahead, I suddenly caught the wink of what looked like car tail-lights appearing and disappearing through the leafy branches which partially blocked my view. I shifted my foot off the brake onto the accelerator and let up the clutch. With any luck, the lights belonged to the woman who had left just before me.

The narrow muddy lane wound around and twisted and turned. Low branches brushed against the soft top of my car as it jolted along the rutted track, sounding uncomfortably like fingernails scraping across the fabric. I raced along as fast as I dared.

The last thing I wanted to do was to fall so far behind that I lost my guide altogether. But I arrived at yet another crossroads to find that I had done just that. All I could see in all directions was darkness and the dim impression of shadowy trees jostling each other and receding into infinity. I opened the window just a crack and listened. Nothing. No distant car engine that might have given me a clue.

There is something very frightening about a wood at night, trees crowding round, blocking the way out, vaguely menacing, indistinct. It is easy to imagine you can see shadows slipping between them. I got a grip on myself. I could go back the way I came but I wasn't even confident that I could find the Hall again. On the other hand, I had seen what I assumed was a car heading in this direction. I couldn't think of any better ideas, so I decided to go straight ahead.

I was driving probably a little too fast when the road suddenly went down an incline then veered sharply right.

My headlights raked the trees, bleached by the dazzling beam, then suddenly flashed back at me as they reflected off something shiny. Instinctively I braked, just in time to avoid hitting a car blocking the road.

The TR skidded in the mud, ending up at an angle, the bonnet inches from a gnarled tree trunk. I gasped and slumped back in my seat, then looked around. The car in front appeared to be empty, the rear and front passenger doors standing open. I felt suddenly fearful. There was no movement in the darkness which surrounded me, no sign of life.

It occurred to me that I might be on the point of disturbing some lovers' tryst. This was a suitably secluded spot. But even if that wasn't the case, it would be foolhardy to investigate out here alone in the dark. I shoved the gear-stick into neutral and was about to turn the ignition when I heard a noise.

The hairs on the back of my neck stood up and I shivered involuntarily. It was impossible to tell if it was my imagination playing tricks, but it had sounded like a human cry, muffled, but distinguishable. I hesitated. It could easily be an animal, I told myself, irritated at my jumpiness. I went to turn the ignition key again and the engine roared into life.

But I could not leave. If that was a human sound, couldn't it mean that someone was in trouble? Couldn't it mean that another woman like myself needed assistance? I could never turn my back on any cry of pain or plea for help.

The only other person I knew of who might be in these woods was the woman who had pushed past me in the Hall. I agonised over what to do. I could leave and try to make my way out of this maze and find a telephone and call the police. But the instant that thought occurred I dismissed it. I would drag the police all the way out here, assuming I could find this place again, with no real evidence that there was anything wrong. And if someone was in trouble, God knows what could have happened to them by the time I got back with help.

I ran one hand through my hair distractedly. All my instincts told me not to get out of the relative safety of my car. If there was some danger out there, there was no sense in walking right into it.

Suddenly I had a brainwave. I switched off the engine and leaned forward to open the glove compartment on the passenger side. Rooting around amongst the old receipts for repairs and other junk that somehow finds its way in there, my fingers finally curled round a small torch.

I switched it on. It has one of those ultra-powerful beams and it pierced the gloom instantly like a knife-blade. Shadowy trunks sprang nearer as they were illuminated and the beam reached through between the trees, moving slickly over glossy foliage, probing the depths of the undergrowth. In a funny kind of way, I felt more vulnerable now I had revealed the endlessness of the forest all around me. The twin eyes of some small animal glowed back pinkly as, with deliberate precision, I swung the light slowly round in an arc.

I probably wouldn't have seen the man at all if he hadn't decided to break cover and make a run for it. As it was, I had a sudden impression of movement to the left, just out of the range of my torch. Swinging rapidly in that direction, I caught a blur of some dull-coloured clothing as he plunged deeper into the darkness. Then he was gone, and there were only branches and leaves, shivering and flirting in the light. I might have dismissed it as a trick of my imagination, except that I could still hear him blundering into the distance. Then it was quiet again.

Something light moved amongst the leaves near ground level and caught my attention. Slowly, I undid my seat belt, opened the car door and stepped out, pausing where

I stood. The wind soughed through the undergrowth, and leaves shifted in the beam of my torch.

I swallowed hard and ran my tongue across my dry lips.

'Is anybody there?' I called, my voice sounding thin and reedy. I trained my torch on the area where I had seen the man emerge. Again I thought I saw something move behind the curtain of leaves. Then I heard it – a guttural, choking sound. I shivered. My mind told me to get back in the car and drive away at speed and notify the police. But something made me stay.

If I could just get a little bit closer, remaining poised at all times to make a run for it, I could see better. Stepping among the low bushes which gathered in clumps around the tree trunks, I began wading through the undergrowth towards whatever it was that was moving. Vines snared my ankles, and my sense of hysteria mounted as I paused to shake them free. When I stood on a branch and it cracked loudly, I gave a stifled scream.

I was within perhaps ten yards of the area where I had seen the man. I glanced round nervously. Anyone could be watching me. Behind any tree could be an attacker. I had no way of being sure that whoever it was I had glimpsed had left completely and wasn't spying on me from some darkness beyond my little enclave of light.

I gave one wild swing round the trees with my torch, as if to drive off any would-be threat, like some primitive human frightening animals with fire. Whatever it was was moving again, struggling. I had got quite close now. I pushed my torch through the tight web of undergrowth and directed it towards the ground. The beam picked out three fingers curled round a slender branch about my waist-height, moving ineffectually, trying to catch a hold, it seemed. There was something so vulnerable and pathetic about their struggle that I spoke out loud.

'Are you all right?'

There was no answer, only the choking sound again, and spasmodic struggling. I leaned forward and pulled away a heavy branch. At my feet lay the body of a woman. A scarf was tied in a strangle knot around her neck.

Automatically, I looked behind me, swinging the torch wildly so that trees and bushes jumped in its syncopated beam. But I could see no one lurking in the dark hollows of the undergrowth. Shaking with fear, I balanced my torch on a nearby bush, so that its light was directed onto the woman. Then I knelt down and began to struggle with the scarf around her neck. But the fabric was so taut that I could not get it free.

Suddenly I remembered the small Swiss Army knife which is attached to my keyring. I fished for it in my pocket, pulled out the blade with fumbling fingers and slid it gently between the woman's neck and the scarf. It was so tight that I could only manage to insert the tip, lying flat against her skin, but as I turned it, the pressure cut through the fabric. Gradually, I continued like this until at last I was able to pull the scarf away. The woman choked and coughed, gasping for breath.

'You're okay. I'm here to help,' I said hurriedly, glancing over my shoulder. 'Can you get up?' I stuffed my knife and the scarf into my pocket and reached down, sliding one arm under her shoulders, pulling her up to a sitting position. Her head slumped forward and she kept coughing.

'We have to get away from here,' I said urgently. 'Can you walk, d'you think?' The woman said nothing, only gulped for air. As her head tilted back, I could see the flood of tears coursing down her face. She was small and light so I was able to support much of her weight as I hauled her to her feet. Her legs buckled under her, but I held her up and she found her footing and took a few stumbling steps forward. When she was balanced, I reached out quickly and grabbed my torch.

'This way.' I pointed with the beam and she swayed in that direction and began staggering through the undergrowth, supported by my arm. We reached my car. I had calmed down a bit by now. If her attacker was watching us, he had evidently decided not to do anything further for the moment. I fumbled for my car keys and unlocked the passenger door.

'Here. Get in.' But she pulled back, resisting weakly.

'My car,' she gasped out. She turned her face to me in the dark. 'I'll take my car.' Before I could stop her she had broken away from me, stumbling towards her own vehicle. She got into the driver's seat, closing the doors behind her. The keys must have been in the ignition. The engine leaped into life and she switched on her headlights. I could see her head lolling back against the seat. Reluctantly, I unlocked the driver's door of the TR and got in.

Rapidly I reversed along the track, keeping an eye on the car in front, which was following slowly. In spite of the twists and turns in the road, she managed to steer her big saloon around the bends until we reached the crossroads where I had taken that fateful turn. I stopped my car and got out, walking back to meet hers.

Opening the passenger door, I said, 'I'm completely lost. Can you find the way back to the barn? Then perhaps they can get into the office at the big house and call the police and an ambulance for you.'

'No!' The cry was heartfelt. Even in the dark, I could see the gleam of fear in her eyes. 'I don't want to go to the police.' She paused, choking, to catch her breath. 'I don't need an ambulance. I'm going home.' She stopped, leaning the side of her head weakly against the back of the seat, watching me, pleading.

I stood there, full of misgivings. 'All right. I can't force you to go. But can you tell me what happened, at least?'

98

'I don't know who it was,' she gasped. 'He was in the car when I got in. Hiding behind the driver's seat. I remember now that I noticed a van or something following me on the way here. I didn't think anything of it at the time. Anyway he took hold of me by the throat, then wound my scarf round so I could hardly breathe.' She held her hands to her throat as if to demonstrate. 'He made me drive along there and stop. Then . . .' She began to weep.

'It's okay,' I said. 'Where do you live?'

Still crying, she blurted out, 'In Hayfield.' That was an area of the city very close to my home.

'Okay. Why don't you drive back towards town and I'll follow to make sure you're all right? When we get to the big roundabout at Barnston, give me a wave if everything's okay and I'll turn left there to go home.'

She nodded. 'Thank you. For everything.'

'No problem.' I straightened up, then on impulse, ducked down to look at her one last time. 'You're quite sure you've no idea who it was?'

She shook her head slowly. 'No.' Her voice was weak but final.

'Okay.' I slammed the passenger door shut.

We set off back towards town, this time with me following her big family-sized car. It occurred to me that I didn't even know her name. She drove very slowly and nervously, pausing for a long time at junctions, until there was no traffic anywhere in sight before proceeding. At the Barnston roundabout, she sounded her horn, and waved from the window. The hand that was illuminated in my headlights was very small and thin and worn-looking. I drove home.

But the incident haunted me – almost more alarming in retrospect than it had been at the time when I had no chance to think about it. I paced around the house, haunted by the brutal images of what had occurred, and hearing again the soughing of the wind in the dark trees overhead.

By midnight, I was still restless. I heard a motorbike draw up outside the house and from where I stood in the darkened sitting room, I could see Lucinda dismount from the pillion, wave goodbye and walk unsteadily towards the front door as her companion roared off into the distance, scarf flapping in the wind behind him.

I was about to meet her at the door when something caught my eye. For a split second, I could swear I saw a pinprick of light, a red glow from the shadows at the side of the house across the street. But when I blinked it was gone.

Lucinda was stumbling about in the hall. I opened the door.

'Bel.' She sounded surprised, peering at me in the gloom. Then she moved past me into the sitting room and collapsed onto the sofa. I switched on a small lamp. She groaned. 'What a night!'

'Do you want some coffee?' I asked. 'Because I really need some help with something.'

Lucinda groaned again. 'I couldn't drink another thing.' She turned onto her side and opened one eye. 'A whole gang of us went out to the pub after the library closed. I didn't have very much but it really seems to have gone to my head.' She rolled onto her back again. 'Fire away. I'm not going to last much longer.'

Briefly, I told her what had happened. Lucinda lay immobile during my account. At the end there was a pause, before she said, 'So?'

I thought for a moment. 'So, it seems such a coincidence. First the nun. Then this. Two attacks on women in the space of a couple of weeks . . .'

Lucinda gave a throaty laugh and pulled herself up onto one elbow to look at me. 'Only two! God, that must be a record.' She looked suddenly nauseous and lowered herself back down. 'It's just a coincidence. The M.O.'s completely different. The man who killed that nun tied her up and raped her. This guy didn't do any of those things.

'My guess is,' she continued, 'she didn't want to go to the police because she knows him. It's a domestic – maybe a jilted lover, an ex-husband . . . something like that. Most attacks on women are carried out by people they know.'

She moved her legs so that her feet touched the floor then heaved herself into a sitting position.

'Look.' She smiled at me kindly. 'Don't give it another thought. The only connection between these two is that you heard about one attack in the news and you were unfortunate enough to interrupt the other. In other words, there is no connection.' She stood up. 'Now I'm off to beddy-byes. Night night.' She moved towards the door and I heard her go upstairs.

After a few moments I switched out the lamp and stood in the darkness, looking out into the street. Across the road I thought I saw a shadow stir. But if I did it was gone in an instant.

I was exhausted. I would deal with it all in the morning.

Chapter Eight

I still felt tired when I woke up next day. On my way down to the kitchen, I bumped into Lucinda. She was fully dressed and toting a large canvas bag which appeared to be full of books.

'Where's George?' she asked. 'He's usually creating a stir by this time on a Saturday morning.'

'He's at Cub camp. I'm sure I told you.'

'Hmm. I thought it was terribly quiet. Well, I'm off to the library. I probably won't be back till late. Have fun.'

I made myself some coffee, feeling curiously at a loose end, then returned to my room. It was a wreck. Piles of clothes lay everywhere. I was about to toss the jeans I had been wearing the night before into the laundry basket when something stuffed into the pocket caught my eye. I pulled at it and a frayed length of red and white woollen material fell out. For a moment I was nonplussed. Then I realised that it was part of the scarf which was used to strangle the unknown woman the night before. I had no recollection of putting it in my pocket.

For a second, I debated whether to throw it away. From what she'd said, the woman was not going to report the attack, so there not much point in keeping the evidence. But something stopped me. One of the advantages and also the problems of having a big house is that one can avoid throwing things out. Besides, it was a Saturday morning. I was incapable of making decisions this early. I stuffed the scarf onto a shelf at the top of my wardrobe.

It was strange having time to myself again, without the responsibility of looking after George. I was completely at a loss to begin with, but quickly adjusted and took the opportunity to have dinner with old friends and also to visit Caroline on my own. She still looked wan but was hopeful that she would get out soon, she confided. Looking at her, I found it hard to share her optimism.

I forgot all about the attack until I went to pick up George from his camp on Sunday. He and Billy were full of tales of their derring-do, most of them far too exaggerated to stand any chance of being believed. My mind strayed as they stowed their bags in the boot, alongside assorted sticks which they thought might come in handy in the future, several stones they'd taken a liking to and various bits and pieces. I scanned the other adults sorting through the swarm of little boys and herding them into cars. The woman I had seen on Friday night was not amongst them.

The thought that she might have been more badly injured than I could tell in the dark haunted me. On Monday evening, I went to pick up George after work as usual. As I waited for him to get his gear together, I chatted to Billy's mother, Barbara. She was the sort of capable, friendly person who knows everyone and is the backbone of all the various extra-curricular activities.

I described the woman I had rescued, although as I spoke I realised how little I had to go on. I had only seen her in the light of my torch at a moment of great duress and then later in semi-darkness. Barbara shook her head.

'No. Doesn't ring a bell. I think I've met all the mums of our lot, too, so it's strange I wouldn't know her. You're sure she was at the Cub camp?'

I sighed. 'I thought I saw her there. Perhaps not. George

and Billy were creating a bit of a diversion so I might have been wrong.'

Barbara waved one hand dismissively. 'Kids! I tell you, you start to think you've got dementia if you're around them for long. It's hard to keep a thought going in your head for more than two seconds. Billy! Stop that!'

Billy and George had been wrestling on the floor. Reluctantly, they obeyed and got to their feet. I drove George to a fast-food place to get him something to eat, because we were going to see Caroline in hospital that evening. I regretted the visit almost as soon as we got there.

'When are you getting out?' George's tone was accusatory.

'Soon, pet. In a few days, if everything works out.' Caroline looked white and tired as she gazed at George fondly. 'But there's something I have to tell you.'

George scowled. Caroline continued slowly, picking her words carefully.

'You know the doctors did an operation to find out what was wrong?' George gazed at her, immobile. 'Well, they've decided I've got something called ovarian cancer.' George visibly flinched at the last word, but his expression remained frozen. Caroline glanced in my direction, to include me in what she was saying. 'Now they're going to operate tomorrow to cut it out and hopefully then I'll be all right . . .'

'Okay.' George broke in. He turned to me and tugged on my hand. 'We'd better be going because I have to look at my badger tapes with Billy. Come on.' He was impatient. I looked at Caroline, afraid of how she might be taking this. Her eyes were misted with tears.

'It's alright,' she said reassuringly, seeing my expression. 'I know what he's like. I know he doesn't mean it. He's just upset.' George was tugging at my hand, leaning towards the door with his whole weight, anxious to leave all this behind.

'Don't worry about George,' I said, wishing there were more I could say. 'He's fine with us. He can stay as long as he needs to.' Caroline nodded, overcome with emotion. 'I'll pop in and see you myself tomorrow during the afternoon if I can get away,' I added. She smiled and waved as we left, but George didn't look back and missed it.

During the drive home, I tried to broach the subject of his mother's illness with George because I was worried at the way he had brushed it aside. I remembered what that was like. When well-meaning people had tried to tell me that my mother was dying, I had stopped them short, not wanting to hear my worst imaginings confirmed. George ignored everything I said.

'Will you watch my tapes with me when we get home?' he asked.

'I thought we should talk about your mummy for a bit, just to make sure you understand . . .'

'I do!' he shouted roughly. 'And I'm talking about my badgers and it's very rude of you . . .' He stopped, suddenly tearful.

'Okay,' I said resignedly. 'I'll watch your tape when we get home.'

But the first thing we both noticed when we arrived back was that the glass was broken in one of the small panes of glass in the back door. Lucinda had said she'd be at the library until late, studying. I turned the key in the lock and pushed the door open. The kitchen looked undisturbed.

'They'd better not have stolen Chipper.' George shot off upstairs to his room. I followed in his tracks through to the hall. The door to the sitting room was open. Nothing had been disturbed, but instantly I noticed that the television and video recorder were missing from their stand in the corner. All the videotapes, at least a couple of hundred of them, were gone too. A quick check of the upstairs revealed that nothing else had been taken. The thieves knew what they were after and had wasted no time on raking through the baubles of jewellery that I possessed.

Reaching for the phone, I called my local police station. Within five minutes a squad car drew up at the front door and a couple of very young-looking bobbies walked in.

'Sixth one this week,' one of them announced cheerfully. The other took down cursory details in his notebook. Then they left. As far as they were concerned, it was just another robbery. There was a gang in the neighbourhood. At least, I thought wryly to myself, the thieves hadn't thought to look under the flowerpot for the key. If they had, my insurance company would probably have taken a dim view of it all.

By now it was almost ten o'clock. I had heard and seen nothing of George since we'd got home, except for a brief appearance to take a look at the police. I mounted the stairs to the first-floor landing and paused, listening for sounds from above. I could hear sobbing. I debated with myself what to do, then quietly I climbed the last flight of stairs to Jamie's studio and knocked gently on the door.

The sobbing stopped abruptly. 'Go away!' he shouted.

I opened the door a crack. 'Can I come in?'

'No!'

I hesitated, then went in anyway. He was hunched under the duvet, with Chipper's cage on the table by the bed. Slowly he emerged and sat up, not trying to disguise his crying now. I put an arm round his shoulders and he leaned against me, shaking with sobs.

'What'll happen if she dies?' he asked.

'Well, there *is* a possibility she might die,' I answered with difficulty. It would have been easier to lie, but I knew from my own experience that children sense when they're not being told the truth. 'But I don't think she will,' I continued. 'The doctors obviously think there's hope or they wouldn't bother operating.'

'You think so?' he managed between convulsive sobs. Gradually, I could feel his weight becoming heavier as he leaned against me and he was no longer shaken by spasms of crying. Finally, there was only a hoarse breathing. Gently I lowered him back onto the bed and pulled the duvet over him. When I glanced back as I reached the door, he was already fast asleep.

I phoned the hospital late the next afternoon. Caroline was still sedated, I was told, but the operation appeared to have gone well. The doctors hoped she could come out in a few days' time.

George reacted to the news without comment. But he was gentler with his mother when we went to visit that evening and hugged her fiercely before we left. Then we set off for one of the late-night superstores to look at television sets.

The burglary was proving to be a major nuisance. I have a personal vendetta against insurance companies, partly because they always double the premium as soon as they hear I work in television and partly because negotiating with them is like dealing with a one-armed bandit which is stacked against you. However, for once, my insurance broker came up trumps and I received a cheque to replace my stolen television and VCR almost at once.

In any event, I had to buy a new set and more videotapes immediately because I need them for work. George was keen to get a very large television like the sort they have in pubs because, as he pointed out, it would be easier to see badgers on it. In the end, I did buy a much bigger set than I would have if George hadn't been with me. It was going to be delivered the next morning while June was at the house.

George was wildly excited when I picked him up the following evening.

'I'm sure we'll be able to see the badgers now,' he confided happily. Then we got into the inevitable wrangle over whether or not I would look at his recordings with him and it took all my ingenuity to put him off again. So he watched them himself. I had expected an enthusiastic response because of the new television, but he was strangely subdued. When I asked him if he'd seen the badgers he merely shook his head and went off to bed looking preoccupied. I couldn't understand what was bothering him. The news about Caroline had been especially good that day and it was virtually certain that she would be home very soon.

The next afternoon, Barbara had to take Billy to the doctor so I left work early to pick George up from school. He said nothing all the way home, which was unusual. No sooner had we got inside than he started again about his tapes.

'Please will you come and look at my tape,' he begged. 'It's really important.'

'George,' I pleaded in turn, 'I've got so much to do I don't even know where to begin.'

A look of anguish passed across his face and he danced a little jig of fury, flinging himself around the kitchen and kicking the table leg. 'You always say that. I just want you to watch one little tape with me. It's been ages now I've been trying to get you to look at it,' he broke into a loud wail, 'and you always say no.'

'It can't have been that long,' I said, stalling for time, wondering if I dared refuse again in the face of this tantrum. 'Anyway, I thought they all got stolen in the burglary.'

'No!' George wailed. 'It didn't get stolen. Billy had it. He watched it at his house.' His fury subsided and he looked at me forlornly. 'Please. You've got

your new television set and stuff now so you can't
say no.'

I gave in. There was a mound of dirty clothes upstairs
waiting to be sorted out but I supposed it could wait.

'Okay. You go and get it set up. Call me when
it's ready.'

A look of pure relief spread over George's face and
he raced off towards the sitting room. Within a few
minutes he was yelling for me to join him. Mentally I
braced myself. Staring at grainy images would give me
a headache.

'I've fast-forwarded it to the right bit,' said George.
I groaned inwardly. If he really had spotted a badger,
life would become hell. He'd probably want to leave
school and carry on a round-the-clock nature watch or
something. I sighed and settled down to view the tape.

The pictures were in black and white and the date and
time of the recording appeared in the lower right-hand
corner. The scene we were monitoring was a wide shot of
a clearing on the other side of the wood. A squirrel flashed
across the background tapestry of trees and undergrowth
which formed a complex patterned backdrop. The squirrel
was hard to pick out, because it was small and easy to lose
sight of amongst the undergrowth and branches.

I was already bored. I began to ease myself out of my
chair surreptitiously, intent on escaping to make a cup of
coffee. But George suddenly reached out and gripped my
arm with such ferocity that I jumped.

'This is the bit that's strange,' he breathed, not taking
his eyes from the screen.

I sank back into my chair. Something much bigger had
loomed amongst the trees. A dark shape came forward
and separated from the background. I could make out two
people, a man and a woman. The woman was stumbling,
being shoved by the man until she fell to the ground in
the middle of the clearing. We could hear indistinct cries

110

picked up by the camera microphone, but it appeared that the woman might be gagged, although it was hard to be sure about that. The man wore dark, loose clothing and a mask which covered his head and face.

As I watched, frozen with horror, the woman's clothing was torn off. Her hands were pinned behind her back. She struggled and there were muffled cries of terror, like the noise of some small animal being tortured. Something was tied around her neck and she was violently raped. Then there was a blinding flash replaced by the white snow of static on the screen. The recording had ended.

'I think that's when the squirrel ate through the cable,' explained George. He looked at me with big eyes full of fear. 'What was going on?' he asked. 'Why was that man making the lady cry? Were they fighting?'

'That's probably as good a description as any,' I said gently. 'A pretty one-sided fight though.' I was relieved that George seemed to have been spared understanding the full horror of what he had just seen. But I certainly didn't want him to view the tape again, however blurred the images might be. So after assuring him that I would deal with it now, I pointed out that Chipper hadn't been fed and he shot off upstairs, apparently relieved to have passed the burden to me.

Then I yelled for Lucinda. She appeared on the upper landing looking fraught, but something in my voice must have got through to her because she descended the stairs and sat down to watch the tape without question.

At first she looked puzzled, but the moment the two figures entered the scene, she sat up, instantly alert. As soon as it was finished, she turned to me.

'Have you called the police?'

'Not yet.'

'Right.' She reached for the extension on a low table nearby and dialled a series of numbers. 'This is Lucinda

Jameson.' she announced abruptly. 'I must talk to DCI Sykes. Tell him it's urgent.'

Twenty minutes later an unmarked police car pulled up at the door and Sykes and another man got out. We played the tape for them.

I'm not sure what I expected Sykes' response to be, but it wasn't what we got at any rate. He and his colleague watched in silence. When the pictures ended and the screen went to static, I switched it off and looked at Sykes. He seemed deep in thought, chewing his lower lip, gazing out of the window. At that moment George returned. He sat on an armchair looking scared, watching the adults around him. Sykes turned to look at the small figure.

'Where was this tape made?' His voice was surprisingly gentle.

George's eyes were wide with alarm. He knew he had started something that was now beyond his control.

'I can show you.' He pointed in the general direction of the wood. 'It's just a little way out at the back of the house in the wood.'

'Have you been back there since then?' Sykes hunkered down so that his face was on a level with George's. The latter nodded warily.

'Did you find anything? Did you see anyone there?' Sykes was watching him closely. George shook his head. 'They'd all gone?' Sykes pressed him. George nodded.

Sykes turned to me. 'Mind if I use your phone?' I gestured that he should help himself and he picked up the receiver and dialled quickly. After a few terse words, he hung up. 'Right. A couple of our people will be here in a few minutes and I want you to show them where it happened.'

A note of caution had crept into Sykes' voice as he turned again to George. 'Why haven't you reported it before now?'

George took a deep breath. 'Well, me and Billy

watched it and we knew there was something wrong but we weren't sure what to do. I asked Bel to look at it but she was too busy till just now.'

He shot me an accusing look.

'Why was that?' Sykes turned to me sharply.

'I thought it was just a tape of little animals. I had no idea it was this,' I answered levelly.

Sykes returned to gazing out of the window, deep in thought. Without moving, he asked, 'Any attacks like this reported over the last few weeks?'

The detective standing next to him shook his head. 'None that I've heard about.'

Sykes grunted. There was another pause, then he seemed to make up his mind. 'Right, well have someone check all the hospitals to see if anyone came in with injuries consistent with such an attack, and also the 999 calls, and just make sure there hasn't been any rape reports we don't know about although I doubt it because,' he turned to Lucinda and me, 'anything like that gets passed to us automatically at the moment in case it's got anything to do with the nun who was killed.'

He stood up. 'I'll take the tape, if you don't mind. We might have some image-enhancing done on that just to see if we can get anything more from it.'

I ejected the tape and handed it to him.

'That's mine!' protested George.

'You'll get it back if it's no use to us,' said Sykes, patting him on the head. George dodged away from Sykes' hand and scowled.

Before he could say anything more and become really obstreperous, I said quickly, 'I'll get you another tape. You can have one of mine.' George said nothing although he still looked mutinous. He got up and stomped out of the room, banging the door behind him.

'One last thing,' Sykes added. 'It might be a good idea to get the boys some counselling, just to make sure they don't have nightmares or anything after seeing this. We can put you in touch with someone suitable.'

'Thanks,' I replied. 'I'll take you up on that.' I paused, debating whether to continue.

'What do you make of the similarities to the attack on Sister Kate?' I asked. 'I thought it might be the same man.'

Sykes shook his head. 'The similarities are no more than has been reported in the press. It could be a copycat attack. Or,' he paused for emphasis, 'it might not be an attack at all.' I looked at him in disbelief, although I could see Lucinda nodding in a 'I should have known,' sort of way in the background.

'I know it looks a rape,' Sykes cut me off before I could say anything, 'but we have no report of an attack. Nor do we have a victim. So unless we come up with one,' he spread his hands out in an expression of emptiness, 'we have no crime.'

'But her hands were tied. She was gagged and she was trying to scream,' I protested.

Sykes shrugged and smiled, a man of the world. 'That's what some women like. You'd be surprised what some people get up to. It could also have been a prostitute with a client.'

'She was being strangled,' I continued. I could hear the mounting hostility in my voice.

He smiled. 'Perhaps it added a little *frisson* to the game.'

Lucinda's voice cut across. 'Leave it, Bel.' She turned to Sykes. 'Let us know what you decide.' She smiled thinly, the barest lipservice to social niceties. Sykes stood his ground for a couple of seconds, but then abruptly spun round and left, tailed by his colleague.

Lucinda shut the door after them, then returned to the sitting room.

'The thing is,' she reasoned, 'there's no point arguing

with him. He's right, in a way. He has no proof that a crime has been committed. You might consider that what we just saw is horrifying, but Sykes works in a world where he does come across people who do things like that for fun.' She shrugged. 'But having said that, I bet he goes over the tape with a fine toothcomb. Anyway . . .' she paused as her eyes alighted on George, who had just wandered in. Her voice rose. 'Are those my crisps you're munching away at?'

'I was hungry!' countered George defiantly.

'But they're mine!' Lucinda sounded indignant. I closed the sitting-room door and left them to it. They had these sort of arguments regularly and for some reason I could not fathom, seemed to enjoy them. I could still hear them from the kitchen, so I closed that door too. Then I dialled Mags' number.

'What the hell is it now?' I was so taken aback, I was speechless for several seconds.

'It's me,' I said lamely.

'Bel.' Mags' anger subsided. 'Sorry. Barry's been on the phone. I got a letter from his solicitor this morning saying that he's going to take legal action to obtain custody of the kids. Plus there's something else happened at work.' There was a catch in her voice. 'I can't tell you about it just now, but I must talk to you tomorrow. Barry's got the kids for the weekend. Can you have dinner with me?'

'Fine.' This was not the moment to tell Mags about the tape. Clearly she had more pressing things to worry about.

'Okay. I must go. Bye.'

The next day, I phoned Sykes to find out what was happening about George's recording, but he was busy and didn't call me back. That evening, Lucinda agreed to babysit. Mags and I took my car to a small restaurant a couple of miles from the studios where we could be sure we wouldn't run into any of our colleagues.

When we were seated opposite each other, I noticed the signs of strain in Mags' face. Her expression was tight and her gestures jerky and nervous, although she had obviously dressed and applied her make-up with the same meticulous attention to detail as always. If she was under pressure, it wouldn't affect her job performance.

'I'm in deep shit,' she began. 'You weren't in the newsroom yesterday, but I really screwed up.' She ran her hand distractedly through her hair. 'I don't know how I did it. I've never made a mistake like that in my entire career. I had to cover that kickback story. Two of the councillors were up in court yesterday and when I was doing the piece to camera in front of the courtroom I don't know what happened but I got the names wrong. I said it was Councillor Jones that was accused instead of Councillor Roberts. I mean,' Mags gestured helplessly, 'the names aren't even remotely similar.'

'So what?' I said. 'You just correct the mistake on-air.'

Mags shook her head. Her food had arrived, but after one bite, she had pushed it to one side. I was starving and tucking into mine. 'Of course. But Jones has decided to make a big production out of it. You see, there's the local elections coming up and he's saying that no matter what we do, it's fixed in people's minds that he's a crook and he's mixed up in this kickback scandal and that doubt will always be there. He's saying that if he loses his seat, he's going to sue.' She paused, rolling her eyes.

'Of course, Trevor's having a field day because at last he's got something on me. He's been stamping around all morning saying that getting the facts wrong is a sacking offence in his book.' Mags looked bitter. 'He makes mistakes every day, but he seems to have forgotten that.'

116

'It'll pass,' I said consolingly.

Mags shook her head. 'No, I don't think it will. Trevor won't let it. We had a huge row yesterday before I went out to cover the court story. He's filed a complaint about my attitude and what was it,' Mags scanned the ceiling for inspiration, 'oh yes, my insubordination.' She gave a wry smile.

'Look.' I reached forward and shook her arm gently. 'Martin knows what's going on. He'll stand up for you. Just hang in there and try not to get in Trevor's way.'

Mags nodded uncertainly. 'It's all I can do, I suppose.' She caught my expression. 'It's okay. I've got a grip on myself. I won't do anything stupid.'

We paid our bill and got up to leave.

'You know the last straw in all this,' she said with ironic humour, 'is that the garage have just told me it'll take ten days to get the part they need to fix my car. You can't win.'

It was dark when I dropped her outside her house. As I drove home, my mind kept returning to what she had told me. I was worried. Everyone in the newsroom knew that Trevor didn't like working with women, but he seemed to be directing all his venom at Mags. The question was, how far was he prepared to go?

I arrived home to find George and Lucinda both upstairs in their rooms, the one studying and the other trying to teach Chipper to sit on command. I wandered into the kitchen. An envelope was propped up on the table, addressed to me and marked *Private* in handwriting I did not recognise.

Filled with curiosity, I opened it up. Inside, printed carefully in tiny neat letters, was a note from June. *Dear Bel*, it read, *I must speak to you urgently. Please phone me as soon as you get in.*

Here we go, I thought to myself. She's going to say

117

she can't carry on cleaning for us. She's had enough. I just know it.

Deciding to get it over with quickly, I dialled her number. June must have been sitting by the telephone because she answered on the first ring.

'Bel,' she breathed in her little-girl voice. 'I thought it would be you.'

'What's up?' I asked, trying to sound nonchalant.

'Something terrible's happened.' There was high drama in June's voice.

'What?' My mind raced through all the possibilities. She'd been hit by a bus? The vacuum cleaner had exploded? 'What is it?' I repeated urgently.

'I can't say over the phone,' replied June gravely.

Oh my God, I thought, that bad. 'I'm afraid I can't come and see you just now, I've got George here.'

'That's okay, I can come round to you. Harry's away overnight on a job up north. But I must talk to you in private.'

She arrived ten minutes later. Her face was solemn and she refused to take her coat off, which made me feel uncomfortable.

'It was nice of you to come round,' I chattered as I led the way into the sitting room and closed the door behind us.

'Oh, it's not a problem,' June said kindly. 'I'm on my own at the moment, anyway. Harry's got a big contract up at Hedgely cleaning all the carpets in one of those stately homes so he's away a lot at the moment.'

She sat down heavily in one of the armchairs, then wriggled into her seat, looking very self-important.

'The thing is,' she began at once, unable to contain herself any longer, 'I found this under George's bed.' She had opened her bag and now she passed across a couple of folded pages from some glossy publication. Bemused, I reached out for them. I could see at once that they were pages from a girlie magazine. The outer page had a picture of a nude woman posing.

'Oh, thank you for letting me know,' I said without much enthusiasm.

'Well, I hope you give him a good talking-to,' June said self-righteously.

I debated what to say to her. 'Well, to tell the truth, June, I don't think I'll say anything to George. In the first place, I'm not his mother. I'm only looking after him for a couple of weeks. In the second place, much as I despise this kind of thing, I don't find it surprising or particularly sinister that a child might be curious about it.' June looked insulted so I hurried on, 'But I'm glad you've told me and I'll mention it to Caroline.'

June stood up, a look of rejection on her face. 'Well, sorry to have troubled you. I must be going. I'll be in on Thursday. Goodbye.' She had left before I could even offer her a cup of coffee.

Sighing, I carried the folded pages through to the kitchen and tossed them onto the table. I had just sat down to eat the pasta I had prepared when Lucinda appeared, looking tired.

'Kettle's just boiled,' I said by way of a welcome. Quickly, she made herself a cup of instant coffee and slumped into a chair with a groan.

'I can't stand any more! If I read one more stupid judge's remarks, I'll go mad.' Idly she reached out and picked up the pages June had brought, and spread them out on the table. I was at the sink splashing cold water on the tomato sauce I had just spilled down my new cotton sweater when I heard her give a low whistle. 'Have you seen this?' she asked as I sat down again.

For answer, I reached out and pulled the pages closer to me. Lucinda had opened them out to look at the inside layout, which contained pictures of two women. In the first set, each was photographed fully clothed, one in a teacher's robe and mortar board, the other as a nurse. Then each was shown stripped, bound and gagged, spread out in a sexual pose, with a look of feigned terror on her face. Invisible hands pulled ligatures taut around their necks as if they were being strangled.

'It's the same setup as in the tape,' I said, feeling puzzled. Lucinda raised her eyebrows and nodded. I scanned the pictures again. Something struck me. 'There's a teacher and a nurse. I wonder if there's one of a nun with her hands bound in prayer?'

'I'd bet any money there is.'

'Is George still awake, do you know?'

Lucinda glanced at the kitchen clock. It was almost nine o'clock. 'Could be. He wasn't making much noise though.' Quietly, I mounted the stairs to the second-floor studio and knocked on the door. 'Don't come in yet!' yelled George. There was a scuffle and the bedsprings creaked. 'Okay!'

I opened the door. George was sitting up in bed surrounded by copies of the *Beano* and the *Dandy*.

'I'll turn the light off in a minute but not yet. It's only nine o'clock,' he said indignantly. I sat down on the bed.

'That's not what I wanted to see you about.' I put the magazine pages on top of the duvet. George eyed them guiltily then looked away.

'What?' He sounded angry, always his first line of defence, I had discovered.

'Where did you get these?' I tapped the pages with one finger. George pursed his lips and I thought he might not answer at all.

But after a few moments he said, 'Who says they're mine?'

'George, cut it out!' I sounded as irritated as I felt. If he started that particular game I'd be here all night before I found out what I needed to know. George looked from the pictures to me, and back again, debating with himself.

Finally he said, 'If I tell you, can I have the money to go and see *Terminator II* on Saturday with Billy?'

'That's got nothing to do with what we're talking about,' I said impatiently.

George heaved a big sigh. 'Oh, all right,' he said with an air of martyrdom. 'I found it in the woods but,' he continued hurriedly before I could say anything, 'it's your fault.'

'George!' I was beginning to wonder if I was going to come out of this even remotely sane. 'It's nobody's fault. I just want to know where you got these pages.'

'It is so your fault!' George was a picture of righteous indignation. 'You wouldn't let me have your newspaper for Chipper so I have to get bits of paper for him in the woods.'

I stared at him, digesting this information. 'So that's where you found it?'

George nodded sullenly.

'Where exactly? Near the badgers' hole?'

He nodded again, adding, 'The second one. After me and Billy moved the camera. It was caught in a bush. I found it about a week ago.'

'Before the squirrels chewed through your cable?'

He shook his head. 'No. After.'

'It's okay,' I said. 'You haven't done anything wrong.'

'Oh.' He visibly relaxed. 'I thought you might be mad 'cos you thought I'd taken your paper again.' He wriggled down under the duvet.

I stood up. 'Night night, sleep tight, watch the dogs don't bite.'

'Bedbugs,' he corrected me sleepily as I turned out the light.

Racing back downstairs, I felt a spurt of elation. These few sheets of paper pointed to a link between Sister Kate's murder and the tape George had recorded. They could also give an invaluable insight into the attacker's mind. And that, in turn, could help track down a sadistic killer.

Chapter Nine

I should have guessed, however, that Sykes would be unimpressed with the magazine pages when I stopped by Police Headquarters on my way to work to show them to him. 'You find that stuff all over the place,' he told me wearily, as in: 'Don't bother me, little girl. I've seen more pornography than you've had hot dinners and believe me this is nothing.' If anything, he seemed to think it confirmed his hypothesis that it was a couple playing games, acting out what they'd seen in a porn mag.

But Sykes did deign to tell me the results of the work they had done on the tape. Image-enhancing had made the pictures much sharper but even I had to admit that there was no way that they could be used to identify either the man or the woman.

Staring fixedly at the two figures, willing them to become clearer, was hard on the eyes. I found my gaze shifting focus and coming to rest on the grey blur of the background. Something caught my attention. Lying on the ground, where it had been discarded on top of the woman's coat, was a long piece of striped material, a bit like a football scarf – a bit like the scarf now lying on the top shelf of my wardrobe, in fact.

It occurred to me that I should mention this to Sykes. But I was tired of the put-downs. He had scoffed at everything I had brought him so far and they had had a much stronger link to the murder of the nun than this scarf. I also knew in my heart that the woman would deny everything. I remembered her terror when I had mentioned the police, her frantic efforts, her hand movements, her desire to physically run away from the very idea. So it was easy to persuade myself to say nothing to Sykes.

But there was now a lot I wanted to talk over with Mags. I hurried into work, impatient to find her, only to be brought up short with the news that she hadn't appeared yet even though she should have been in at least two hours ago.

'Late again,' said Trevor pointedly when he overheard me asking for Mags. 'I need all the help I can get to cover that big pile-up on the motorway we had this weekend – grieving relatives, why it happened, all that stuff. She's no use to me if I can't rely on her.' There was a glimmer of malice in his eyes as he ostentatiously pulled down a hardbound notebook from the shelf above his desk and made a note in it. Then he slammed it shut and grinned mirthlessly as Ron Polly and I stood watching.

'And what about that documentary you two are supposed to be doing, eh? When am I going to get to see that?' There was a sneer on his face as he turned away.

'Bastard!' muttered Ron under his breath.

But when my friend did appear half an hour later, I quickly realised that it might have been better if she'd stayed at home. Mags has the sort of small delicate features the camera loves. Normally, her make-up is applied in such a way as to lift her from being merely pretty into the realm of the beautiful. We are all so used to her good looks in the office that no one gives her a second glance.

But today we could not help staring. Her eyes were red-rimmed and bloodshot so that the make-up which she had applied merely looked grotesque. When she caught sight of me, she tried to smile as usual, but it was a reflex, I could see that.

As she crossed to her desk, I noticed that her black

tights were laddered and that the hem of her skirt had come down at the back. Such things would have been par for the course where I am concerned. But Mags had been appearing on television for ten years; immaculate grooming was second nature to her. I had never seen her in such a state before.

'And where the hell have you been, Missy?' Trevor's voice boomed out across the newsroom. Everyone stiffened and studiously carried on with what they were doing. We had all known this was coming from the moment Mags had put one foot over the threshold. She had sunk into her seat. I couldn't understand what was wrong. Her usual spirit seemed to have deserted her. There was something profoundly weary about the way she brought her hands up and clasped them in front of her on the desk. Like an animal waiting helplessly for the slaughter.

Trevor's portly frame had crossed the room by now and was standing before Mags.

'I'm sorry,' she said quietly. 'I've been ill. I came in because I knew you would be short-staffed already since John's on holiday.'

'Oh, thanks *very* much,' said Trevor with leering sarcasm. 'It's wonderful to have you here – especially looking like shit, with your tights ripped.' He placed his hands on Mags' desk and leaned forward. 'What's the matter? A night on the tiles? Didn't make it home before you came to work this morning?'

'That's quite enough!' Ron Polly strode across the short space separating his desk from Mags' and stood beside her. His face was livid with fury and his grey eyes sparked behind his glasses. This was support from an unexpected quarter. I had been standing on the sidelines in a state of anguish, wishing I could go to Mags' aid, but feeling instinctively that if I did so, I would be subtly undermining her, letting Trevor know she wasn't a match for him, she couldn't handle him herself.

But Ron was a contemporary of Trevor's. I had seen them standing shoulder to shoulder at the bar many a night after work, even before Trevor joined RTV. They had come up through the ranks on the newspapers together and they talked the same language. Ron speaking up like this was a statement that Trevor was out of order, that he had broken even their code of behaviour.

For a moment there was a stand-off. Ron's outrage against Trevor's malice. Then, almost imperceptibly, there was a slackening in Trevor's muscles, a sort of scaling down of his threat.

'Well, she can go and get herself tidied up so she at least looks like a professional,' he tossed out, spinning round and heading for his office, slamming the door behind him.

Ron shifted from one foot to the other. 'Are you all right?' he asked Mags roughly, awkward in this unaccustomed role as defender of women. Mags nodded, her eyes on her whitened knuckles.

'Thank you,' she said very quietly. Then she stood up, and, eyes downcast, reached for her handbag and started to walk towards the door. She looked so lonely. There was total silence in the room. We watched helplessly, none of us with the gumption to know how best to react. As she neared the door, one foot skidded on a sheet of paper lying on the carpet. We all tensed, willing her not to fall, not now.

But she recovered, pausing for a second to collect herself before walking with dignity out of the room. There was a sudden rush of activity as everyone returned to what they had been working on. I slipped out quietly and walked along the hall to my office at the far end, to check if Mags had taken refuge there. But the room was empty. I debated. The next place to try was the loo. There was a large one near the lifts, with a powder room and a chaise longue and tinted mirrors all around the walls. But that was too public, I decided. Next to my office was a firedoor leading onto some back stairs. At the top was a small toilet.

Mags was collapsed in a corner.

'Mags, Mags, what's going on?' I bent down and tried to help her to her feet. As soon as she reached a standing position, she turned away from me and vomited into the wash basin.

'Wait here!' I said urgently. 'I'll be right back.'

I did a mental recce of the layout of the building and decided that the most discreet route to the ground floor was down the back stairs and across the alley to the adjoining wing. Within a couple of minutes, I had burst into the office of the Occupational Health nurse. She was bandaging the foot of one of the props men and looked irritated when I entered.

'Sorry,' I said breathlessly. 'Joan, this is an emergency. I need some help.'

She relented visibly and stood up. 'What should I bring?'

I shook my head. 'Nothing. Just come quick.'

Together we raced back the way I had come and into the ladies' loo off the landing. Joan instantly assessed the situation, quickly checking Mags' pulse.

'What's happened? Has there been an accident?'

Mags shook her head. 'No. I don't feel very well, that's all.' I stared at her. I couldn't believe that that was all there was to it. Joan turned to me.

'She arrived this morning not looking too good and then Trevor put the boot in,' I answered her unspoken question tersely.

Joan put an arm round Mags' shoulders, supporting her to an upright position.

'Right, Mags,' she said gently. 'Nothing's hurt, is it?' Mags shook her head wearily. 'Okay. I'm going to take you down the back stairs and across the alley to my office. I don't think we'll bump into anyone on the way.'

Joan turned to me. 'I'll have her lie down for a bit. She can't go home in this state. Come back in an hour or so when you're free and if she's better you can take her home then.'

I nodded, then leaned forward to hug Mags gently. 'I'll tell Trevor you're sick.'

Joan nodded approvingly, as she gently led Mags towards the stairs.

'Sick!' yelled Trevor in tones of derision when I gave him the news. 'Sick!' He shook his head in disbelief. 'If you can't take the heat you should get out of the kitchen, is what I say.' He looked around him for an audience. 'I'm supposed to take it seriously when someone's a bit weepy, am I?' He walked towards me, beating his chest for emphasis. 'Well, what about me?' He glanced round him to make sure everyone was listening. 'I was taken to Casualty on Friday night. The doctors wanted to keep me in but I wouldn't let them. This place would be in a fine mess if we all stayed off for that time of the month.' He ended on a falsetto, a sneer on his face. I gave him a look of pure hatred. Over his left shoulder, I caught sight of Ron Polly giving Trevor the finger.

I got a call from Joan after lunch to go and take Mags home. She looked pale and tired with all her make-up washed off, somehow ordinary and vulnerable without the armour of her usual glossy finish. But she had slept for a couple of hours and did look slightly better.

I drove her home, offering to accompany her inside and make her a cup of tea. She refused.

'I'm fine. Really,' she insisted. I was unconvinced. Making a visible effort to pull herself together, to seem normal, she asked, 'How's the documentary coming along? You mentioned something had happened when I spoke to you on Friday.'

'George picked up some pages from a porn magazine in the wood near where the attack took place. It showed women tied up like the nun and the woman on the tape. I took it to Sykes, but he's not interested.' As I spoke, Mags shuddered involuntarily.

'Look, I don't think you need to be thinking about work just yet,' I said gently. 'Joan's right. You need a complete rest for a few days. Are you going to call a doctor?'

'No!' Mags' vehemence took me by surprise. 'I can't cope with anyone asking me questions or telling me what to do. I just want to stay in my own house in peace for a while.'

I nodded, taken aback. 'I understand. Promise you'll call me if you need anything? Even if you just want to talk. Even if it's the middle of the night.'

'Fine. I think I'll take one of those pills Joan gave me and go to bed for a couple of hours.' She got out of the car and walked up the path to her door without a backward glance.

I drove home, brooding over the way Trevor had treated Mags. The awful thought had now entered my mind that he might actually try to have her fired, or transferred permanently out of News. That would leave her devastated, particularly if she wasn't well.

I paced around the house. There was also Trevor's jibe about our documentary. If only we could somehow finish that and make a good job of it, then Trevor would find it very hard to sack either of us.

The only new lead we had was the magazine pages, even if Sykes dismissed them as irrelevant. I think I had some half-baked idea that if I could see the whole layout, it would give me a clue to the identity of the attacker, or at least take me inside his mind so that I could understand how he operated. At any rate, I had to do something and that was all I had to go on.

There was an adult bookshop in the city centre, near

the station. Restlessly, I got in my car and drove down there. Since it was late afternoon, I expected the shop to be more or less empty, but when I walked in, there must have been at least half a dozen men browsing through the merchandise.

There was an entire section devoted to bondage. Some of these, I was sure, must be illegal. They were also surprisingly expensive – at least four or five times the cost of one of the women's glossies. I began leafing through the pages, trying to find the magazine from which the pages George had found had been torn.

But although I must have scanned at least thirty magazines, none contained the pictures I was seeking. In desperation, I turned to the grizzled-looking man behind the counter, who was eyeing me sourly.

'Need any help?' There was a hint of derision in his voice. I produced the magazine pages.

'Ever seen any of these before?'

He glanced down at them quickly then looked me in the eye with an insolent, combative expression. 'And what if I have?'

'Can I buy the magazine, please?'

'No.' He smiled and waited for my response.

I sighed. So we were going to play games. 'Why not?'

'Because,' he leaned forward on the counter and spoke with exaggerated slowness, 'we don't have it.' He straightened up and continued in a normal tone: 'It's from a mag called *Tartlets* which isn't published any more. There was only a few issues. Them pages are from number two if I remember correctly. All right? That do for you then?'

'What were the rest of the pictures like?' I was determined to persevere.

Anger flickered across his face. 'Look, how should I know? It was basically more of the same but I can't give

130

you a blow by blow account, if you'll excuse the pun. Now if you don't mind I'd appreciate it if you'd leave. You being here has run off all my regulars.'

I glanced round the shop. He was right. It was empty. 'You mean they won't be in the same shop as a woman?' I asked incredulously.

He shook his head. 'Nah. They don't like women much. Just the ones in the pictures.' He grinned. I turned to leave without another word. But he must have relented because as I got to the door he spoke again.

'The people who buy these type of mags tend to be specialists. Your best bet is to try to find someone who's a collector – a real connoisseur. Someone like that would probably have it in their collection.'

I nodded curtly. 'Thanks.'

After that, I hurried home because I had to help George pack his things. Caroline had been released from hospital and although she still wasn't completely in the clear and would be visited daily by nursing staff, she had been desperate to get her son back.

As I raced up the garden path towards the back door, I was waylaid by Emmet, the retired fisherman who takes care of my garden. He insisted that there was something he had to show me and led me, seething with impatience, across the garden to some shrubs outside the kitchen window.

'Look at that!' He pointed accusingly at a pile of four or five cigarette butts lying on the ground. 'I think you need to have a talk to that young lad. Looks to me like he's been smoking on the sly.' I looked at the cigarette ends helplessly. They were right under George's bedroom window. I decided on the easy way out.

'He's going back home today, Emmet, so I think we'd best just leave it,' I tried to placate him, before telling him what a fine job he was doing and rushing indoors.

George seemed very moody as he stuffed his belongings carelessly into his holdall. He said nothing all the way home. When I stopped the car, he got out, dragging his bag onto the pavement. Caroline appeared smiling happily and waving at the window of their flat on the first floor. At the last moment before he slammed the car door shut, George muttered in a rush, 'Thank you very much for having me and Chipper. Bye.' Then he walked slowly up the path, Chipper's box under one arm, dragging his holdall by the handle with the other. I was caught off gaurd by a stabbing sense of loss.

I got home just as Lucinda arrived back from the grocery store. She seemed in good spirits. I knew that two of her exams were already over although she still had two to go.

'Where's George? she asked cheerfully.

'Gone back to his mother. I told you two days ago,' I answered tersely.

Lucinda frowned, looking down at the plastic bag of groceries she was carrying. 'That's a pity,' she said. 'I've just bought him a lifetime supply of crisps.' She shrugged. 'Oh well. I suppose he can have them when he comes to visit.'

Next morning, I propelled myself out of bed as soon as the alarm went off, psyched up for the scrummage of getting George ready for school. It wasn't until I was halfway through my first cup of black coffee that I remembered he wasn't there.

'Goodness. It ain't half quiet around here without old George,' commented Lucinda when she appeared ten minutes later. I hadn't expected we'd miss him so much. It meant that I got to work in record time, however, to find Mags already there. She was very pale and tired still, but resolute. I walked over and perched on the corner of her desk.

'How are you feeling?'

She tried a smile. 'Much better.' I caught a sudden scent of something alcoholic. Gin? Vodka perhaps? Mags was rattling on. 'I decided I was better off back at work. It takes my mind off things. I was just sitting brooding at home. I had a good sleep last night so I feel okay and,' she shot a furtive glance towards the closed door of Trevor's office in the corner, 'I didn't dare stay away too long in the present circumstances.'

'Hmm.' I was very dubious. 'I still don't think you should be here although I understand why you're worried. None of us can be too careful where old Trevor is concerned.'

'What's this about Heavy Trevy?' came in a stage whisper from behind us. We turned to find Julian's grinning face.

'Just the usual,' I sighed.

Julian became serious. 'Yes, I heard about that.' He patted Mags on the back as he moved off. 'Never mind. We're all right behind you. If it comes to a showdown, he'll lose.'

Mags smiled sadly. 'I wouldn't be too sure of that.'

I changed tack. 'Listen, I've decided to follow up on those magazine pages George found. I still think they could be a clue to what the rapist might do next.'

Mags tried to look interested, but there was a profound weariness in her manner. It worried me. She had always thrown herself into each new assignment with gusto. She loved her job. Now I got the impression it didn't matter much to her any more. Something very fundamental had changed but I didn't know what or why.

'Have you thought of asking Lucinda?' Mags suggested lamely, as if to pass the buck, when I'd finished the account of my attempts to track down the magazine.

'Of course! I must be losing my mind!' I slapped my forehead with the palm of one hand. 'Why didn't I think of that? I'll ask her tonight.'

Lucinda had been so distracted by her exams that I had

stopped trying to interest her in the documentary and the lack of progress with the police investigation. But she had been in the local Vice Squad when she worked as a detective. She was the obvious person to locate a copy of the magazine.

'Alan,' she said.

'*Alan*?' I repeated incredulously. 'I didn't know he worked in Vice.'

'He doesn't.' She gave me a wry grin. 'He *is* Vice.' Then seeing my look of mystification she relented. 'If you recall, one of the things we fought about all the time was his collection of porn. I'm sure he'll have what you want.'

I telephoned Lucinda's former home, where Alan still lived, but only got the answering machine. Then I remembered what he'd said to George about overtime, and called Police Headquarters instead. Alan came on the line in a couple of minutes, affable and friendly. After all, I was the one who'd let him into my house over Lucinda's dead body.

I didn't waste time on the preliminaries. 'Alan, I'm trying to track down a particular bondage mag.'

There was a slight cough on the other end of the line and a pause. I could imagine him shuffling from one foot to the other, wondering how to deal with this one. If it had been Lucinda, she'd have let him stew, but I needed information badly, so I decided to help him out. 'Lucinda thought that you might have seen it somewhere, since you're out and about so much.'

'Oh, right.' There was an audible lightening in his tone of voice. 'That's highly possible. What is it you're looking for?'

'Back numbers of a magazine called *Tartlets*.

'Yes.' Alan sounded cautious. 'I remember that one. I don't think they got much beyond about six issues before it folded. I'll see what I can do. When do you need it?'

'As soon as possible. Tonight would be great.' I sank to low cunning. 'If you can lay hands on it, stop by and have a drink with us,' I paused momentarily to let the plural sink in, 'on your way home.'

Three hours later, at ten o'clock, the front doorbell rang. Alan stood on the doorstep, smiling, with half a dozen magazines under his arm.

'Where's Lucinda?' he asked, looking round expectantly as I showed him into the sitting room.

'She's upstairs,' I prevaricated. 'I'll call her down in a minute. You've got the magazines, I see.'

Alan looked disappointed. He laid the half-dozen issues on a small table. 'Do you know which one you want?' I produced the torn pages.

'I'm trying to find where these came from.'

Alan glanced at them, then without hesitation tossed aside the top two magazines in the pile and picked up the third. He flicked through the pages, then folded one over and passed the magazine to me. Lucinda had been right.

'What do you want it for?'

Having got him there under false pretences, I felt I at least owed him the truth on that. 'George found these pages near where that woman was attacked out back. I think they belonged to the rapist.' I was scanning the pages before and after the ones I already had. As Lucinda and I had guessed, they were part of a series of photo essays – if you could call them that – showing a range of female stereotypes. All of them appeared fully clothed on the first page, looking haughty and unobtainable. On the second page of each sequence, they had been stripped and bound and their genitalia displayed; rendered powerless, an exaggerated look of fear on their faces. Apart from the teacher and the nurse, there was an air stewardess, a schoolgirl, a cheerleader and a policewoman. The very last one in the sequence was a nun. Her hands had been tied in prayer.

I showed them to Alan. 'What if our man is following this pattern? What if he's finding women who fit these stereotypes, then attacking and raping them? Couldn't that help track him down?'

Alan looked thoughtful, but after a couple of seconds, he shook his head. 'Nah. You wouldn't be able to predict who he would go for next so you couldn't trap him that way. And I doubt very much if you could find him through the mag – you know, by finding out who bought it locally. These things are collector's items. They get passed around amongst select groups of people and it's all a bit secretive. I bet most of the people who sell them don't know their customers' names.' He looked at me kindly. 'Good try, though. Have you mentioned this to Sykes?'

I nodded despondently. 'He didn't think there was anything in it.'

Alan began to gather his magazines together. 'Yeh. It's like I said. I wouldn't lay much store by it either.' He straightened up, visibly changing the subject. 'Now, what about that drink? And did you say Lucinda was coming down?'

'I'll go and call her. Can I keep this?' I held up the issue which contained the pages I'd been seeking. Alan hesitated.

'Sure,' he said, but he sounded a little uncertain. I went upstairs and twisted Lucinda's arm to come down for a drink with Alan. She agreed, but before we had taken even one sip, she made some acid remark about Alan's predilection for porn, they got into a raging argument and he stormed out, slamming the front door so hard I really thought the glass would shatter.

Chapter Ten

I couldn't wait to tell Mags what I had discovered. I wanted to convince her that progress was being made, to get her back to her old self. The TR was acting up, however, and it took ages to get it to start, which made it all the more surprising that, when I walked into the newsroom, her desk was empty.

'Where's Mags?' I asked Ron quietly. He shrugged as if to say, 'Don't ask me.'

'Has she called in sick?'

He shook his head. 'Not that I've heard.' He glanced about him quickly then leaned closer to me. 'You'd better get on to that girl. You'd think she was deliberately trying to ruin her career.'

Quickly, I returned to my office and dialled Mags' number. There was only the answering machine and I hung up without waiting to leave a message. It was totally unheard-of for Mags not to show up for work without letting someone know why. Wild thoughts flashed through my mind. She'd been so upset lately. Supposing she'd done something stupid, like mixing booze with the pills Joan had given her? What about her children, where were they? The more I thought about it, the more frantic I became.

But I couldn't leave the building. I had a crew booked to go to City Hall to interview the Mayor about the corruption scandal. I couldn't cancel that without drawing attention to Mags' absence – not to mention jeopardising my career into the bargain. But I was worried stiff.

In desperation, I phoned June. I must have sounded frantic when she picked up the phone because she instantly became alarmed.

'What is it? What's wrong?'

Quickly I explained that Mags hadn't shown up at work and I was worried because she'd been ill. Could June take a taxi over to Mags' house and see if she was there and if everything looked normal?

'Harry can take me, that's okay,' June volunteered. 'Is there a key I can get?'

'There is,' I said, mentally cursing my lack of organisation, 'but I can't remember where I put it. Just ring the doorbell and see if she answers. If she doesn't, have a look through the windows and see if anything looks out of place.'

I had to run to meet up with my crew and we arrived at City Hall ten minutes late. But the Mayor was a genial man, the consummate politician, gladhanding everyone, and although his PR lady scolded us for being late, the only thing that upset him was that I would be doing the questions and not the glamorous Mags.

It was noon before we emerged and I could use the mobile phone in the camera car. Impatiently, I dialled June's number. She answered on the first ring.

'Bel, I've been waiting for you to call,' she breathed. 'Harry came with me and we rang the doorbell then Harry had the bright idea of going round and knocking on all the windows because the curtains were still closed. But no one answered. Either she's really fast asleep or she's not there. Harry wouldn't let me call the police or an ambulance until I'd spoken to you because he said the papers would have a ball because Mags is so famous.'

'Thanks, June.' I was gabbling my words. 'You're a pal. I must go. Thanks again.'

I replaced the phone. Fear gripped me. 'Could you drop me at my car round the corner?' I said to the cameraman as we approached the studios. He swung the car obligingly past the main gates and drew level with my TR6 parked on a side street.

'D'you mind leaving the tape on my desk?' I swung myself out of the passenger seat.

'No problem.'

'And,' I stuck my head back into the car, 'don't say anything about Mags not being with us, okay?' I glanced round to include Andy, the sound recordist sitting in the back.

'Is she okay?' he asked, frowning. 'Someone said that bastard Trevor has been giving her a hard time.'

'You can say that again.' I withdrew my head and made to close the door.

'Aye well, send him out with us. We'll show him what a really hard time is.' Andy winked and gave me a cheery wave as they did a smart U-turn and headed back to the main gate.

I drove home and rummaged through the kitchen drawers, cursing the whole time. Finally, when I was nearly hysterical, I found the key to Mags' house in a little wooden box marked *Keys* on the hall table – the last place I would have looked. It took me five minutes to reach Mags' home, a detached house of grey stone, half-hidden from the road by thick bushes and shrubbery. As I wended my way up the narrow path, I could see that the curtains were still closed, as June had described.

I was so nervous that I fumbled as I tried to insert the key in the lock. Swearing vehemently, I finally got the door to spring open and walked in. Mags' home is often untidy, littered with children's toys and paraphernalia, but beneath the superficial layer of playthings, it is always clean. The house I now entered looked as if someone had trashed it completely. Clothing was strewn around the hall and over the bannisters. There was a cup of coffee on a small table growing mould. A thick layer of dust lay everywhere and seemed to hang in the air. Something was very wrong.

'Mags!' I yelled at the top of my voice. 'It's me, Bel!' There was a leaden silence. I shivered, filled with foreboding. I began a rapid trawl of all the rooms, not bothering to keep quiet, banging doors carelessly behind me.

A cursory survey of the downstairs revealed nothing except further signs of neglect, so I raced up to the first floor. I knew where Mags' bedroom was. I pushed the door open.

'Mags!' I called, loitering outside. There was silence. I walked into the room. The curtains were drawn, but I could make out an antique dressing table facing me, a line of built-in wardrobes receding along the wall to my left and a large bed beneath the window to my right. The duvet was heaped up on the bed.

Gently, I drew it back. Mags lay curled up beneath it, in the foetal position. She was wearing the same clothes I had last seen her in the night before, right down to the high-heeled shoes. Her eyes were closed. A sense of foreboding almost overwhelmed me. I bent to shake her, but before I could do so, she spoke very slowly, as if she were far away in some deep pit.

'Leave me alone.'

My relief was palpable. In those first wild moments when I saw her lying there, I really thought she might be dead. I sat down on the edge of the bed.

'Mags,' I said gently. 'Something's wrong. I don't know what it is and I don't know what to do.'

Mags turned onto her back. Tears rolled down her face as she said, 'Nothing's wrong. I've got a bug of some kind. Just leave me alone.'

Something struck me. 'Where are the children?'

After a pause, Mags answered reluctantly, 'They're at

school and daycare as usual. They spent the night with Barry. It was his birthday so he had them.' She began to weep.

'What about tonight? D'you think I should call Barry? Maybe he and his girlfriend could take them for a few days to give you a chance . . .'

Mags propelled herself to an upright position. 'No,' she wailed. 'No, no, no.' She was sobbing hard now. Weakly, she dragged her legs over the side of the bed.

'I'm fine. I'll come to work, if that's what it takes.' She stood up, swaying, then collapsed back onto the bed.

'You'd better change your clothes,' I pointed out. 'Do you want me to get some out?' She was crying too hard to talk but she shook her head.

I left her to get dressed and went downstairs. I was in a quandary. Mags was clearly having some sort of breakdown. She obviously thought the best thing to do was to keep going but I had serious misgivings. What if she made more mistakes and Trevor got what he needed to fire her?

The living-room door opened and Mags appeared. She wore no make-up and she had dressed carelessly in a sweater and skirt and an old pair of shoes which were caked in mud.

'Get your navy jacket and that navy and white spotted scarf,' I ordered. 'And we need to find another pair of shoes.'

Listlessly, Mags did as she was told and I did my best to make her look her usual smart, professional self. Then I drove us both to the studios, praying that the TR wouldn't pack up on me now.

Being back in the building produced a reflex action in Mags and she adopted the ghost of her normal efficient manner. She even managed to wave as she walked past Eric, the security man on duty in Reception.

'As far as anyone knows, you did the Lord Mayor's

interview this morning,' I briefed her as we climbed the stairs. 'Stick your head in the newsroom as if you've just come back from lunch and then go and sit in my office or Julian's room. That's where I'll be editing the interview. We may need you to voice it.' Mags nodded, obedient as a zombie.

I went upstairs, picked up the tapes from my office and headed towards Julian's editing room. He was standing on his head when I entered.

'Just getting some blood back to the old grey cells,' he explained cheerfully. I gave myself a shake. I was beginning to wonder if I was going mad. Quickly, I told Julian that Mags was unwell, but that we didn't want to let Trevor know that.

'Oh, he's a creep,' agreed Julian. 'People like Heavy Trevy are dinosaurs. They don't belong any more.'

'Well, they're still here,' I commented sourly. 'Let's get this piece put together and then I'll see if Mags is okay to voice it.' Julian set to work. He was fast, his fingers flying across the buttons operating the machines.

Forty-five minutes later, we had cut the interview together with some library footage of council meetings and the exterior of City Hall. Not the most exciting piece of work I'd ever done, but the best we could manage under the circumstances. I walked along the corridor to the far corner of the building, knocked on my office door and poked my head in. Mags was sitting lifelessly in a chair by the window, gazing out with an expression of profound sadness and despair on her face.

I came in and closed the door. 'We've cut the Mayor's interview. I've written the links for you. Can you manage to voice them, d'you think?' I asked quietly. She turned her head slowly towards me, as if she were far away, underwater.

'Yes.' It seemed to take an immense physical effort for her to stand up. I prayed that we wouldn't meet anyone on the way. We did, but it was one of the graphics artists and he clearly had his mind on other things because he nodded to us absently as he rushed past, murmuring, 'Hi, Mary.' So much for working in the same building for eight years.

By the time we got back, Julian had set up a microphone to record the links. It was a bit rough and ready, but then news always was. We got away with things that wouldn't be acceptable on any other programme. Mags read the links lifelessly, but fortunately they were short and since I didn't think asking her to do them again would produce much improvement, I nodded assent to Julian's questioning look.

Mags was quiet and withdrawn. 'I'll take this down to the newsroom,' I told her. 'You go back to my office and stay there. I'll tell Trevor we're working on something to do with the documentary and they can call you there if they need you.'

Somehow, this ruse worked. Trevor was totally preoccupied talking on the phone to his 'sources' getting what he considered to be hot leads on the council corruption case which seemed to be mushrooming. At any rate, he didn't appear to notice Mags' absence and accepted the interview of the Mayor without comment.

We waited until ten minutes after the evening programme had ended so that most of the news team would have left for home or the pub before we ventured forth from my office. But as luck would have it, my car wouldn't start. None of my usual tricks worked. Reluctantly, we returned to Reception so that I could phone a garage.

Mags suddenly seemed to come up out of her lethargy. 'Ten to seven!' There was panic in her voice. 'I have to pick the kids up from the babysitter by seven at the latest.' She stumbled towards the door.

'Wait!' I put down the phone. 'I'll call a taxi.'

'No chance.' Dave, one of the security men leaned on the counter. 'There's a big concert on at Bellingham Hall tonight. Taxis are all busy. I tried to get one for Ron Polly ten minutes ago and they said there'd be an hour's wait.'

'Hold on!' I caught Mag's arm as she headed towards the door. She struggled feebly to get free.

'I have to get there before seven!' She was starting to cry.

I looked round distractedly. At that instant, Trevor came down the stairs. On impulse, I called out to him.

'Trevor!' He turned towards me and I stood so as to block his view of Mags. 'My car won't start. I don't suppose you could do us a favour, could you, and drop us off on your way home?'

I had expected a show of surly reluctance, but Trevor nodded jauntily and said, 'No problem. This way, ladies.'

Perhaps it was because he wanted to show off his smart new car. I pushed Mags into the back, so that Trevor couldn't see the state she was in.

'It's a Cosworth,' Trevor murmured with studied casualness as he pulled out of the car park. Then when I looked at him blankly, he added, 'Only one of these in town,' as he put his foot down and the car roared to the end of the street.

We arrived at the babysitter's within minutes. As Trevor drew into the side of the road, Mags leapt out, without waiting for him to come to a complete stop. I was about to follow her to see if she was all right but she had already disappeared up the path.

'She's got to get her kids by seven,' I tried to explain, seeing Trevor's puzzled expression. He shrugged and pulled out into the traffic again. I hardly listened to his conversation as he drove the couple of blocks to my home. He seemed to be relishing this opportunity to be sociable. I think he was still talking about his car.

The house was empty when I got in and there was nothing to distract me from my thoughts. I was intensely worried about Mags. On the spur of the moment, I telephoned June and asked her if she would be able to help Mags out some evenings with the children. She seemed to jump at the idea. Perhaps she was lonely, because she mentioned that Harry was still working out of town several nights a week.

As soon as I hung up, the phone rang, making me jump. It was Mags, her voice thick with tears.

'I need to talk to you,' she said, and hung up.

The house was in darkness when I arrived and there was no answer when I rang the doorbell. I still had her key in my pocket from earlier in the day, so I let myself in, calling out to announce my arrival. Two of the children appeared briefly in their pyjamas at the top of the stairs, then shot off again. I walked along the hall, checking rooms as I went, nearly killing myself when I stumbled over a couple of coats and a schoolbag which had been dropped on the floor.

Mags was sitting in darkness in the living room. She remained completely still as I fumbled around until I switched on a lamp. She didn't even flinch as the light hit her. She was staring blindly into space. She knew who it was although she didn't look my way.

I sat down nearby. 'It isn't just Barry, is it? Or Trevor. You've coped with that sort of thing before.'

She turned and looked at me dully. Her first attempt at speaking made her cough and choke, but she seemed determined not to give up. The words came slowly and unemotionally, in a dead voice.

'Do you remember that Friday night when you and I went out for dinner to talk about work? Barry had the kids that weekend.' I nodded. 'Well.' Her voice was very quiet. I could see it was a tremendous effort for her to talk about this. 'That night when you dropped me off, I walked

145

up the path and I was looking in my bag for my key when someone grabbed me from behind. He put his hand across my mouth so I couldn't scream. He used my scarf to gag me then something, it felt like handcuffs, to hold my wrists together. I was so taken by surprise that I froze. I didn't fight back, I couldn't do anything.' She looked at me with a puzzled expression, strangely detached. 'It was like a very primitive reaction, like an animal mesmerised by fear.' She stopped, seemingly lost in thought, gazing down at her hands twisting in her lap.

I watched her helplessly. There was something eerie about her account, as if it hadn't happened to her, but to someone else.

She started talking again, picking up where she had left off, her voice low. 'I was bundled into the back of a car. I don't know why he didn't force me to go into the house – perhaps he didn't know the kids weren't there. He drove for a while, fast. It was a very powerful car, I could hear the engine. He stopped at a crossroads or something. Anyway, there was a street-light shining in. I was trying to note everything I could that would identify him. There was a funny blue stain on the upholstery. It was shaped like a raised umbrella. Could have been ink – a pen that had leaked or something. Well . . .'

There was a long pause, as if she were preoccupied by this detail, as if it were important. But she was so obviously on the brink of not telling her story at all that I was afraid a word from me might shatter her fragile resolve, break the spell. So I said nothing. Just waited, my eyes never moving from her face. She looked distant and removed. She was alone in a world of her own pain.

After several minutes, something seemed to bring her back to the present. She turned to me, frowning a little. 'I was taken to a wood somewhere, tied up and then raped.' She said it matter-of-factly, then carried on as if afraid to dwell too long on those words, afraid to let them gather too much power in the silence.

'Afterwards, he shoved me back in his car and dropped me off at the roundabout as you come into town at Barnston. He threw my clothes after me.' She was beginning to lose her composure now and, had started to weep. 'I got dressed and walked home. My handbag was still lying on the path outside the front door and I let myself in. By that time it was about three in the morning.'

'Why didn't you call me? I'd have come over.'

She shook her head dismissively. 'I couldn't. I just wanted to crawl into a hole. As it was,' she gave a funny half-sob, half-laugh, 'I curled into the tightest ball I could. I got into the cupboard.' There was a note of hysteria in her voice. 'I was looking for somewhere safe.'

Her large green eyes had jagged edges of pain. There was a long pause. Then she said, 'Tonight when I got into Trevor's car, there was a blue stain identical to the one I saw that night, on the upholstery of the back seat.'

I stared at her, not quite able to take this in. She waited patiently, not looking at me, as if she didn't want to influence my response, as if she needed me to reach my own conclusions, to validate what she was saying, to prove she wasn't mad.

As the full significance hit me, I looked at her incredulously. 'What are you saying? That Trevor was the man who abducted you! That he *raped* you?' The last words were whispered, as if by speaking them quietly, I could defuse some of their devastating impact.

Mags gazed at me impassively for several moments, then she nodded almost imperceptibly. 'That's what I'm saying.'

I ran my hands through my hair distractedly. 'But why didn't you say something at the time?' I had blurted that out before I stopped to think and I could hear the implied accusation.

Mags looked at me sadly, as if I too had failed her. 'Until it happened to me, I always thought I would report it if I were raped. But I felt like *shit*. I couldn't bear for anyone else to know I'd been so humiliated. I couldn't bear to be exposed. It was like being hung out naked for the world to see.

'I didn't know what indignities they would put me through at the hospital. What the police would ask. I was terrified of being at their mercy. It would have felt like the rape all over again. I couldn't bear the thought of another strange man, even if he did call himself a doctor, poking at me. All kinds of people would have the right to look at me. My private parts would become public, open to scrutiny. I would have been examined by all kinds of people. I wouldn't be able to refuse, not once I was in the system. And my kids – how would I keep it from them? What would it do to them to know I'd been raped?

'I know a lot of the police officers, remember. I couldn't stand the thought of them looking at photographs of me. Those pictures get sent to the defence team. Lots of people see them. And then the press.' She closed her eyes and leaned back. 'Our dear friends in the press. Some of them would hold back because they know me.' She opened her eyes, gazing at me wearily. 'But it's a hell of a story. Local celebrity raped. They wouldn't be allowed to name me, but they would say enough so people would guess. And this town is so small that it would be common knowledge within days.

'Someone would slip them copies of the evidence pictures. They wouldn't publish, but it would be a collector's item, wouldn't it?' Her voice was harsh with anger. 'They'd pass it around amongst themselves. It happens. We both know it does.

'I've worked hard for everything I've got. I've put

in twelve, fourteen-hour days as a matter of course. Regardless of how tired or under the weather I've been, I've got up every morning and put on my make-up and carried on as if I'm invincible. I've fought every inch of the way to be taken seriously as a journalist, to be allowed to cover the big stories, the boys' stories, the murders and the juicy court cases. And in one night, in the space of two hours, all of that was destroyed. Everything. My whole life. Everything I've built up.'

She was silent. When she spoke again, it was quietly, with certain knowledge. 'No one would ever forget. Every time they saw me on television, the public would remember I'd been raped. I would be a rape victim for the rest of my career.'

I had been sitting riveted to my seat, unable to take my eyes off her for a second. 'And now?' I ventured.

'I don't know. I thought I could just push it all down. I could carry on as usual. I would let no one see what had happened to me – not even my friends, not even you, Bel – because it was the façade that mattered and once it cracked, I would be done for. I wanted to push away that swamping feeling of being a piece of shit. But it doesn't work.' She put her head in her hands and began to weep. 'I'm scared to be out alone on the street. I'm scared to stay alone here at night. I can't sleep. I hear noises. I'd lock myself in my room except I'd be shutting out the kids. I imagine what he might do to them. I am frightened the whole time. I never was safe, but I carried on my life because I could ignore the dangers. Now I can't. I see them everywhere.'

She closed her eyes and took a deep, sobbing breath. When she looked at me again, her gaze was steady. 'It's probably too late now. But it's finally dawned on me that the only way to regain my peace of mind, my self-respect, is to fight back.'

'Do you want me to call Sykes – or Henderson?'

149

For a moment, I could see in Mags' eyes that she was wavering. Then she said, 'Henderson. He'll understand.'

She was right. No one could have been more sympathetic or attentive than Henderson. He knew Mags well from her work as a reporter and did not doubt her integrity. She might have been his own daughter, from the way he reacted. You could see that this threat to her life and well-being cut him to the quick.

Sykes moved fast, at Henderson's instigation. Somehow, as always, the press got hold of the story. They were waiting outside Police Headquarters when Trevor was brought in for questioning. Mags went for an examination by a woman doctor – although she had to insist on that. The police officer making the arrangements kept saying, 'But he's a *doctor*,' referring to the male police surgeon, as if that made any difference.

But so much time had passed since the rape had happened that all trace of semen was gone, and any stray pubic hairs or forensic evidence had been washed away in the shower. When the police asked to examine the clothes Mags was wearing that night, there was nothing to give them. She had thrown every last item in the rubbish bin and it was long gone, incinerated.

Martin came to visit Mags, feeling remorseful for being so unsupportive but vehement in his condemnation of Trevor. When the police had picked the latter up, he had been full of bluster, threatening to sue. One of the detectives involved in questioning him told us he was still loudly maintaining his innocence, claiming he had an alibi.

I took my crew down to Police Headquarters to record the mood in the Incident Room while this was going on. The investigators seemed tense but cautiously optimistic. It was clear they were all hoping that they had finally caught their man.

So I was present when Sykes broke off his interview with Trevor to call a meeting of his team. Everyone stirred expectantly. Perhaps this was news that he had confessed, or that he had irrevocably incriminated himself.

Sykes addressed the group. 'Well,' he said with a twisted smile, 'the bad news is that he has a cast-iron alibi. We've checked it out and it's solid. We know he couldn't have driven his car that night and he swears the vehicle was parked outside his house during the entire weekend, and that he had the keys with him. Trevor Gates is not our man.' He turned and headed for his office, calling over his shoulder: 'Commander Henderson and I would like to talk to Ms Lawson at once, if you don't mind. Someone get her. *Now.*'

Twenty minutes later, PC Burke came up to where I was standing with my crew in a state of shock, awaiting developments.

'Ms Lawson has requested that you be present at the interview,' he whispered discreetly. He led me upstairs to a large room. Henderson and Sykes were ranged along one side of a long table, their faces grave. Mags was already there. She looked devastated.

'I don't understand,' she was saying, bewildered.

Sykes' eyes were hard. 'It's very simple. Trevor Gates has a cast-iron alibi for the night you say you were raped by him. We've checked it. On the night in question, he called an ambulance at eight pm and was taken to St Luke's complaining of chest pains. Doctors there did some tests and decided to keep him in overnight for observation.'

Sykes paused to let that sink in before continuing: 'He owns a Cosworth – the car you say was used to abduct you. According to the manufacturers, it is virtually impossible to break into it and drive off. Mr Gates swears it was standing outside his front door when he left and was still there when he returned the next day.'

151

I could see Mags casting around for something to clutch on to. 'What about Sister Kate?' she said finally. 'What about that day?'

'That one is a little less conclusive, I'll grant you,' Sykes replied smoothly. 'He left the office about eleven a.m. to go for a meeting with a friend of his called Tigger Benyon. Tigger can't recall the meeting but that isn't surprising since he was unusually drunk that day, according to his colleagues.' Sykes leaned forward on his desk, clasping his hands. 'Which brings us to the point, Ms Lawson. Why didn't you report this sooner? Your description of the vehicle you say was used to abduct you would carry more weight if you had never been in Trevor Gates' car. But you didn't make your accusations until after you had been driven home in it and knew what the interior looked like. What's to say you didn't make the story up then? What's to say you aren't accusing an innocent man?'

'He's not innocent. What I told you was true,' Mags answered hotly.

'But it can't be. Simple as that.' Sykes opened a file lying in front of him and consulted several loose sheets of paper with closely-typed script. 'Mr Gates suggests that this may have been vindictive. That you hold a grudge against him because he got the job you wanted. That you've made everything very difficult for him and been extremely rude to him in front of colleagues. He thinks this may have been triggered because he publicly admonished you for a bad slip-up you made on a recent court report.' Sykes leaned his chin on his hand in an expression of boredom, as if waiting for Mags to trot out the usual excuses.

Mags was white. When she spoke, her voice shook. 'Everything I told you is true. I *was* abducted. I *was* in that car – I saw the same stain. But if you say he has a cast-iron alibi, then I will withdraw my accusation.' She stood up, swaying slightly. 'But I know I was kidnapped in that vehicle and then raped.'

Sykes smiled thinly. 'I'm afraid it may not be as simple as retracting your statement. You can't just accuse an innocent man of a heinous crime, then when you are caught out say "Oh sorry, forget it." We have spent a great deal of time and effort on this, interrupting a serious and complicated murder investigation. God knows what might have happened if Mr Gates hadn't had a good alibi – if he'd just gone home and watched telly on his own all night like most people. He could be facing a murder charge now, and I could have had my men tied up on a wild goose chase for weeks, months even. Oh no, it's not that simple.'

Mags sank weakly back into her chair. She was staring at Sykes, eyes wide. 'It wasn't malicious,' was all she could say.

Henderson had been watching her closely. Now he spoke for the first time. 'You must understand, Mags, that this is a very serious situation. We don't know yet how Trevor Gates will want to proceed. The best thing may be for you to go home and we will have a think about this. I don't know how your employers will react, but I strongly advise you not to go to work in the meantime. It would be very difficult under the circumstances.'

I had expected Mags to be upset, to start crying perhaps as soon as we got out to the car. But she seemed to be in shock. I drove her home in silence.

'D'you want me to come in for a while?' I asked when we reached her house, but she shook her head slowly.

'No.' Then she gave her head a sudden intense shake. 'I'm going mad,' she said. She got out of the car and disappeared in the direction of her front door without another word.

Chapter Eleven

The next few days were a nightmare. Mags was suspended from work almost immediately.

'Why didn't the police do a DNA test on Trevor?' I moaned to Lucinda over coffee late one night. 'That would have proved whether or not he's the rapist!'

'They wanted to.' Lucinda looked at me helplessly. 'But he got on his high horse and said he wouldn't be treated as if he was guilty, and refused to cooperate.'

'Well, why didn't they force him to?' I was almost shouting in my frustration.

'They couldn't. He had an alibi which checked out. He wasn't a suspect any more. They couldn't insist unless he was.'

I still clung to the hope that it would all blow over, that Mags could plead that she had been under a lot of pressure and eventually be reinstated. I lobbied Martin to this effect, knowing that he was sympathetic.

Then the news broke that Trevor had filed a lawsuit alleging defamation. Mags had repeated her accusations to a local journalist in what she thought was an off-the-record conversation. The next day her words had appeared in an article about sexual harassment in the workplace. Trevor wasn't actually mentioned by name but he was furious, nevertheless, claiming that most people would be able to put two and two together and realise he was the man she was accusing of rape. If his lawsuit was successful, it would be the end of Mags' career.

As if that wasn't bad enough, the tabloid press were staking out her home. It was the worst possible nightmare. Now not only did everyone know that she claimed to have been raped . . . but she had been branded a malicious liar into the bargain.

As soon as I heard the news, I went to see her. She answered the door only after I had called out to identify myself. The green eyes were cloudy, she wore no make-up and she seemed painfully thin, dressed in an old pair of baggy jeans and shapeless grey T-shirt, which made her arms seem like sticks. There was no sign that she had been crying, but as I looked at her I had a sense that she was dangerously close to the edge.

'I'm finished,' she said flatly, with no trace of emotion. 'I'll never get another job, not in journalism. And if I can't earn the money, I can't keep this house. And without a home for my children, Barry will take them.' She turned to me with eyes that were vacant as a bombsite. 'It's all over.'

'I believe you,' I blurted out. 'I know you're telling the truth about being raped. I'd never seen you like that before, not in all the years we've worked together. And Martin believes you too. The problem is that there's no proof that your attacker was Trevor.'

'What's the use?' She held out her hands in a gesture of emptiness. 'There's nothing we can do. It's finished.'

'Look,' I pleaded. 'You can't give up. If the police won't pursue this, then we have to. All the time we've been making our documentary, we've heard them saying that the best hope is to find a link between victim and attacker. As far as the police are concerned, they've only got one rape/murder to go on. And then one malicious accusation. But we know that there have been three attacks – Sister Kate, you and the woman in the videotape – and it may have been the second time for her. The investigators have only got clues from one case to work on. We've got three.'

Mags was looking at me with a dubious expression. I could see it was going to take a lot to convince her.

'Let's start with your case,' I said with a brisk confidence I did not feel. 'You've got to remember everything you can, every little detail.'

Mags regarded me for a few moments, and I wondered if she was going to join me in this or not. But then she began to speak, reluctantly, it seemed, her voice listless.

'I can't describe him. He grabbed me from behind and he wore a mask. But he was about Trevor's height and build.'

'What about his voice?' I prompted.

'That was muffled by the mask. Quite light for a man, though, I would say. He wore aftershave, but not one I recognised.'

I grasped at that straw. 'Could you identify it, do you think, if we went to a department store and tried them? Was it one you remember Trevor wearing?'

Mags shook her head. 'I don't particularly recall any cologne or anything that Trevor wears. I'm not good at remembering scents. It's not one of my things.'

We sat in gloomy silence. I could not avoid the thought that we were trying to accomplish something that the whole police force with all its resources had been unable to do.

'Did he use a striped scarf, like a football scarf?' I asked. Mags thought for a moment, then shook her head dispiritedly.

I tried again. 'Do you know where you were taken? Perhaps he always goes to the same area.'

Mags sighed. 'I have no idea where he took me. It was dark. It must have been away from houses because I didn't see any lights. It took about fifteen minutes to get there.'

'That could have been almost anywhere,' I commented. Mags nodded in wry agreement. She was looking at me as if to say that this was a waste of time and we both knew it. She stood up, went to the fridge and got out an opened bottle of wine. Without asking, she placed a glass in front of me and another at her own place at the table and sloshed wine carelessly into both. She took several sips from her own glass.

'There *is* one thing I forgot to mention,' she said. I looked at her sharply. Apart from anything else, this was the first sign that she was willing to be more than a passive participant.

'I've been trying not to think of it because in some ways it's the worst thing of all,' she added.

I waited, my eyes locked onto her. She reached out and began tearing the label off the wine bottle, strip by tiny strip. Finally I could stand it no longer. I grabbed her hand to hold it still. 'What?'

Her face flushed and I suddenly felt her humiliation. It struck me painfully how damaged she had been by this experience, that she should feel ashamed with me, her friend.

She was gathering herself to speak. 'I think he took pictures,' she said abruptly, 'when he had me tied up. He took one before he raped me and then one afterwards. He had a flash. That's why it's so bad.' She had twisted her hand free and was now tearing the label again with avid intensity. 'It's the thought that there are photographs of me to be gloated over by him and whoever. Supposing he sells them?' She looked up at me, her eyes fathomless. 'There could be hundreds of copies on the street by now.'

For a moment I could think of nothing to say. But I rallied quickly. 'No,' I said emphatically, sounding more confident than I felt. 'If he has pictures he'll keep them to himself. If he sells them, they can be traced back to him and he'll be done for murder and rape. He must know that.'

There was something niggling at the back of my mind. 'There was a flash on George's videotape,' I said. 'The man had his back to the camera so you couldn't see what he was holding but there was a flash, just before the tape ended. I wonder if he took a picture of the other woman too? Perhaps that's part of the ritual, taking photographs.'

Mags shrugged despondently. I bit my lip, desperately trying to think of a way through all of this.

'Let's suppose they were in colour – he'd want them in colour, no doubt about that,' I thought out loud. 'It's quite complicated to process and print colour pictures, but he couldn't take them to a shop or a lab because someone would spot them and tip off the police. So they were probably Polaroids.' I stopped and spread my hands in a gesture of defeat. 'Wherever that gets us.'

Something flickered in Mags' eyes. 'Someone sent me Polaroids in the post, you know. I'd forgotten.' She was speaking almost to herself. I kept quiet. There was something so fragile about Mags at the moment that I dared not interrupt.

She hid her face in her hands, as if deep in thought, then lifted her head slowly. 'The rape put it out of my mind. It put everything out of my mind. But for a couple of weeks – maybe three – I got a series of Polaroid photographs in the post.' She looked directly at me. 'They were shots of me, sometimes on my own and a couple of times with the kids. They'd been taken in the street when I didn't know about it.

'I was annoyed because they seemed intrusive, but I thought it was just another fan who'd seen me on television, trying to show me how close he'd got, trying to make contact. You know,' she shrugged helplessly, 'if you appear on telly, people think they know you.

They think they've got rights to you. I get letters from old ladies telling me about their cats. People write to me because they've got problems with the council and they think I can wave a magic wand. Lonely men send me proposals of marriage. And some men send me obscene fantasies. You get used to it. Most of it you just bin.'

She paused, a faraway look in her eyes. 'I didn't think of it at the time, but I suppose the thing about these pictures was that they weren't addressed to me at RTV. They were sent here. It felt like a real invasion of privacy, a power trip for someone: "I can see you but you can't see me".'

'What did you do with them?' I spoke very quietly.

'Well, I did find them disturbing but I didn't have time to dwell on them very much or do anything about them. It would have meant interviews with the police, perhaps having my mail intercepted, questions about anyone I knew who might be doing this – all kinds of stuff. I had so much on my plate with Barry and everything else that I ended up chucking them out. Then they stopped anyway.' There was a long silence. Mags gazed out of the window.

'Do you think it was him?'

'Could be. I don't know.' She looked at me with a glimmer of hope in her eyes. 'D'you think there could be other things like this – clues that we've missed?'

I suddenly threw my arms wide, leaning back in my chair.

'Perhaps. We have to find the woman in the videotape. We have to find her and compare notes to see if we can figure out who this man is.'

Mags nodded but she looked exhausted. 'I won't be much use to you, I'm afraid. Every time I step outside the door, the news hounds chase me. They've taken it up as a personal crusade. You know – how it's really men who are victims. They love it when they can say a woman has falsely accused a man of rape, because then they can imply that all rape charges are suspect, that women are asking for it and that we're only raped when we let it happen and that really we love it.'

'Not all of them, surely,' I remonstrated gently.

She gave me a sceptical look, then shrugged dismissively. 'It feels like it. Anyway, there's the kids.'

'Why don't you go to your sister's for a few days? I could help you get away without them knowing.' I jerked my head in the direction of the front of the house where the press were staked out. 'You could sneak over the wall into your neighbour's back garden as soon as it's dark and I could pick you up on the next street.'

Some of the tension drained away from Mags' shoulders. 'Oh, I can't imagine what it would be like to get away from all this.' She closed her eyes, savouring the idea, then opened them again abruptly. 'Could you fetch my car for me? It's still at the garage. They finally got it fixed two days ago, but I haven't been able to stir from the house.'

'No problem – I can do that this afternoon. I'll park it on the next street over. You could leave tonight.'

'Done.' Some of the colour had come back to Mags' wan face.

I left the TR at home and took a taxi to Corders', a large family-owned garage in the centre of town. They had a reputation for honest, reliable work and were used by almost everyone I knew. Mr Corder himself was on duty at the service desk when I arrived and he gave a discreet nod when I told him why I was there.

'She just telephoned,' he said. 'If you wait here I'll bring it round to the front.' While he was gone, I paced up and down the small office restlessly. I was nervous that someone might have tipped off the press about Mags' car being here, and wanted to be gone as quickly as possible.

Someone had obviously made great efforts to smarten up this area – to remove from it any hint of engine grease and grime. The walls had been painted a pale blue-grey to match the carpet. There was a smart, modern grey desk with a swivel chair. Behind it was a board studded with hooks on which a series of blue clipboards hung, one for each job order, the keys hanging neatly alongside. Above the board were various framed certificates showing the mechanics' qualifications. And right bang in the centre of them was an enormous blow-up of a now familiar photograph.

Of course – I'd thought I recognised him. The man presenting the cheque to Sister Kate was none other than Mr Corder. I stepped around the desk to get a closer look. Suddenly, something caught my eye. Standing just behind him, half-hidden by his right shoulder, was Trevor, clearly visible for the first time in this enlarged print.

'Did you know Sister Kate?' Mr Corder had returned.

'I know *of* her, that's all,' I replied. 'What was the cheque for?'

Mr Corder smiled. 'It's a group of local business leaders. We like to raise money for deserving causes in the city centre where we're based.'

I pointed to Trevor. 'Why is Trevor Gates there? He's not a businessman.'

'Oh, he came along from the newspaper. I think he was Father of Chapel for the NUJ or something like that.' He held out Mags' car keys. 'I left it just across the street. Tell her we think we've got it sorted out now. She can settle up with us later.'

I drove across the city and parked in the quiet residential street behind Mags' house. Then I walked home and telephoned Mags to let her know her car was ready. She had made arrangements with her neighbours. As soon as it was dark, they would help her and the children over the wall into their garden, then out to her car. She would be with her sister by midnight.

I felt restless when I had done that, spurred on by what I had discovered that afternoon. It was a small victory, but at least I'd proved a link between Trevor and Sister Kate. Under the circumstances, I needed to clutch at every straw.

I found the torn scarf in the wardrobe upstairs where I'd left it. When I had first realised its significance, I had thought about putting an ad in the paper, asking the owner to come forward. But then I had decided that that was dangerous. If it *was* the same woman who had appeared on the videotape, she had already been attacked twice. By drawing attention to her, I could be putting her at risk a third time. In any case, I knew enough about her to predict that the first hint of publicity would send her underground.

George had Cubs that night. I phoned Caroline. She was recovering well, although she was still weak and tired easily, she said in answer to my queries. She could do with a holiday but chance would be a fine thing.

'Would it be all right if I picked George up from Cubs?' I asked. 'There's something I want to have a chat to him about.'

'Oh, he'll like that,' she said, sounding pleased. 'He talks about you and Lucinda all the time.'

It looked as if World War Three was in progress when I walked into the Scout hut. Little boys were running around everywhere. In the middle of the room a stout woman I recognised from before as Beryl was shouting orders. She smiled vaguely when she saw me and motioned me to the side. I dodged through the flying bodies and reached her in one piece. Quickly I introduced myself. Then I held out the scarf.

'I believe this may belong to the parent of one of the

boys. I found it at the Cub camp at Round House,' I explained briefly.

She held the scarf aloft and yelled at the top of her voice, 'Boys, pay attention!' Instantly the noise quietened down and the activity slowed and finally stopped. Tangles of bodies unravelled until about twenty little boys stood staring at us inquiringly. George made a face at me and nudged the boy standing next to him.

'Does anyone recognise this scarf?' Beryl asked in stentorian tones. There was a murmur of 'No' from the crowd.

'Are you sure?' She turned round from side to side so that everyone could get a good look at the scarf. Then she lowered her arm and held it out to me. 'None of this lot, I'm afraid.' She frowned. 'You know, there was another group of Cubs at Round House that same weekend. They were in tents out behind the house. I've got the number of their Akela somewhere.'

She rummaged in a large rucksack and produced a dog-eared notebook. 'Here we are. Joey Lauder – 753092.' She snapped the book shut and smiled. 'Very nice woman. She might be able to help you.'

Shortly afterwards the meeting ended and George sauntered over with Billy. I drove them both home via a hamburger chain because they insisted they were starving, so they were both dozy from stuffing themselves by the time I handed them back to their parents.

'What have you been eating?' I heard Barbara ask her son suspiciously as I made my getaway.

Once home, I dialled Ms Lauder's number. I explained about the scarf.

'Funnily enough,' she said when I'd finished, 'someone did ask about that. Now, who was it? One of the boys asked if anyone had found it in the woods and handed it in. Said it belonged to his brother. Just a minute.' There was a long pause and the sound of pages being turned.

'Here we are. His name is Danny Simpson. Would you like me to mention it at our next meeting on Friday?'

I thought quickly. We didn't have any time to lose. 'Would it be possible to give me his address – or his phone number might be better?' I asked.

'No problem.'

Within seconds, I had the information and was faced with the dilemma of what to do now. The boy had told Joey that the scarf belonged to his brother. I had been working on the assumption that it belonged to the woman. Stupidly, it hadn't occurred to me that it might be the attacker's. If it was his, I certainly didn't want to hand over anything that might be considered evidence against him.

The best thing to do would be to tell everything to Sykes and let him deal with it. But I was doubtful, as always, that he would take it seriously. Besides, if it did belong to the woman, then the arrival of the police on her front doorstep would probably make her clam up for ever.

The address I had been given was close to where I lived, so I decided to stop by there on some pretext, but to keep the scarf hidden in my pocket, in case it turned out to belong to the attacker.

Number 57 Kingston Avenue was a small house in a quiet, tree-lined street. I parked my car some distance away and approached the front door. A young boy with a heavy fringe of dark hair which he had to keep sweeping back out of his eyes answered the doorbell. I could hear a television blaring in the background.

Giving him a friendly smile, I explained that I had found a scarf which I thought might be his. For a moment, he looked puzzled, then his face cleared.

'What's it like?' he asked eagerly.

'It's wool. Red and white stripes,' I answered, watching his reaction closely.

He smiled broadly, tossing his hair back out of his eyes. Turning round, he yelled at the top of his voice, 'Mum!' The woman who emerged from a doorway at the end of the hallway was small and dark, as I remembered. When she saw me, she stopped in her tracks. I had pulled the scarf out of my pocket and now held it up. I saw her hesitate, as if she might retreat, only her eyes were held by the scarf and I understood that she could not bear to let it go.

Reluctantly, she stood aside to let me enter. She indicated a half-open door to my left and I walked through into a small, overheated sitting room. A comedy programme was playing on the television in the corner. Behind me, I heard her tell the boy to go upstairs and play with his computer. That didn't seem to please him much, because he stumped off up the stairs, kicking each tread as he went.

The woman, presumably Mrs Simpson, followed me into the room, picked up the remote control for the television and switched it off.

'Sit down, won't you?' She pointed to one of the velour armchairs on either side of the fireplace and took the other one herself. 'Thank you for bringing me back the scarf. It belonged to my son. I was really upset that I'd lost it.' She sounded nervous, pulling her navy cardigan tighter round her body. I looked at her closely. She had a worn, soft face, devoid of make-up, so that I could see the traces of old scars and pockmarks – a map of a woman who had had a hard life.

I handed her the torn scarf. 'I'd have got it back sooner but I didn't know how to find you. I'm Bel Carson, by the way,' I said.

For a moment, she looked as if she wanted to hold back, but then she responded, 'Paula Simpson.' There was an awkward pause. Clearly she wasn't going to bring up what had happened if I didn't mention it.

'That was the scarf I cut from around your neck that night, if you remember,' I said as gently as I could.

She jumped to her feet, wringing her hands. 'I remember. That was very kind of you. You saved my life, I've no doubt of that. But I'd rather not talk about it if you don't mind.' She stood waiting, silently willing me to stand up and take my leave. But I was impervious to such pressure. I had more urgent things to worry about.

'I came here because a friend of mine was attacked and raped by a man about ten days ago. We think we know who it is, and believe it's the same man who attacked you.'

Paula seemed to go limp. She collapsed back into her armchair and buried her head in her hands. Her voice was muffled but I could hear the anguish as she said, 'Oh God. I was afraid that would happen. But I told myself he'd had his jollies. He'd stop with me.' She looked up at me, her eyes flooded with remorse. 'Was it that story I saw in the papers – the one about that television reporter?' I nodded and a spasm of pain crossed her face before she continued. 'How's your friend now? He killed that nun, you know.'

'She's not too good,' I replied. 'She's a pretty strong individual but it happened at a bad time. The worst thing is that she thinks she knows who did it and told the police but there's no evidence so now he's suing her.'

She shook her head despairingly. 'But how can he? He's a bastard.'

I shrugged. 'It's my friend, Mags' word against his. I want to believe her, but even I have to admit she has no proof. That's why we need your help. You see, there's a tape, Paula. It shows a woman being raped in the woods near my home. There's a scarf like yours round her neck. I thought she might be you.' I was watching her carefully. All the colour drained from her face and the muscles went slack as if the power had gone out of her.

'It wasn't me,' she whispered. 'You'll never get me to say any different.'

'All right,' I agreed. My mind was racing. If I botched this up, then Paula might be lost to us for ever as a source of information. 'I'm not asking you to go public.' She was watching me warily, sizing up every word and intonation, every fleeting expression on my face.

'I won't go to the police.' Her voice was stony and resolute.

'I'm not asking you to,' I said hurriedly. Something relaxed in Paula's demeanour. I took a deep breath. 'I just want you to tell me anything you can that might help us nail this bastard.' She was looking at me sceptically. I remembered her earlier anguish. 'So he doesn't do this to anyone else,' I added with a flash of inspiration.

That got to her. Her defensiveness gave way and she nodded weakly. 'Okay. Come through to the kitchen. I'll make us a cup of tea.'

As she set about boiling water and setting out cups and saucers, she continued her story. 'I won't go to the police because they wouldn't believe me. I used to be a prostitute, so they know me. Getting raped went with the territory, but we'd never have reported it because we knew no one would take us seriously.' She heaved a long sigh.

'I've been off the game for about nine years, ever since I got married to Dan, my husband. That's the main reason I can't go to the police. He used to be a client of mine when his wife was ill. She was quite young and they had a little baby, Danny, but she died. Cancer. Dan's a long-distance lorry driver and he had to get back to work, but he didn't have anyone to look after the baby and he couldn't bear to have him adopted, so he made me an offer. He needed someone quick so he said he'd marry me, but I had to give up the game.'

She laughed wryly. 'He didn't have to ask twice. I

had a little boy myself at that time. A bit older he was. Eight. His name was Andy. He got himself killed in a motorcycle accident when he was a teenager. Sort of thing you have nightmares about.' She wiped away a tear and busied herself pouring tea. 'That was his scarf you brought back.

'Anyway, if I marched off to the police with this and it went to court and it came out I used to be on the game, the lawyers would make mincemeat out of me. I've seen it happen. And Dan would throw me out. He can put up with me being an old whore and all, as long as I behave myself now and I don't let people know and I don't do anything to rub his face in it or shame him in front of his friends. I'm here only as long as I'm useful and I don't cause any trouble. It's not like I'm flesh and blood, not like him and Danny.'

She smiled sadly. 'I'd just go somewhere quietly and kill myself. Not because of Dan. He's been all right by me – he's treated me well, I have a nice home and a car and everything. But I lost Andy. I couldn't bear to lose Danny as well. I've raised him from when he was eight months old. But he's not mine – I don't have any rights. If he was taken away from me I'd have nothing left. Nothing.'

'I understand,' I said sympathetically. 'My friend didn't report it either – not until she realised who did it. But I need you to tell me what happened.'

Paula had replaced her cup in its saucer. She seemed to be gathering her thoughts.

'I go to an upholstery class on Tuesday night,' she began. 'It's held at the school.' She shuddered. 'I was walking home when he grabbed me from behind. The lights are out on that part of the road so I didn't see him. He used handcuffs and he shoved me into the back of a car. He drove to a wood somewhere and dragged me in. Then he bound and gagged me. He tied something round my neck so I could hardly breathe. I thought I was going to die.' She stopped and looked me in the eye. 'Do I have to go into the rest if you've seen it?'

I shook my head. I didn't want to cause her unnecessary grief. But there was one thing I had to know. 'There was a flash on the tape. What was it?'

She considered that for a moment. 'Something happened. There was a sort of explosion . . .'

'I know about that,' I interjected. 'Some little animal ate through the electric cable so there was a short-circuit. The tape ended then.'

'Ahh.' There was a look of dawning comprehension on her worn face.

'Was there anything else?' There was an urgent undertow to my voice.

She paused for a moment, frowning, then said with sudden remembrance, 'Oh, just the pictures. He always took pictures.'

My surge of elation gave way to confusion. 'Always? He raped you more than once?'

'No.' She had made no attempt to drink her tea and now she pushed the cup and saucer away from her. 'But he attacked some of the other girls. We all knew about him. It would start out like a normal job, then he would use his handcuffs, tie the girl up, nearly throttle her and take a Polaroid before he raped her. I think he took another picture afterwards, but I'm not sure. He knew we wouldn't report it. We were easy pickings. I think he was just practising on us,' she snorted. 'Now he's trying it on real women.' There was heavy sarcasm in her voice.

I was struggling to take all this in. 'You mean he used to rape the prostitutes?' Paula nodded. 'When was that?'

'Oh,' she leaned back and scanned the ceiling, eyes narrowed. 'He'd stopped before I gave up, but not long before. It must have gone on for about four or five years.

He'd do half a dozen girls every year – some times more, sometimes less. But he stopped, let's see, must be about ten years or so ago.'

'What did he look like?'

'Don't know. Always wore a balaclava, like he does now. That's what would tip us off. But a lot of times when it was dark you couldn't see that until it was too late. The girl would be in the car before she noticed and then quick as a flash he'd have the handcuffs on and that would be that. He used to have a little Mini van in them days.'

'Did he kill anyone?' I asked.

She shook her head. 'I don't think so, although you can't really be sure. Not when you're talking about whores, because we come and go and no one really notices – not unless a body turns up. There was several girls over the years who disappeared and we just assumed they'd moved on somewhere else. But there was a lot of his victims lived to tell the tale so I don't think he was into killing then.'

'Well, he is now,' I answered dryly, 'although he let you go the first time. Why d'you think he came back to try and kill you?'

Paula shivered. 'I don't remember much before you arrived. Just trying to breathe. Just trying for one more breath of air. But one thing stuck in my mind. I didn't notice it at the time but I remembered later.' She looked at me with wide haunted eyes. 'He said things had changed. He said I was dangerous now.'

I could feel my neck tensing up as I readied myself to ask the crucial question. 'Can you remember if there was anything that happened in the days *before* the rape that made you uneasy?'

She laughed mirthlessly. 'Oh yes, you bet there was. He was stalking me, I'm sure of it now. It must have been him, had to have been. He sent me pictures in the post. They'd been taken of me as I went about the neighbourhood. One was of me in the butcher's, taken through the window when I wasn't looking. Another when I'd just nipped into a little alley because my underskirt was riding up and I wanted to pull it down – he got that. Picking Danny up at school . . . the bastard had followed me everywhere. I knew what he was trying to say. He was saying I couldn't get away. He'd got me in his sights. I was his prey.'

'But you did nothing.'

She shook her head wearily. 'No, how could I? Same thing as I've just said. I didn't want to draw attention to myself. I stopped going out at night unless I absolutely had to or else Dan was with me. I just hoped he'd got what he wanted and he'd go away.'

She looked at me with eyes fractured by pain. 'But he didn't. He just destroyed everything I had. In one go. Reduced me to being a whore again, at the beck and call of anyone, to be used and thrown away.'

I hardly dare ask. 'What happened to the pictures?'

'I threw them out. I didn't want Dan finding them and asking questions. Anyway, they gave me a funny feeling and I hated it. I didn't want them around.'

I couldn't hold back a heavy sigh.

Paula stood up. 'Look, I wish I could be more help but I'm really busy. Dan's due back home tomorrow.'

I nodded as I too got to my feet. 'Paula, we need to find out if there are any things that you and my friend who was raped, and Sister Kate have in common that could help us work out who this man is. Would you meet us sometime to talk about it?'

She looked undecided for a moment, then: 'Okay. But I need some warning because of Danny. And it must be somewhere really private and you must promise never to pass on my name to anyone.'

'I promise.' I made to leave, then turned back. 'And thanks.'

Chapter Twelve

I awoke at five o'clock the next morning, after a restless night. As I sat up in bed drinking coffee, I realised that Paula's testimony had in some ways only added to my sense of frustration. She had backed up Mags' story and convinced me we were on the right track. It was the same man who had attacked both women. But we still couldn't prove a connection to Sister Kate's death, nor did we have any evidence to confirm Mags' accusation that Trevor was her attacker. Sister Kate was dead and could provide us with no clues. All we had to go on was Mags' story. Either I had to come up with another suspect or somehow I had to link Trevor to the photographs and the attack on my friend.

The obvious problem was his alibi. It was that which had stopped the police investigation of him in its tracks. The witnesses to his story were doctors and nurses. It was hard to see where there could be a crack in the fabric of his lies. I dragged myself out of bed. I had to try.

It was about seven o'clock when I started up my car. The streets were quiet and damp with rain from the night before as I drove towards the hospital. St Lukes' was a modern district general, with graceless boxy buildings laid out in the midst of car parks and patchy lawns. It was where my husband, Jamie, had been treated when he was dying of cancer, so I knew my way around it only too well. I hadn't been back since his last visit.

Large blue and white signposts directed me to the Accident & Emergency unit. I walked into the reception area, past the trolleys lined up along the wall, each with its white honeycomb blanket neatly folded at the foot. A young woman looked up as I approached the desk. She had a frizz of blonde curls, pale skin, pink lipstick and round blue eyes. A name tag on the white coat she wore loosely over her red jumper announced that she was Melanie, receptionist. She had a telephone receiver held at one ear.

'Yes? Can I help you?' she asked, putting one hand over the mouthpiece.

'I hope so.' I tried hard to give her a winning smile. 'My name's Bel Carson and I'm a director at RTV.' There was a flicker of interest in her eyes. 'I'm following up on a case you had a couple of weeks ago, a Mr Trevor Gates, and I wondered if I could talk to any of the staff who dealt with him that night?'

She shook the blonde mane and straightened up into professional mode. 'You'll have to go through Public Relations and anyway, no one will discuss a patient's case history. Confidentiality.' She looked suddenly alert and turned her attention back to the telephone. 'Well, we haven't got his records here. He says . . .'

I wandered away. I knew from experience that I'd get nowhere by going through official channels. I had no right to any of the information I was seeking. My only hope was to find someone willing to bend the rules. A burly female nurse was standing on the far side of the reception area, consulting a clipboard which she held in her hand. It was worth a try.

'Excuse me,' I said tentatively. She looked up with a faint air of resignation. I got the impression she was perpetually being accosted by other people. 'I wonder if you could help me?' She sighed and lowered the clipboard

174

slightly as if she might just consider it. I took that as permission to continue.

'A man, a Mr Trevor Gates, was brought in here a couple of weeks ago on the night of Friday, eighth May complaining of chest pains. He was kept in overnight.' The nurse was preparing to rebuff me, I could see, so I pressed on quickly: 'I don't suppose you know who would have been working that night?'

Her eyes narrowed. 'Why do you want to know?'

I decided to come clean. Glancing round quickly to make sure we were not overheard, I noticed the receptionist watching us curiously, but when she caught my eye, she suddenly busied herself with her files.

I took a deep breath. 'A friend of mine believes that Trevor Gates raped her that night but he says he was here. I need to know if he could have left and come back without anyone knowing.'

'No. I wasn't on that night because I was on my holidays, but there's no way if he was a suspected heart attack that he'd have been allowed to leave the building. No way.' She was quite definite. Her gaze shifted past me. 'Yes, what is it, Jo?'

I turned to see a young nurse hovering just behind me. She sounded apologetic. 'Dr Selby would like to see you in Room Three.'

'Right.' The first woman looked back briefly at me. 'Sorry, but I don't think anyone will be able to tell you any more than that.' I nodded resignedly as she rushed off. The young nurse gave me a curious look before following her.

Feeling very dejected, I walked slowly back to the exit and across the road to the parking lot. I had just reached my car when I heard a shout.

'Miss! Miss!' Turning I saw the receptionist hurrying across the car park towards me. She was still wearing the white coat but now I could see that she had on a tight black skirt and a pair of white stiletto shoes which made her progress difficult. She was gasping for breath as she reached my car.

'Oh,' she moaned, putting one hand on the bonnet and leaning against it. 'Excuse me. I heard what you said to Sister just now.' She paused to catch her breath before continuing more calmly. 'I was here that night and I remember that man because I took his details and he told me he was the news editor at RTV. Then later on I read about that television reporter who said she'd been raped by a colleague and I wondered if it might be him.' She paused to take another deep breath.

'I'm just out on my teabreak so I have to be quick. I couldn't say anything in there or I'd get myself fired, but I read about them not believing your friend at the time and I thought to myself, what a load of codswallop. I bet she's telling the truth. You see, I was raped two years ago one night when I got off work.' She turned and nodded towards a clump of trees on the far side of the car park.

'It happened just over there. I was taking a short cut to the bus.' She turned back to me and I could see the anger in her face. 'They caught the man and we went to court and they put me through hell. And I mean hell. But he got off. He had been sentenced for rape once before and accused of rape another three times though the women didn't press charges, but they couldn't bring that up in court. I went through all that and he walked free! So I know there's not many women who would face all that unless they were telling the truth. So I'll help you if I can, but I won't stand up in court again.' She had blurted all this out in a rush and now she stood gasping for breath.

'Can you tell us anything, anything at all that would let us know we are on the right track?' I could hear the pleading note in my voice.

She swallowed hard and appeared to be collecting her thoughts. 'Right. Well, what Sister said about him not being able to leave the building would be true on a normal night. But that night wasn't normal.

'The ambulance brought Mr Gates in, complaining he'd had chest pains. But he was feeling not too bad by the time he got here. It was nine o'clock on a Friday night, so none of the big wheels were on, none of the consultants. They'd all gone home or off to their weekend cottages with instructions for us not to disturb them except in an emergency. So he was seen by one of the new junior doctors who'd just come on rotation.

'But just after Mr Gates arrived – minutes, really – there was that big crash on the motorway. An entire family of four kids wiped out. Lorry jack-knifed. Four other people killed. Ten people in Intensive Care. Eight people with serious injuries. We were up to our eyeballs.

'Mr Gates was put in a side room out of the way. The doctor who saw him should probably have done a bit more than he did, but he got called away to help with the other stuff almost at once and Mr Gates seemed not too bad, as I said. He was left there until early the next morning.'

She shrugged as if apologising. 'There's been an internal investigation about what happened because it was a bit of a cock-up, really. We didn't want to advertise it.'

'So,' I said, trying to sort through this information, 'Trevor could have left and come back.'

'Could have done,' she agreed, 'although it would have been *unusual*. You see, that little room is next to a flight of stairs that leads to a fire exit. You could get out that way and onto the road and find a taxi, I suppose.' She glanced at her watch. 'Look, I'm sorry. I have to go. Is that what you wanted to know?'

I smiled. 'That's brilliant. Exactly what I wanted to know.'

I was jubilant as I drove back to the studios. But as I thought about what to do with this information, reality set in and my triumphant mood began to evaporate. If I told

177

Sykes, it might just be enough to get him to reopen the investigation into Trevor, although the police might be put off by the receptionist's refusal to testify if the case went to court. But that would reopen the inquiry for Mags as well. In spite of all her current troubles, she was showing signs of recovering from the trauma of the rape. Reviving her allegations against Trevor could set her back.

Perhaps what we were talking about now was damage limitation. As I parked my car and headed for the entrance to the studios, it occurred to me that the best thing might be to use what I had discovered to pressurise Trevor into dropping his court case – to let the whole thing die down.

Martin was clearly getting ready to depart when I knocked on his open office door. He wore a smart grey suit, the dark hair streaked with grey was clipped short and he was darting around the room gathering files and sheets of paper and stuffing them into an expensive-looking black leather briefcase. He stopped as soon as he saw me standing in the doorway.

'Bel. Come in – close the door. What can I do for you? How's Mags?'

'How do you expect she is?' I answered dryly.

Quickly, I filled him in on what I had discovered at the hospital. He listened attentively as he pulled a cigarette out of a packet lying on his desk. Lighting up, he sighed blue smoke into the air.

'I don't know,' he said slowly. 'This is a terrible business. What in God's name possessed her to accuse him in the first place? Why didn't someone stop her? Why didn't *you* stop her?' he added, rounding on me.

'Because I had no reason to doubt her.'

Martin sank into his seat and eyed me sceptically.

'Martin,' I remonstrated with him. 'You know Mags. She's not some hysteric. If she says Trevor raped her, then we have to take that seriously. It might seem far-fetched to you, but she wouldn't have made up something like that.'

He sighed heavily and began playing with the cigarette packet on the desk before him. 'Oh God. I wish I knew. The thing is, she did lose that job to Trevor and I know she found that hard to take. She was under a lot of pressure at the time. We had a talk about it one night in the pub. I was telling her about Laurie and me splitting up and she was talking about Barry wanting the kids.' He inhaled deeply. 'I just don't know.'

There was silence. Martin swung his chair round to gaze out of the window on his left. Finally, he turned his head to me and said, 'Even if she is right – and believe me, Trevor's no friend of mine – she can't prove it can she?' He rubbed his eyes, then continued in a more conciliatory tone.

'What are you thinking, that he slipped out of the hospital somehow? That he had a heart attack and then went out and raped Mags?'

'It's possible, if it was a very minor heart attack. You know what state the hospitals are in these days. There was a big pile-up on the motorway that night, so the staff were very busy. Perhaps he got fed up with waiting and went out for some fresh air. Or perhaps he decided to leave. He lives near Mags. He could have got in his car, driven round there, waited till she came home and struck. Then, realising he needed an alibi, he went back to the hospital, lay down again and waited to see if anyone had noticed his absence. If someone did, he could have said he'd tried to find the canteen for a cup of coffee and got lost, or he'd been at the loo. As it turns out, no one would have realised he was gone.'

Martin picked up a pen and began doodling on the leatherbound blotter before him. 'The problem is, my hands are tied. Trevor is insisting on a court case and he's within his rights. I can't show favouritism by supporting Mags.'

I leaned forward. 'Martin, there has to be evidence.

179

The police didn't go any further with their inquiries as soon as they found out about the alibi. They didn't even search his house. I bet if someone did, they'd find all kinds of incriminating stuff.'

Martin looked at me sharply, understanding dawning in his eyes. He pointed at me with the pen. 'Don't even think of it! Good God!' He slammed the palm of his other hand down hard on his desk. 'What the fuck is going on in this newsroom? I've got one reporter accusing the editor of raping her, I've got him countering with a lawsuit for defamation, and now my director is taking up breaking and entering!' He sighed and shook his head. 'I wish, I wish,' he muttered half to himself, 'none of this had ever happened.'

'Martin, I'm desperate. Mags is going to be ruined. She'll lose her job, her house, maybe even her kids. If Trevor wins, she'll never work again. This is the only job she's trained for and it's what she's good at, you know that,' I wheedled.

He was staring bleakly out of the window. One hand was at his forehead. Finally he spoke, very quietly.

'No breaking and entering, please.' He slowly swung his chair round to face me. 'This Saturday, Trevor's invited some of us *boys*,' he made an ironic face as he uttered the last word, 'to watch the football game at his house. He's done this before. He has a big screen telly in a sort of games room built on at the back. We make a hell of a din, quite apart from the noise of the game. I shouldn't wonder if the front door was unlocked and I know we wouldn't hear a thing.'

For a moment, a level look of mutual understanding passed between us.

'Thanks, Martin. You're a pal,' I said, standing up.

He got to his feet, another cigarette between his fingers. 'Just don't get caught and if you do, you didn't hear anything from me.'

I was strangely calm about the prospect of raiding Trevor's house. I thought through the consequences if I got caught. He would possibly call the police, although with Martin there, I was pretty sure he could be talked out of that. He might try to fire me – but I had already thought up various lame-brained excuses which might just be enough to make the senior management too afraid of an industrial tribunal to give me the sack.

I had decided that if I were caught, I'd claim I'd gone there to talk to Trevor to try to persuade him to drop his lawsuit against Mags. When no one had answered the bell, I'd stuck my head round the door and then ventured further in, calling for Trevor. I'd assumed he must be at home because the door was unlocked. It was a weak story, but I intended to stick to it and hope it would cause enough confusion to keep me out of police custody.

Of course, I didn't ring the doorbell. I waited until five minutes after the match would have started, then, not wishing to delay any longer and waste precious time, I approached Trevor's front door. He lived in a small terraced house in one of the smarter streets not far from my home. I had walked over there, so as not to draw attention to myself in the TR6.

I had a moment's misgiving as I caught hold of the handle. This was the first time in my life I had entered someone else's home uninvited, and knowing that it would be against their wishes. It was also the second time in my life I had entered the home of someone I believed to be a murderer.

I found myself in a chilly, empty-looking hall. Ahead of me was a closed door and there was another to my right. A large grandfather clock in the corner between the two doors ticked loudly. To my left was a flight of stairs. There was a sudden roar of voices from somewhere at the rear of the house. A goal, perhaps. I had taken the trouble to find out how long each half of the game was. Ten minutes had gone by. That left me only another half hour or so, to enable me to be well clear before either Trevor or one of his guests appeared. I had no time to waste.

I had already formulated a plan of action, reasoning that Trevor was unlikely to hide anything incriminating in the more public areas of the house. He would either choose somewhere upstairs or a garden hut or garage. I didn't have access to those, but I could search the upper rooms.

I was wearing trainers and so I mounted the stairs with no sound except for a few creaks from loose treads. At the top of the stairs was a small square landing, with three doors opening off it. The one on the left was a bathroom.

I searched that quickly. There was a small wall cabinet above the washbasin, containing several bottles of prescription tablets and indigestion remedies. Apart from a few ancient toothbrushes with splayed bristles, there was nothing else. The cabinet under the washbasin proved equally uninteresting. I felt the enormity of my task. It was impossible for me to start tearing off the panelling around the bath, for example. There were lots of places where Trevor could have hidden things like handcuffs or clothing without me being able to find them.

But I was banking on the fact that a camera was a very ordinary thing to have lying around and that Trevor would have felt no need to hide it. I emerged from the bathroom, taking care to close the door quietly. To my left, opposite the stairs, was another door. Tentatively, I opened this one and entered what appeared to be the spare bedroom. There were a couple of single beds with scratched oak headboards dating from the fifties, but no bedding and nothing under the beds. Against the far wall, next to the window, was an old-fashioned dressing table with lace doilies and a woman's battered hand-mirror and hairbrush set. Gently, I prised the drawers open. They were all completely empty, except for a couple of mothballs which rattled around like billiard balls.

Emerging from the spare bedroom onto the landing, I glanced at my watch. I had only fifteen minutes left. From down below came the distant intermittent cheers of Trevor and his guests. The last door opened onto a large room spanning the whole of the front of the house. To my left, along the same wall in which the door was set, was a row of built-in wardrobes. The headboard of a double bed was placed against the wall at right angles to them, so that the bed came out into the room almost to the doorway. To my right was another fifties-style dressing table, again with lace doilies, and on the wall facing me were two windows with a large desk between them. Panic surged through me. There was still so much ground to cover.

Quickly, I opened the cupboard doors. They were stuffed full of clothes. Some of them had fallen onto the floor and been left there. Others were crowded onto hangers, three or four shirts on top of each other so that the ones underneath were heavily creased. There was a faint odor of sweat. Old hand-knitted cardigans and sweaters jostled for space next to a variety of tweed sports jackets and suits. Several looked as if they could do with being cleaned but there was nothing suspicious that I could see.

I checked the floor, pushing back the hanging clothes and lifting up garments to see more clearly. Apart from a large collection of shoes and ankle boots in various stages of disrepair, there was nothing of interest except for a plastic bag in the corner. Inside was a pair of old trainers, covered in mud, a dark grey sweatshirt with a hood and a worn pair of navy tracksuit bottoms. The only thing missing from the description of the killer's outfit was the balaclava.

A shelf ran along the top of the wardrobe and clothes spilled off it onto the shoulders of the clothes hanging below. Standing on tiptoe, I moved along, lifting piles of clothes, prodding to see if there was anything hidden amongst them, pulling down anything dark for further examination in case it might be the missing balaclava.

But there was nothing else which was in any way incriminating. Feeling desperate and conscious that I had very little time left, I opened the single drawer of the dressing table. It was full of rubbish – old tickets, receipts and knick-knacks such as studs, nails, badges of one kind or another.

The desk was the only thing left. I could hear a change in the noise from downstairs. I glanced at my watch. The first half was nearly over. I should leave now, before Trevor and his guests ventured into the main part of the house for drinks or came upstairs to go to the loo. I pulled open the top drawer. It, too, was full of junk – odd pens and pencils, rubbers and rulers. The drawer below contained old chequebooks and income-tax records and piles of loose receipts. Frantically I jerked open the last drawer. It contained a 35mm camera and film. I was in despair. If Trevor owned a Polaroid camera, he kept it well hidden.

But I couldn't stay any longer. I gave a last look round the room. Something – it looked like a newspaper – was peeking out from under the bed. Dropping down onto my hands and knees, I peered underneath. The debris which had fetched up there told a sad story. There was a half-eaten tin of beans with a spoon sticking out of it, several empty tortilla packets, two cartons of ice cream scraped clean, and, nestling amidst the dust balls, a stack of magazines, well-thumbed and dog-eared.

Quickly, I flicked through the pile. I was now so convinced of Trevor's carelessness that I didn't worry about keeping them in order and putting them back exactly where I found them. In any case, I didn't have time. I was so inured to disappointment, so resigned to the fact that my search had been virtually useless that when I uncovered issue number three of *Tartlets* second from the bottom of the pile, it almost didn't register for a moment. When it did, I froze, then as a final whooping came from downstairs and continued in a grand finale, I grabbed the magazine, stuffed the others back under the bed and got to my feet.

Excited voices sounded down below. Clearly the match had ended. I stepped out onto the landing. Somewhere at the back of the house, I heard a door open. Springing into action, I raced down the stairs, not even worrying about keeping quiet. My goal now was to get out with the evidence.

I reached the front door and grappled with the handle. For a moment, the door seemed to jam then it lurched open as I heard voices in the kitchen. I leapt outside and pulled the door behind me. The sound of it closing merged with the sound of another door into the hall opening. I had just made it. And I finally had some concrete evidence.

Chapter Thirteen

I delayed looking at the magazine until I had got home, made some coffee and settled down in one of the armchairs in the sitting room. After I had savoured the first two or three sips of coffee, I took a deep breath, like someone preparing themselves for an ordeal, pulled a low table over in front of me and laid the magazine on top. I looked at the cover for a moment, the woman in tawdry vampish underwear, bound and gagged, her eyes blank. Then I began to turn the pages. I was in for a shock.

It was the right magazine, okay. There were the pictures of the nun, the schoolgirl and all the others. Including the nurse and the teacher. That meant the pages hadn't been ripped from this magazine. I had accomplished nothing.

I leaned back in the armchair and closed my eyes. All my efforts to help Mags had led nowhere. The most I could do was testify that Trevor owned an outfit like the one worn by a man who might have been the rapist – but so did thousands of other men. I could show his alibi was shaky, but I couldn't prove that he did, in fact, leave the hospital that night. I could demonstrate his interest in sado-masochistic sex, bondage and violence, that he was familiar with the scenarios acted out by the rapist. That was all. There was nothing that would stand up in a court of law – or that would convince anyone, frankly, that Trevor was our man.

The phone rang. For a moment, I contemplated not answering, just curling up into the foetal position and nursing my wounds. But I have been trained to answer phones on the first ring, always to think in terms of emergencies and deadlines. So I dragged myself unwillingly into the hall and picked up the cordless receiver, carrying it back to my comfortable armchair.

'It's Mags,' a voice said as soon as I answered.

'Mags! How are you?' I tried to sound bright and breezy, but she wasn't fooled.

'What's wrong?'

I sank into the armchair, curling myself into a ball with the phone. I couldn't pretend any longer.

'It's been a bad day. I don't seem to be getting anywhere.'

There was a moment's silence, then Mags' voice, with an edge of panic: 'You're not going to stop, are you? You're not going to give up? Bel, if—'

I broke in quickly. 'No. No. It's just that I haven't a clue what else to do. Trevor's alibi isn't as solid as the police think, but that's a long way from proving he wasn't where he said he was.'

'We can't stop, Bel. We can't!' Mags sounded so desperate that I felt guilty. 'Can I meet this other woman – Paula – the one who was attacked?' she asked.

Of course. She was right. 'I should have thought of that before,' I said quietly. 'I'll call her now.'

'Phone me right back.' Mags was high on panic. Everything that made her life worth living was at stake. It was selfish of me to have even thought of giving up.

Paula hesitated only for a moment. 'I'd like to meet her too,' she said. 'She's probably the only person who can understand how I feel right now. Can it be tonight? You see, Dan's home at the moment. He and Danny are watching a video so I can slip out for an hour or so and it won't matter. Another night I'd have to find a babysitter.'

Mags made it to my house from her sister's in fifty

minutes. I didn't dare think what speed she must have been driving at, particularly since she was already as high as a kite. She looked fraught.

Paula arrived shortly afterwards. She seemed awkward and shy in Mags' presence. I poured wine for all of us and we sat down round the kitchen table, a notebook at the ready. I launched in at once.

'First of all, have you ever seen each other before now?'

Mags shook her head, but Paula said shyly, 'I know who you are, of course, but not personally, no.'

'Did either of you know Sister Kate?' They both answered in unison in the affirmative, then looked at each other, slightly surprised by this coincidence. Mags, it turned out, knew her because she'd done a news feature a couple of years back about the drop-in centre. Paula's link was more unexpected.

'I got to know her about three years ago.' She fidgeted, drawing a pattern on the oilskin tablecloth with her fingernail. 'My son, Andy. He was on drugs. That's how he got himself killed.' She darted a glance up at us to see how we were taking that, then looked down again. 'I saved up for a motorbike for him because that was all he ever wanted and I said if he came off the drugs he could have one for his seventeenth birthday. He went to the Centre. Sister Kate was there and she was ever so kind and helpful; she took a special interest in him. Andy hoodwinked us all into thinking he was clean, but there was someone dealing at the Centre. They never found out who it was. Andy took some stuff and went out riding on his bike. Got himself killed,' she ended simply.

Mags and I were both silent for a moment. Paula saw our looks and shrugged. 'It's okay. I thought I wouldn't go on living after that but you do.' She sighed heavily. 'The sad thing is, you always do.'

189

There was something in Paula's tone of voice and level delivery that warned us off giving sympathy.

I thought it best to change the subject. 'You were both stalked,' I pointed out. 'But we don't know if Sister Kate was. You all live in the same area, but he attacked you at your homes, while she was murdered at her place of work. It was as if he knew you and her in different ways.'

On impulse, I got to my feet and left the room. A few minutes later I returned with a map of the city and several sheets of Cellophane. I spread out the map, then laid one sheet on top, securing it with a couple of spring-clips. The other two women had been chatting quietly to each other. Now they looked at my little setup with interest.

'What's this?' Mags leaned forward.

I proffered a red marker pen. 'Mark out the routes you take every day – to work, or dropping off your kids, to go shopping, the hairdresser's, all that sort of thing.'

Without another word, she set to work. When she had finished, she removed her sheet of Cellophane and I attached another one. I handed a green pen to Paula. 'Now you.' Both women had already understood what I was up to. As soon as Paula had finished, Mags laid her sheet over Paula's and we all bent over the map, comparing the red and green lines. Although Mags and Paula lived within a mile of each other, their daily travels hardly overlapped at all.

Mags sat back, frustrated. 'I suppose it's not surprising,' she remarked. 'My kids go to different schools so they've got different friends and none of them is the same age as Danny.' She consulted the map again. 'We don't even go to the same supermarket, do we?' She stabbed a finger at a point where the red and green lines converged. 'That's where I go to the butcher's – Romford's.'

Paula turned the map slightly to view it more clearly. 'Yeh, I go there too. But I doubt very much if Sister

Kate did. Someone else always does the shopping for the convent.' She shook her head despairingly. 'There's hardly any point where our lines cross. It's amazing really how little they do.'

I was clutching at straws. 'Can we narrow down the times when he followed you? Was it weekends, or evenings only, or was it during the day when most people would be working?'

Paula and Mags considered for a moment, then answered almost simultaneously. 'During the day,' said Paula.

'All hours. Weekends, evenings and a couple of times on my day off,' answered Mags.

'So,' I doodled on my notebook, 'he's someone who isn't accountable to anyone else for large chunks of his time. He can be gone following his victims around without anyone noticing.'

'Trevor,' said Mags simply.

'Trevor,' I agreed. 'He disappears during the day. Once the assignments are given at the morning conference, he goes off to meetings, he says, or to PR bashes or whatever. And he has days off during the week. He could have arranged his time off to coincide with Mags' – which brings me to my next point.'

I fished in my folder and produced a brochure for RTV which I had lifted off one of the tables in Reception. I flicked through until I found what I was looking for. I held the page open with one finger and swivelled the pamphlet so that Paula could see what I was pointing at. 'That's Trevor. Do you recognise him at all?' Paula leaned forward and peered at it for a second. Then she sat back, shaking her head. 'Sorry. He doesn't look familiar.'

'So you don't think it's the same man who attacked you and raped the other women?' I wanted to be quite clear.

She hesitated. 'I couldn't be really sure one way or the

other. I never saw the one that did the other girls. And it was dark and he wore that mask thing when he raped me, so I can't say for definite. I didn't think of anyone or anything except getting out of there alive, just survival, whatever happened. But I don't think it's him.'

I glanced at my watch. Eleven o'clock. Paula noticed and looked at her wrist too. Then she stood up.

'I have to go. I'm sorry I haven't been able to give you anything useful.' She smiled awkwardly. 'I'm glad you asked me though. It helps to speak about it. Makes it seem less huge and horrible and menacing. It's funny – once you talk about it, that's it. It doesn't get any worse. That's the limit set on it; that's what happened. If it goes round and round in your mind it just grows and festers.'

I stood at the front door waiting to make sure she got into her car safely. She could drive straight into the garage at home, she had told me. Dan would probably be in bed. He wouldn't have waited up for her but he was a light sleeper. It would just take one scream if anything went wrong and he'd come running.

Perhaps it was watching her tail-lights disappear that reminded me of that night in the woods. And perhaps it was thinking of that, that made me scan the bushes and trees on the opposite side of the road. For a moment I thought I saw a movement in amongst the shrubs, but it was hard to tell.

Mags left soon after. I switched off the lights, then tweaked the curtains in the sitting room to one side and looked out. Nothing. I knew that it was only too easy in these circumstances to lose my nerve and start being afraid of everything and nothing.

Wearily, I climbed the stairs. There was a light on under Lucinda's door. I paused and knocked. 'Come in.' She sounded as tired as me. When I opened the door, it took me a moment to adjust to the gloom. The only light in the room came from a reading lamp. Lucinda was seated at the desk in the corner, surrounded by heavy books piled up on the floor around her, her hair tousled, her eyes red-rimmed and weary-looking.

'Sorry to disturb you.'

Lucinda smiled. 'Don't worry. The die's probably been cast already. If I don't know it now, I never will.' She sat sideways in her chair and leaned back against the wall so that the front two legs lifted off the floor. 'What's up?'

I sank down onto the bed. 'Is it easy to get hold of handcuffs?'

Lucinda shook her head in mock reproof. 'Still worrying away at that, eh? There are all kinds of places you can buy them. You can even get them mail order, I think.' She shifted her weight, bringing the chair onto all four legs again with a crash. 'You can have a look at mine, if you like.' She stood up, stretching stiffly, then walked over to the cupboard by the fireplace. 'There.' She tossed a small circular black leather case onto my lap.

I unzipped it carefully. Inside, the rings nestling one on top of the other, was a set of shiny metal handcuffs. I pulled them out and examined them, holding them up to the light. Lucinda was raking around in her desk drawer.

'Here are the keys.' She threw over a keyring in the shape of a large metal 'L'. I caught it awkwardly. Attached to the ring were what looked like two small metal cylinders of different diameters. Each had a small nick in the rim.

'Funny-looking keys,' I commented, turning them around and examining them from all angles.

'Those will open almost any set of handcuffs.'

I looked at her curiously. 'You mean they're all the same?' She nodded. 'But I'd have thought that each one would be unique,' I commented. 'Anyway, I suppose that answers my question. There's nothing unusual about owning a pair of handcuffs, so there's no chance of tracking the bastard down that way.' I stood up and yawned. 'I'm knackered. Good night.'

I stumbled up the remaining half-flight of stairs to my room. As I got ready for bed, I resolved that first thing next day I would go to visit the convent, just to see if Sister Kate had complained to anyone that she was being followed. It was our last chance. Nothing else had worked.

It was cloudy when I awoke next day. Nine o'clock. I leapt out of bed, remembering my resolve of the night before. The nuns would be up early, I was sure, so I showered and dressed quickly, swallowed a cup of coffee and a roll, and raced out to my car.

I was right about the nuns being up early, but what I – as a confirmed heretic – hadn't taken on board was that every one of them who was capable of movement would be at church. There was only one caretaker and a couple of very old women sitting in the garden who didn't even look in my direction when I arrived.

If I came back in an hour, then Sister Pauline would be here, I was told. Seething with impatience, ready to go with this renewed energy which the day had brought, I made my way to a nearby café and ate a proper breakfast.

Sister Pauline was calm and patient with my request when I returned. We sat in her office with its worn furniture. She folded her hands in front of her, while she thought about my question.

'Kate mentioned nothing to me about anyone following her, or "stalking her" as you put it. And I think if she were worried about something like that, it is me she would have come to. Many of the older sisters find the stories in the newspapers and on television alarming enough. Kate wouldn't have wanted to worry any of them, I'm sure.'

This was not very encouraging. I tried one more approach.

194

'Did she ever receive any photographs of herself in the post – or any unusual letters that you're aware of?'

The Mother Superior considered carefully, then shook her head slowly. 'No. I can almost swear to that.' She moved closer as if to impart some confidence. 'Kate did get letters from former pupils or other nuns who had gone on to do different things elsewhere, but she always shared them. Mail isn't something which is taken away and savoured in secret here. And there were never any letters that seemed odd or out of place, and certainly no photographs – not of Kate herself, at any rate. There's been the odd picture of a former pupil's spouse and family that they've sent over the years, but that is all.'

There was a smell of Sunday lunch wafting into the room. I stood up, thanking Sister Pauline yet again for her patience, and took my leave. I got into my car and drove around aimlessly for a while, even though the convent was only a couple of streets away from my home. Then, on an impulse, I headed for open country, found a quiet, straightish road and let the old TR rip. The wind seemed to blow right through me. As I slowed to a stop after twenty minutes, I felt completely relaxed and refreshed.

That was when it hit me. I had been so stupid. Of course, Sister Kate wouldn't have received any letters or photographs at the convent! Paula and Mags had received mail at their homes, and that was where they were attacked. But Sister Kate was murdered at the place where she worked. The photographs, if there were any, would have been sent there.

As far as I knew, the drop-in centre was closed on Sundays, but I was so impatient that I drove down there anyway. The big double front doors were closed and firmly locked when I tried the handle. I stepped back until I could survey the front and side of the building. It could just have been a trick of the bright sunshine, but there appeared to be a light on in a first-floor room at the side. Either it had been left on accidentally, or someone was in the building.

I began to try to find a way in. Eventually, I discovered another, smaller door round the corner, hidden behind a screen for the dustbins. It was unlocked. The soles of my trainers squeaked on the linoleum as I walked along the corridor.

'Hello! Anybody here?' I called out. There was no answer. I passed several closed doors, not stopping to try any of them, hoping that I would either hear someone moving about or find an office that was open. I reached the stairs and began to climb up. The corridor at the top stretched empty and narrow. Light flooded from an open doorway at the end. I called out again but there was no answer, so I walked towards it. I was beginning to feel uncomfortable. I was now so far into the building without any invitation that I had really no excuse.

I stepped over the threshold, looking round me gingerly. The overhead light was still on, presumably because the trees outside made it rather gloomy. It was a small office with a Formica-topped desk in front of the window. Two or three empty manilla files were scattered across it. A grey filing cabinet stood against the wall to my left. The top drawer was open, as if someone had been interrupted in the middle of looking for something.

I was suddenly aware of the smell of burning. I walked further into the room, and looked around me. There was an iron fireplace in the corner, which had been hidden by the open door. In the grate were the charred remains of burnt papers, still smoking. I could see that some of them were photographs, large eight-by-ten prints. The blackened husks still retained their shapes, the ghosts of their images quivering in an invisible draft.

'Can I help you?'

I yelped. With one leap I turned to face the speaker and at the same time moved a couple of feet further into the room. Andrew Marmot stood in the doorway, eyeing me coldly. One part of my mind registered that he was blocking my exit.

'I saw there was a light on,' I stammered. He continued to look at me, unmoved. 'I had a couple of questions about Sister Kate,' I carried on nervously. 'I really wanted an answer as soon as possible. I knew it was a long shot, but I came down here anyway and then the door was open . . .' I tailed off.

His gaze flicked past me. Automatically, I twisted slightly to see what he was looking at. Behind me was the desk. Now that I was closer, I could see the files lying on top of it quite clearly. The top one was labelled B and the one beneath it was M. I couldn't see what the third one was. Were these the files Tammy said were missing from the cabinet at the murder scene?

Andrew spoke again. 'What are the questions?' Then, without waiting for my answer: 'You'd better come downstairs to my office.'

He stood aside to allow me to leave before him, and I heard him closing the door and turning a key in the lock. Nothing was said until we reached his office off the main lobby. He felt in the pockets of his jeans.

'Damn! Wait here a minute – I won't be long.' He disappeared back the way we had come and I heard him racing up the stairs. Apparently, he had left something behind.

It occurred to me that I could leave right now, and for a moment I was tempted. But then I might never find out if Sister Kate had received any photographs. I could hear Andrew's footsteps overhead. Restlessly I paced around the hall, coming to a stop in front of the staff bulletin board. I gazed absent-mindedly at the picture of Sister Kate. Then, as if waking up, looked at it more closely.

It had been cut down from a larger photograph, as I'd noticed the last time I was here. But now I examined it carefully, prying the edge away from the board with my fingernail. It had the tell-tale black underside of a Polaroid photograph. The edges had simply been trimmed to fit the space on the board.

'Here we are.' He was back, jangling a set of keys in his hand.

'We don't actually need to go into your office. Out here would do,' I said. 'It's only a couple of simple questions.'

'Oh?' He sounded wary.

'I'm trying to find out if Sister Kate received any unusual mail during the couple of weeks before she died, especially photographs of herself.'

Something passed across his face, but I couldn't decipher what it was. He shook his head. 'I wouldn't know. She opened all the mail for the Centre. I wouldn't see anything that was addressed to her.'

'When was this picture taken?' I pointed to the snapshot on the wall.

Again he shrugged. 'No idea. We put this board up not long before she died. I asked everyone for a photo. At first Sister Kate said she didn't have one, then a couple of days later she produced this.'

'Were there any others? Anything in her desk, perhaps?'

'No. The police removed anything in the office that was hers. You'll have to ask them, although I was present when they cleared everything out so that I could make sure there was nothing vital belonging to the Centre that we'd need, and there weren't any pictures. Why do you want to know this?' He was eyeing me suspiciously.

'Oh, nothing. Someone said something about pictures that had been sent to her. I thought we might be able to use them,' I murmured vaguely. He looked as if he was about to press the point.

'I have to go,' I said hurriedly. 'I'll see myself out.' Before he could say anything more or make a move to stop me, I shot off down the hall towards the door I had come in by. The sunshine outside felt reassuring and safe. I made my way back to my car and, just in case he was watching, drove off down the street.

I needed somewhere to think. I found myself heading for the beach. Since it was a Sunday afternoon, it was busy with families and dogs and kites, but they petered out at the far end, near the river estuary. The only people who hung out here were dedicated anglers. I parked so I could look out to sea and leaned my chin glumly on the steering wheel.

So Sister Kate had come up with a Polaroid picture for the staff bulletin board some time just before she died. A few days earlier she had said she didn't have any photographs of herself. Unless she had simply forgotten about this one, she had come by it only days before her death. She had lived frugally all her life, so it was second nature to her not to waste a perfectly good photograph. Could she have kept any of the others and used them in some way too?

I racked my brains. Ordinary Polaroid pictures have the wrong dimensions for passport photographs and anyway she didn't need a passport. I tried to think of all the times when I'd been required to supply pictures of myself. My I.D. card for RTV had a photograph but that had been done by a special machine which produced a laminated card at the end of the process. In fact, as I thought about it, I realised that all my picture identity or membership cards had been made by the same process.

I had seen no photographs displayed at the convent. Sister Kate had no family, except a niece in New Zealand. Could she have sent any of the other photographs to her, assuming Sister Kate had received any more? Or could the nun have mentioned them to a friend — perhaps passed on any suspicions she might have had? I thought of Mrs Bellamy.

She was seated at her window, watching the world go by, when I arrived. Clearly I was a welcome diversion in an otherwise lonely afternoon. She was determined to keep me there for as long as possible and bustled off to make afternoon tea.

'This is the time I miss Kate most,' she sighed as she returned with a tray, leaning back against the living-room door to close it. 'It gets so lonely on these long Sunday afternoons. When I was younger I could go out for a walk, but I'm not really up to it now. And when you get to my age, so many of your friends and family are gone. Passed away. Well, never mind.'

She laid down the tray and turned briskly to pouring the tea.

'What was it you wanted to ask about?' she questioned me, after the first few sips.

'I wanted to know if Sister Kate received any Polaroid photographs of herself in the weeks before she died. They might have arrived in the post.'

Mrs Bellamy nodded assent. I almost choked on the mouthful of tea I was about to swallow.

'Oh dear, dear. I'll get a cloth,' she fussed, and before I could stop her, she had disappeared from the room. She returned a few moments later and methodically dusted me down. When all trace of the tea had been mopped up, she returned to her seat.

'Yes, now – the photographs. Kate mentioned them to me the last Sunday she came for tea. She said it was a bit of a mystery. They came in the post like you said and there was no letter or anything to explain what they were for. She thought it might be one of her former pupils playing games with her. We had a chat about who might do that sort of thing.'

'And did you come up with anyone?' I hardly dared to hope that the solution to all our troubles might now be handed to me on a plate.

She grimaced delicately. 'Oh, not really. We got into talking about all the mischievous little monkeys we'd taught over the years. But we'd lost touch with all of them.'

I tried another tack. 'Do you recall a pupil called Trevor Gates at all?'

Mrs Bellamy frowned with concentration. 'The name's sort of familiar, but I couldn't swear to it, no.'

I felt despondent. 'So Sister Kate said nothing that would indicate who sent her these photographs or where they came from?'

Mrs Bellamy shook her head regretfully. 'No, I'm afraid not. But you could take a look for yourself.'

I stared at her. 'You've still got some of them?' I half-rose to my feet and looked urgently round the room as if they might be on display on the walls. Mrs Bellamy placed her china cup and saucer carefully on the little table by her side and levered herself out of the armchair.

'There's only one. I had stuck it in the album, but then I decided to take it out and frame it and have it by my bed. Kate gave it to me that last Sunday. She'd never given me a picture of herself before. I thought afterwards that it was sort of an omen. As if she knew.'

Mrs Bellamy left the room and I could hear her laboured breathing as she slowly mounted the stairs. Her footsteps crossed the room overhead, then with painstaking care she descended again.

'Here we are.' She sank exhausted into her armchair and proffered a small silver frame. As I took it from her, I could see that it contained a blurred Polaroid photograph. It was the wrong dimension for the oblong frame, which was shaped for a more conventional 35mm format. The white border surrounding the image was clearly visible.

It showed Sister Kate walking along the street, wearing her black headdress and a grey coat. She was carrying an old-fashioned shopping bag. Her head was turned slightly

201

to one side and she was looking away from the camera with a distracted expression. Like all the others, she had been the photographer's unwitting prey.

I examined it minutely. At the top right-hand corner there was a clear pinprick, edged with blue and tailing off until it merged with the picture. A flaw of some kind, perhaps.

'Could I borrow this?' I asked.

Mrs Bellamy was reluctant. 'It's all I've got,' she whispered.

'I'll take good care of it,' I promised. 'I think it may help find whoever killed Sister Kate.'

She had reached out and put a gentle hand on the other side of the frame. It was almost as if she thought we might tussle over it. I let go and she held it to her chest, gazing at me as if searching for my motive. Finally, she held the photograph out to me.

'All right. But please don't take it out of the frame unless you absolutely have to. I don't want fingermarks all over it.'

I stayed for a little while longer, listening to her tearful reminiscences. It was five o'clock before I left, but the day was not over. I felt I had to follow this through as far as it would go. There'd be no camera shops open at this time on a Sunday, so I headed straight for Police Headquarters.

Sykes was working in his office; Alan had said his boss was ambitious. When I was shown in, there were photographs of the crime scene and folders of interviews strewn around the DCI's desk. I had become used to his dismissive comments and was half-prepared to be sent away with a clever put-down yet again. But to my surprise, Sykes was immediately attentive and stretched out a hand for the photograph. Of course, I reasoned: Sister Kate was a proven victim. He was clearly willing to take seriously anything that might shed light on her case.

'If it was put into this frame straight away, then maybe there'll be fingerprints from the murderer, if indeed you're right and the picture came from him,' he said, looking up from the photograph to give me a thoughtful look.

'By the way,' he said, as he accompanied me downstairs to the exit, 'I checked up on what you told me about that chappie you say was raping whores. Some of the girls hanging around the docks do actually remember someone like that, but he disappeared years ago, they said, and we couldn't actually pin down anyone who said he'd attacked them. Just a lot of pros who'd heard about him attacking someone else. So who knows' – we'd reached the main door – 'perhaps it's just one of these stories that go around and around.'

He sniffed the air like a connoisseur savouring a fine wine. It was still warm and balmy. He turned abruptly to face me.

'She didn't ever exist, did she, the mystery woman who was attacked but won't come forward?' Then, as I gazed at him with a mounting sense of outrage: 'You just invented her to try and make your friend's story look a bit better, didn't you?' There was a taunting glint in his eye. 'It's all right, you can tell me. It's nothing I didn't figure out a long time ago for myself.'

I shook my head. 'You're wrong, completely wrong.'

Sykes gave me a knowing smile. 'Pull the other one,' he said, then turned on his heel and disappeared inside so that the doors swung violently behind him.

Chapter Fourteen

I had felt quite elated to have finally got hold of one of the photographs – to have concrete proof that Mags' story was true. But my meeting with Sykes had set my success in perspective. Now I knew that I had proved nothing which would stand up in court, and probably nothing which would lead anywhere – certainly not to the murderer. If the police found a suspect and he had a Polaroid camera with a flaw which produced marks like the one I had seen . . . perhaps the photograph might help with his conviction. But alone, it was not enough, and was unlikely to take me or anyone else to the man who had attacked Mags and Paula and killed Sister Kate.

The phone was ringing as I unlocked the back door and I skidded across the kitchen floor to get to it before it stopped. The voice on the other end was incoherent, but I recognised it as June's. She was hysterical and weeping. Wild thoughts flashed through my mind. Could Harry have had a heart attack? Then a horrible premonition took a cold grip on me. Had June – God forbid – had another miscarriage? I couldn't make out a word she was saying.

Finally I said, 'Look, Lucinda's not here. I'll be right round.'

She was watching at the window as I pulled into the narrow drive of the Evans' small bungalow. She had stopped crying, but her eyes were red-rimmed and I could see that tears were not very far away. She was choking for air the way small children do when they have been sobbing for a long time. Silently she led the way into the small, immaculate sitting room and sat on the pink velour sofa. She tried to say something then started to cry again.

'What is it? What's wrong?' I moved across and sat down next to her. June had always seemed so placid and I found it disconcerting to see her fall to pieces like this.

She took off her glasses and ran a finger under each eye, wiping away the tears.

'Something terrible happened,' she managed to stammer. I gazed at her helplessly, then looked round the room for inspiration. There was a cocktail cabinet in the corner. I went over and opened it. On the mirrored top shelf stood a bottle of sherry and one of brandy. Down below were several glasses.

In the absence of any better idea, I poured June a stiff brandy and handed it to her. She held out a shaky hand for the glass and took a few sips. It did seem to calm her down because she began to talk again, more coherently this time.

'Harry's away.' That brought a fresh flood of tears, but she rallied and continued a few moments later. 'He's been away for two weeks. He's got a big job cleaning the carpets and upholstery at two stately homes up north.' She took another sip of the brandy, this time choking on it. I slapped her back gently.

'I went to visit a friend this afternoon and stayed for tea. I caught the bus home. I was walking back, when—' she stopped and looked down at her glass.

A cold feeling of apprehension came over me. I gripped June's arm tightly, unable to say anything.

She gave a heavy sigh, then looked at me, her eyes tired behind her thick lenses. 'I was raped. I think it was the same man who got Mags and that nun.' Then she started to sob again.

I put my arms around her and she leant against me heavily, her whole body shaking. I tried to collect my thoughts. Once upon a time, I would have reached for the phone without a second thought. But the events of the last few weeks had taught me otherwise.

'June, would you like me to call the police?' I asked gently. She pulled away so that she could face me and then nodded.

'Yes. I want him caught.' I looked at her with new respect. I understood how brave a statement that was now. She wiped away the tears again. 'Could you call Harry first, please? Tell him I'm all right really, but I need him.'

'Of course.' I got to my feet, glad that there was at least something I could do.

A woman with a very smart accent answered when I rang the number June gave me and then there was a wait of several minutes before Harry came on the line.

'Yes?' He sounded hostile and I was taken aback.

'Harry, it's Bel.'

'Oh, Bel.' There was an audible change in his tone. 'Nice to hear from you. What can I do for you?'

I stammered, casting around for words that would make this easier. 'Harry, I think it would be a good idea if you could come home as soon as possible – immediately, in fact,' I began.

He sounded very tetchy. 'Well, that's a bit difficult under the circumstances, Bel. I'm sorry June's got you involved. It'll just make it more difficult if I come home now. The sooner she gets used to me being away—'

'No, Harry. You don't understand,' I interrupted. There was a pause. 'June's very upset. She's been attacked.' I ended dangerously close to the truth.

There was a long pause, during which I could imagine Harry's shocked response.

'What d'you mean?' His voice was gruff.

207

I took a deep breath. 'She's been raped,' I said simply.

There was an almost inaudible gasp, 'Good God!' then an even longer pause than the last one. I had almost begun to wonder if he had fainted, except that I could hear harsh breathing on the other end of the line.

Finally he said,' Can I speak to her?'

I relayed his request to June. She stood up and walked slowly across to the telephone.

'Harry,' she said, and burst into tears. I left the room and went to find the kitchen with some dim idea of making June a cup of tea. But before I could track down the cups and saucers I heard June shouting for me. I ran through to the sitting room. She held out the receiver.

'Harry wants to talk to you.' She looked calmer.

Harry's voice was urgent. 'I'll come right away. Tell her to wait for me, to just sit tight till I get there.' He hung up.

June had returned to her seat on the sofa and was sipping at her brandy again. I bit my lip, not sure what to do next. Then I dialled my own number. Lucinda picked up the phone on the second ring.

'Yes?'

'Lucinda, it's me.'

'Bel?' She sounded surprised. 'Where are you? I thought it was Alan calling me back just now. He's already been on the phone twice and I've only been home ten minutes.'

'I'm at June's,' I said. 'Something's happened. Can you come round now?'

There was a slight pause before she answered. 'Sure. I'll be right there.'

I felt immense relief when Lucinda walked into June's small sitting room. Not only did she know June better than I did, but she had also worked on rape cases when she was a detective. She radiated calm. And I wanted someone else to take charge.

'We should call the police,' was her instantaneous reaction when she heard what had happened.

'But Harry said to wait till he got here,' whimpered June.

'Harry's wrong,' retorted Lucinda. 'Even if you decide not to proceed, you ought to talk to them now. This man may still be in the vicinity. There might be a chance of catching him.' She moved to the telephone and seconds later was talking to someone she obviously knew. She spoke for only a couple of minutes before hanging up.

Sykes arrived shortly afterwards, accompanied by two other detectives. June kept repeating tearfully that she wanted to wait for Harry, but Lucinda was adamant. With a sigh, June began her account.

The story she told matched the previous attacks that we knew about in every detail. She had been grabbed from behind and handcuffed. She held out her wrists, which clearly showed red marks where something hard had cut into them. She was bundled into the back of a car and taken to a wooded area. She was vague about where that could have been and had lost all sense of time so she couldn't even guess how far they had driven.

Her attacker had worn dark clothing and some sort of hood and a mask. She couldn't identify him. His voice was muffled. She had been stripped and raped. He had tied something round her neck. We could see the raw marks. Later, he had let her go and she'd put on her clothes and walked home.

At this point, Lucinda, who had been sitting with an arm round June as she spoke, glanced sharply at Sykes.

'She should go to hospital.' He nodded in agreement, but June shook her head vehemently.

'No. I'm not going till Harry gets here. I want Harry,'

she ended plaintively. She started to weep again. Lucinda held her closer.

'It's okay, June. You don't have to do anything you don't want to. But you need medical treatment now. At once. For your sake.' June looked at her in bewilderment.

'That's right,' agreed Sykes. 'If you became ill or something because we didn't get you to a doctor ASAP then we'd really have been failing in our duty.'

Lucinda helped June to her feet and guided her to the door. The WPC moved to her other side. June turned away, but stopped abruptly on the doorstep.

'Bel, will you wait and tell Harry where I am?'

'Of course.' I watched as she was helped out to the waiting police car. Half an hour later, Harry's red van drew up at the door. He leapt out with surprising agility for a man of his build and burst into the house. He entered the sitting room looking distraught.

'Where's June?'

'She's doing okay,' I said in as soothing tones as I could manage. 'The police decided—'

'Police? I told her not to talk to them . . .' He had already turned and was heading for the front door again.

'Wait!' I yelled. He paused and looked over his shoulder. 'She's not at the police station. They've taken her to the hospital. I'll drive you down there.'

All the way there, Harry talked incessantly, rubbing his hands together in anguish. 'I don't want her making a report. I just want her home. I'll cancel that contract up north. I can stay and look after her. I don't want this to be in the papers and everyone knowing.' He sounded desperate.

We were directed to wait on some chairs in a corridor when we arrived at the hospital. Within a couple of minutes, the WPC joined us.

'It'll only be a little bit longer,' she said comfortingly.

She looked at Harry and asked tentatively, 'Mr Evans? Hello, I'm Detective Sergeant Jones. I've just seen your wife. She'll be fine. Lucinda Jameson is with her while they finish the examination.'

Harry leaned forward, poking a finger aggressively at the WPC. 'She won't file a complaint. I don't want this in the papers or going to court. I don't want people knowing what happened to June.'

The WPC recoiled, disconcerted. 'Okay, okay. You can discuss that with your wife.' She went on: 'It appears that Mrs Evans may have been attacked by the same man who raped and killed Sister Catherine – that nun who got killed at the drop-in centre a few weeks ago.'

Harry had gone white and his eyes seemed huge behind his glasses.

'The murderer?' His voice was faint. He closed his eyes for a second, then opened them again. 'The same man?'

The policewoman nodded sympathetically. 'That's what it's sounding like. That's why we're so keen to talk to her, because she could provide us with important leads.'

But Harry was shaking his head vehemently. 'No, no, no! I won't have it. He might come after her again. If he killed that nun, then he could kill June and I don't know . . .' His voice trailed away as he shook his head and clamped his mouth shut, as if to stop himself from crying.

The policewoman looked undecided, but after a few moments she reached out and touched his hand gently. 'We can talk about that later. For the moment, let's just concentrate on seeing your wife's all right, okay?' She gave him a reassuring smile and he nodded reluctantly.

'I want to see her now, I don't care whether they're ready for me or not. I want to see my wife!' He had stood up and his voice had risen. As if on cue, a nurse appeared through a door further down the hall. She beckoned to us.

We filed into the room. June was dressed in a pair of slacks and a sweater which didn't quite fit her and which were obviously not hers. She had an air of profound weariness, watching as we filed into the room. Then she spotted Harry. She looked up at him piteously and held out her arms. Harry walked over and enveloped her in a big hug, burying his face in her hair. After a few moments, he pulled back to gaze into his wife's face.

'Come on. I'm taking you home,' he said hoarsely. June nodded and leaned her head against his shoulder in a gesture of trust and vulnerability. Lucinda had been standing at June's side as we entered. Now she moved across to me.

'Let's go. They need to be together. The police will give them a lift home when they're ready.' Turning to June and Harry, she said, 'We're off. But we're on the other end of the phone if you need anything. I'll call in the morning, June, just to see how you are.'

Harry looked at Lucinda with gratitude shining in his eyes. 'Thanks, Lucinda. And you, Bel. I don't know what we would have done without friends like you.'

I stepped outside and sniffed the chill night air. It felt good after the recycled atmosphere of the hospital with its thick chemical smells. I felt suddenly exhausted and when I glanced at Lucinda, I could see she felt the same. In silence, I led the way to my car and drove us home.

The next few weeks passed in a haze of tension. Mags was still suspended and the atmosphere in the newsroom was strained and miserable. My attempts to find the rapist had reached a dead-end.

Throughout this period, I didn't see June at all. Harry was keeping her sequestered with him and had insisted that his wife drop her complaint. The police were pretty dejected about it, Lucinda reported, but at least they were now convinced that they were dealing with a serial rapist.

It was Lucinda who also brought home the news that the DNA tests on the semen sample taken from June after her rape matched that taken from Sister Kate.

'At least the bastard's got a low sperm count. It would have been the ultimate irony if June had got pregnant from a rape and had to have an abortion,' remarked Lucinda wryly.

As it was, Harry had been deeply shaken by the news that his wife had been attacked by a killer. He had responded by barring his front door against everyone, not even allowing the police to see his wife. He had grudgingly permitted Lucinda to visit, however, and she reported that, far from feeling trapped, June seemed to be revelling in it.

'You'd think they'd just got married. Harry flutters around her all the time. It's "Junie-Moon this" and "June-bug that". I must be getting old and cynical but it gets a bit embarrassing after a while. I mean they're not sixteen any more,' commented Lucinda, rolling her eyes.

I had gone to visit Mags as soon as possible the day after June's rape, to tell her what had happened in case it was reported in the press. In the event, it wasn't; Harry saw to that. Apart from a veiled reference to a rumour that another woman had been raped by the man who'd killed Sister Catherine, which appeared in Tigger's column, nothing was ever mentioned.

Mags' reaction when I told her the story was a complicated mixture of sheer horror threaded through with rage and guilt.

'If only I'd had the guts to report it sooner,' she groaned, pacing restlessly up and down. 'Then I might not be in such a mess and June would have been spared all this.' She tried to telephone June to console her, but Harry said that he didn't want his wife reminded of the attack and refused to allow her to come to the phone.

'God, he sounds like a right old woman.' Mags shook her head in disgust as she hung up.

Her own situation was going from bad to worse, and yet there was a kind of calm about her, which in some ways I found more disturbing than the near-hysteria of before. It was the numb hopelessness of a woman who was about to lose everything and who could do nothing more to defend herself. Trevor had refused an offer to settle out of court.

'Not that I'm sorry,' Mags snorted derisively. 'It would have turned my stomach to have paid that bastard anything after what he did to me.' But her solicitor had warned her to expect to lose the case. Mags was looking financial ruin in the face.

'I wish it were all over,' she commented sadly, staring blindly away from me out of the window. 'It can't get any worse and the waiting is hell.'

I hesitated, wondering if I dare ask what would happen to her children, but before I could say anything, she turned to look at me directly and said, 'I might have to let Barry have the kids.' Tears formed in her eyes but she didn't seem to be aware of them trailing down her cheeks, because she carried on without a tremor in her voice: 'What could I offer them? We're going to be homeless soon. I certainly wouldn't get another job in television, or in journalism for that matter.'

She gave a sudden, heaving sob. 'How could I live without my kids? How could I bear to see them pass by with Serafina in the park, being her children, when they're mine?' She turned a tearstained face up to gaze at me questioningly, as if somehow I might have the solution.

That evening when I got home I sat down at the kitchen table with my notebook. Lucinda had finally finished her exams and had flown off to Spain for a week of blissful romance with Ian, her new boyfriend, so the house was

completely quiet. It seemed we had lost the fight. I had
followed every lead I could think of and got nowhere. I
had tried to follow the police investigators' example and
find every link between the attacker and his victims in
an attempt to identify him. I had failed miserably. I felt
weighted down by half-truths and facts that didn't fit
together. They orbited meaninglessly round and round
in my head.

I decided to try my old trick of writing everything
down, to see if on paper the facts assumed a shape which
I had missed before.

First there was Sister Kate's rape and murder. The next
item, after much deliberation, I wrote down as Paula's
rape, although I noted in brackets that only she and her
attacker knew about that before the videotape came to
light. Then, several days later, someone tried to strangle
her in the woods.

I thought about George's videotape for several minutes,
doodling all over the facing page. It had survived against
the odds, only because he had taken it to show Billy.
That's where it had been when the burglary took place. I
had never given the break-in a second thought, assuming
it was just one of a series in the neighbourhood. But the
thieves or thief had taken all my tapes. Why bother? They
were virtually worthless to anyone but me . . . unless that
was what the burglar was really after all along . . .

Had the rapist somehow known about the videotape
before I or the police did? Was that why Paula had been
attacked a second time – because he knew there was
evidence that might incriminate him and that Paula's
testimony might be enough to make it stand up in
court? Was that what he'd meant when he said things
had changed – that she had become *dangerous*?

I continued doodling, my designs becoming ever more
intricate, the lines turning back on themselves in elaborate
swirling dragon tails. The rapist might have guessed in

retrospect that the flash had to do with something electrical and concluded it might be a camera. But how could he have found out who had set it up?

My brain was reeling. Who knew about George's surveillance operation – apart from Alan, Harry, Billy and me? Billy and I could be ruled out. So could Alan and Harry, because anyone who knew about the camera wouldn't have been so stupid as to have taken a victim to that spot.

I struggled to make something coherent out of all this information. In the end, everything pointed to one conclusion. The rapist couldn't have known about the taping in advance, but he had to have found out about it just after it happened. And he could only have got that information from George.

I reached for the wall telephone, almost dislocating my shoulder in my haste. George was busy right now, Caroline reported, sounding embarrassed, after she had gone to pass on my request to talk to him. I looked around desperately for inspiration. The door to one of the kitchen cupboards had swung open and I could see the tins and packets of food Lucinda had bought on her last trip to the grocery store.

'Tell him,' I extemporised, 'that I have twelve bags of cheese and onion crisps for him if he'll come over to see me now.'

Caroline chuckled. 'I expect that'll do the trick.' A few seconds later, George himself came to the phone. He sounded cheerful.

'Okay, I'll be over in a little while. I'm just finishing a game of Dungeons and Dragons with Billy but he's got to go home soon and then . . .'

'Fine. I'll look forward to seeing you,' I interrupted, realising that this was one of George's stories which could go on for ever.

While I waited for him to arrive, my thoughts turned

obsessively to Trevor. Could he have found out about the taping? Or had I been chasing the wrong man all along? Frantically, I began to review the evidence I had collected against him. He had a job which allowed him to be gone without questions being asked. He liked pornography, particularly bondage magazines. His alibi for the attack on Mags was dubious. Mags claimed to have been abducted in his car. I tossed my notebook aside in despair. We had nothing that tied Trevor to these crimes except Mags' testimony. And that, by her own admission, was not because she could identify Trevor himself, but because of his car.

Had I been blinding myself to the truth all along by concentrating on Trevor, by refusing to consider any other suspect? Suppose he *had* been telling the truth. Suppose he *had* been in the Accident & Emergency ward all night, like he said. That would have meant his car was standing outside his house – possibly all weekend – *unused*.

He sounded irritated when he answered the phone. I could hear the television blaring in the background, but it was silenced almost at once.

'Trevor, it's Bel.'

'Oh, that's nice,' he replied acidly.

'Trevor, I've been thinking about this thing with Mags—'

'Look, I've had enough of this,' he cut in. 'I know you lot have got it in for me.' I could hear his voice becoming more distant as he said this and I suddenly realised he was about to put the phone down.

'Don't hang up!' I shrieked. 'Trevor! You've got to help!' There was silence, but no dial-tone, not yet. He was still listening, albeit reluctantly. 'Trevor,' I pleaded. 'Please help. Could someone have taken your car the night that Mags was attacked, while you were in hospital?'

There was another long pause, then the sound of someone fumbling with the receiver. His voice was gruff.

'That car cost a fortune. I never let the keys out of my sight. The manufacturers have made it practically burglar-proof. Good night.' The line went dead.

I replaced the receiver and slumped back into my chair, exhausted. I folded my arms on the table and laid my head on them. The endless questions and scraps of information began their circuit again. Trevor was linked to two of the victims – he worked with Mags and he was part of a group of businessmen who had given Sister Kate money for the drop-in centre.

I thought about the photograph. I have a very visual memory. I recall things in still-frames – chunks of my life captured. I saw a clear image of myself, standing there in the reception area at the garage, looking at the wall. Seeing the picture of Sister Kate accepting the cheque. And beneath it, all those clipboards, with work orders. The keys for each vehicle attached.

'*What!*' The voice when he picked up the phone was so hostile that it was almost as if Trevor had known it would be me.

'Which garage do you use?'

There was a heavy sigh. 'Corders'. Like everyone else.' He hung up.

I replaced the receiver, my mind racing. Was that how it had happened? Could it be that Mags' attacker was not Trevor, but someone who could have got hold of Trevor's keys when the Cosworth was at the garage being serviced – and copied them?

I was suddenly aware of an insistent banging and George's voice yelling, 'Bel!' I got up and unlocked the back door.

George stood there scowling. 'I've been knocking for hours,' he moaned, scuffing his shoes on the floor as he entered and giving the place a quick once over. He turned to face me.

'Where's the crisps?' he snarled. It was the shootout at the OK Corral.

I opened the cupboard door to show him. A smile lit up his face and he reached out a hand.

'Uh-uh!' I stood in his way. 'You can have *one* packet now and the rest *after* we've had our little talk.' He knew when he was beat. He hoisted himself up onto the kitchen counter, pushed his glasses further up his nose and tore open the packet.

'What do you want to talk about?' he asked in the manner of a kindly psychiatrist about to solve all my problems.

'I don't like reminding you of this, George, but do you remember that tape you had, which showed the woman being attacked?'

George looked away and fidgeted with the packet in his hands. 'Mmm,' he muttered.

'Who knew about that tape before you showed it to me?'

George began to swing his legs, so that his feet kicked rhythmically against the cupboard below him. 'Me and Billy showed it to some of our pals.'

I felt my heart sink. 'How many?'

George counted silently on his fingers. 'Three,' he announced. 'There would have been five but the twins had to go home for their tea sharp because their mum was mad with them about something.'

'Were there any adults who knew?'

George shook his head and looked at me slyly. 'Can I have another bag of crisps? Please?'

I groaned and fetched one more bag. 'Do you have any idea who your pals might have told about it?'

George ripped the packet open and stuffed a handful of crisps into his mouth. Then he mumbled something.

'I can't hear a word you're saying,' I snapped irritably.

He swallowed. 'No one. We all took an oath. I was scared he might try to murder me so I didn't want anyone knowing. He might creep up behind me some night when I was coming home from school and it was dark and he might stick a knife into me and there would be blood everywhere and it would run down all over the place.' He grinned cheerfully and swallowed another handful of crisps. 'Are you going to give me a lift home, Bel?'

I nodded. I wasn't going to get any more out of George and a change of scene would do me good. 'Come on. Let's pack up these crisps of yours. My car's in the lane.'

We loaded the ten remaining packets into a large plastic bag and stashed it behind the driver's seat. There was an audible crunch when I leaned back.

It wasn't far to George's house. As I drew to a halt outside the front door, something else occurred to me. 'I suppose you always did your filming in the same place, didn't you?'

George nodded. 'Most of the time.'

For a second I was misled by the nod into thinking that was an affirmative. Then the words sank in.

'What do you mean, "most of the time"?' I asked.

'Well, *most* of the time,' said George with added emphasis, as if he were explaining something to someone who was hard of hearing and stupid into the bargain. 'Remember, I told you. Billy and me decided to move the camera one time when we were on our own because we weren't getting anything at the other bit. We had a look around and there was a hole on the other side of the wood that looked like it was a badgers' sett. Actually it's a fox's den we found out later,' he confided.

I was staring at him, transfixed. I was finding it hard to breathe. 'Did you tell anyone else about that?' I managed to get out.

George frowned, deep in thought. 'I can't remember.

220

Alan nearly blew a gasket when he did find out because he said we could have electricated ourselves. But that was when the police came about the tape afterwards.' He shrugged and reached for the door handle. 'I've got to finish my homework or I don't get to watch telly,' he announced, scrambling out onto the pavement. He slammed the door. 'See you soon.' I watched him run up the path.

I started up the engine and drove to the end of the street. Glancing in the rearview mirror, I noticed George energetically waving goodbye, so I rolled down the window and absent-mindedly waved back as I swung round the corner.

I was in a state of shock, but I forced myself to think as logically as I could. I had always assumed that other people had known where the taping was carried out. I had forgotten that the last location of the camera had been George and Billy's little secret. No one else had known it was there until after the attack – not me, not Harry, not Alan, no one. My mind baulked at the implications. Harry's contribution had simply been to provide the power supply for the recording. But Alan fitted our profile of the rapist very closely. I had never even considered him before, but the more I thought about it, the more it all slipped into place. There was the link to the pornography, the stalking of his victims, for all the world like a police surveillance operation, plus the freedom to come and go at odd hours.

The crucial question, the one which would prove his innocence or incriminate him of rape and murder, was whether he *knew* the camera had been moved. But how could I find out?

I swung into Garnet Street. This was the most direct route back to my home from George's but it was also the street where June lived. Harry's red van was parked in the drive. On impulse, I pulled in behind it.

As I expected, it was Harry who answered the door. He looked less than thrilled to see me but I could tell that we had both reached the conclusion that an outright refusal to let me cross his threshold was too impolite to be tolerated. He opened the door wide and stood aside to let me step into the small hallway.

He began talking as if he was braced for an argument. 'I'm sorry, but I'm not going to let you see June. She's still in a very fragile state.'

'It's not June I've come to see,' I said as soothingly as possible. 'I just wanted—'

I was interrupted by the door next to me opening and June's voice saying, 'Who's that . . . Bel!' There was no mistaking the pleasure in her voice. She reached out and grasped me by the elbow, drawing me into the overheated sitting room.

'Is that you playing Rottweiler again, Harry Evans?' she scolded. She wagged a finger at him before saying in a confidential tone to me: 'He's terrible. Won't let me out of his sight since the,' she stumbled over the word, 'the attack. Have a seat. Harry, love, could you make us a cup of tea, or would you rather have coffee?' She looked at me inquiringly.

I sneaked a glance at Harry. There was an air of alarmed helplessness about him, as if things were getting out of his control.

'I'd love some coffee,' I said, smiling at June. She settled herself in the armchair on the opposite side of the fireplace from mine. 'Oh, I'm so pleased to see you,' she continued. Then she mouthed with a sideways glance in the direction of the kitchen, 'Harry's driving me crackers. He's just been lovely, but he won't let me out of his sight.' Then in her normal voice, abandoning any attempt at secrecy, she added, 'I think it's the idea that I could have been murdered like that poor nun. He's terrified of losing me now.'

She smiled as Harry entered, pushing the door open with one foot and balancing a tray in both hands. 'I think it's made us both realise how lucky we are to be together, hasn't it, Harry?'

'Yes, of course it has, honey bun. Now where do you want me to put this tray?'

I thought I detected a slight edge to Harry's voice. Either he was irritated at the manner in which I had wangled my way into his sitting room and an audience with June, or the enforced intimacy was beginning to wear on him. When he had handed us both our cups of coffee, he settled himself heavily on the sofa in front of the window. There were a few minutes of inconsequential chat during which Harry's foot twitched irritably. Finally he could stand it no longer.

'What is it you wanted to ask me then?'

I placed my cup and saucer on a nearby table. 'Harry,' I began tentatively, 'you remember that videotaping that George did?'

Harry looked grave. 'Awful business.' He shook his head disapprovingly.

'Did you know that George and Billy moved the camera?' I held my breath.

Harry thought for a moment, pursing his lips. 'No. Not till it all blew up, that is.' He looked at me with a puzzled expression.

'Alan never mentioned it?' I pressed him.

He shook his head. 'Not that I can recall. No.'

The disappointment must have shown on my face.

'Was it something that you thought might help Mags?' June asked sympathetically. I nodded, feeling too dejected to speak. She sighed. 'Well, you know, if there's anything I can do . . .'

I shot a covert glance at Harry. He looked ready to intervene. But June seemed to be remarkably recovered from her ordeal, not at all in the fragile state Harry had implied. This was the first chance I'd had to really talk to her about the attack since the night it happened.

'There is one thing,' I said, keeping a wary eye on Harry.

He moved forward in his seat. 'June, my love . . .'

'Harry, it's fine.' She waved him away with one hand, then smiled placatingly. 'It's the least I can do.' Harry looked sceptical, but said nothing more. He sat there as if poised for action. June turned back to me. 'What was it, Bel? Fire away.'

I launched straight in. 'Before the attack, June, was there anything unusual that happened, anything that made you suspicious or gave you a funny feeling in any way?'

June looked perplexed, furrowing her brow. 'No, I don't think so.' She shook her head. 'No, nothing that I can think of. Why, did Mags mention anything?'

I shrugged. 'Oh, she thought someone might have been following her for a few days before the attack.' I hesitated, then decided there was no turning back. 'Did you get any unusual mail before that night?'

June looked at Harry as if for guidance. He remained impassive. She looked back to me and shook her head. I tried again.

'June,' I said carefully, 'when you were attacked, did the man take any photographs?'

June frowned. 'I don't think so, no.' Then she said with a note of anxiety in her voice, 'The police didn't say anything about this. Is this something new?' She bit her lip. 'You know, I did get a funny feeling sometimes when I was walking over to your house to do the cleaning. Like maybe someone was watching me.' She looked at me, oddly tentative.

'Did anyone send you photographs in the post before the attack?' I pressed on. June turned quickly to Harry for support. He got up and stepped across to her and put an arm round her shoulders protectively.

'I think June's told you everything she knows, Bel. I don't want her getting upset again, especially with me having to go back out of town.'

June looked up at him sharply. 'You're leaving? Where are you going? You said you'd stay with me, Harry.' Her mouth trembled and I could see she was near to tears. She tugged on his hand and gazed up at him beseechingly. 'I need you, Harry.'

He sighed helplessly. 'I know, love.' He squatted down so that his face was level with hers and stroked her hair with one hand. 'I got a call from those people I was working for up north. I have to finish that job or they're going to have to get someone else in. They really have no choice because they're opening to the public in August and all the carpets have to be done.' His voice took on a cajoling tone. 'I have to, Junie. It'll mean a lot of work for me if I do this job right.' He whispered the last words. 'It'll set us up. I want you to be able to get over this and for us to have kids and just forget all this and be happy.'

June bent forward, leaning her forehead on Harry's chest. When she spoke, her voice trembled. 'Oh, Harry. I can't bear it when you leave.'

He gripped her gently by the shoulders, pushing her away. 'Best get it over with, Junie. I was going to leave tonight so I can be ready to start first thing in the morning.' She was weeping now. 'Look, you've got Bel here and Lucinda – she'll pop round whenever you want, I'm sure. It'll only be for a few days, just to finish the job.' He bent his head to look up into her face, as he wiped away her tears. Then he glanced at me. 'You'll keep an eye on her, won't you, Bel? It won't be for long.'

'Of course.' I stood up, feeling that I was intruding on something very personal. 'But I'll go now and leave you two to get sorted out.'

Harry saw me to the door. 'I'm just off in a couple

of minutes myself. I'm glad you came round. I've been trying to break the news to her all day. It made it easier to tell her somehow with you here. You know, I could remind her she wouldn't be all on her own.' He looked weary.

'Lucinda or I will stop by and see how she is tomorrow,' I promised. I could hear June's voice raised in anguish as I walked down the path.

Chapter Fifteen

Something didn't make sense. I drove all the way home, walked into the house, paced round it, read the notes I had written earlier then sat down and stood up again. Why had the rapist suddenly changed his mode of operation? Why hadn't he taken any pictures this time? I kicked a chair across the kitchen floor in disgust. We were being outwitted by a worthless piece of shit.

I couldn't bear to be inside any longer. Picking up my keys, I went out to my car, got in and reversed down the lane, intending to find somewhere to drive fast and furiously and work out some of my frustration. I headed out of town in the direction of Round House, choosing quiet country roads. The car dipped under overhanging branches. I thought about the attack. Why hadn't June been treated like all the other victims? Why was she different? There was no rhyme or reason to it. Unless . . .

I screeched to a halt, skidding on the loose surface of the country road, raising a spray of grit. Leaning my forehead on the steering wheel, I cursed my own stupidity. Why hadn't I thought of this before? It might already be too late. The rapist might have been tipped off by my investigations and destroyed any evidence. I swung my car round and headed back into town.

June's house was in darkness when I arrived and Harry's van had already gone. I parked the TR askew in the road and raced up to the front door. It took several minutes of leaning on the bell before I saw the living-room curtains twitch and then June opened the door.

I understood as soon as I saw her why she hadn't answered at once. She was sobbing hard, so hard she was on the verge of hysteria, gasping for breath. Without saying anything she turned and led the way into the living room. It was in darkness. I switched on a light, then, mindful of the man who stalked women, who watched them unawares, I drew the curtains.

'Has Harry left?' I asked.

June nodded, still sobbing. I guided her to the sofa and sank onto it sideways, pulling her down next to me so that we faced each other. She looked away miserably, ashamed of her tears. I gave her shoulders a little shake.

'June,' I said urgently. 'You have to help me. It's important. I think you can lead us to the murderer.'

She looked at me dully. 'No, I can't,' she said, and began to sob afresh. I braced myself. If I handled this wrongly, we might never know the truth.

Quickly, I outlined the chronology of events I had written down in my notebook. In spite of herself, June was interested and her crying stopped.

'But that wasn't a crime – the police said it wasn't,' she objected when I mentioned the videotaped attack. 'It was just people having funny sex.' And later, when I pressed on in spite of her arguments, 'But I thought the papers said Mags was making it up to get even with Trevor.'

I shook my head. 'Mags *was* raped. So was Paula. And both of them, quite independently of each other, told me they had received Polaroid photographs taken of them in the street in the two weeks or so before they were attacked. So I went back and I found out that Sister Kate got some too, only no one had known about it.' I paused. June was gazing at me with a perplexed look on her face. 'Only you, of all his victims,' I said pointedly, 'didn't get any.'

June stared at me. Then suddenly, she jerked back to

life. 'I threw them out,' she said. She looked away, unable to meet my eye.

I grabbed her by the shoulders and shook her hard. 'Stop lying!'

Something in June collapsed. She was weeping again. I closed my eyes and tried desperately to think how I could make this work. I gripped her shoulders harder.

'June, look at me,' I begged. 'Please look at me.' But she kept her head turned away. I heard myself say very quietly, 'You weren't raped, were you?' Her silent weeping burst into loud sobs.

'No,' she choked. 'I made it up.' She gulped back her tears and looked at me with reddened eyes. 'Harry's left me. He's got a girlfriend up north. He's moved there for good. He did it once before, but that time . . .' She broke down again. I looked round wildly and spotted a box of paper hankies. With one wild lunge, I grabbed it and thrust it into June's trembling hands. She plucked at one and blew her nose with it.

'That time,' she continued, sniffing, 'I told him I was pregnant.' She rubbed the tears from her eyes, calmer again. 'He came back because he always wanted children. But it was a lie. I faked a miscarriage the day before my first doctor's appointment. But now he's got another girlfriend. He's gone back to her tonight. I thought the being pregnant thing wouldn't work again.' She took a deep sobbing breath.

'That night, I persuaded him to go to bed with me. I thought that would help, he would stay. But he didn't. He made love to me then he just got up, put on his clothes, said cheerio and left. I was desperate.' June paused, looking at me, pleading for understanding. 'Then I remembered how worried he was about Mags and what had happened to her. He kept asking about it. I knew all about the rape from you and Lucinda and what was in the papers. So I just made it up.'

She sat looking down at her hands miserably, twisting the paper handkerchief to shreds. There was a long silence. She still didn't get it.

'June.' I spoke very slowly and deliberately. 'Remember those samples they took at the hospital that night? The police had those tested. The semen matched the semen of the rapist. The man you had sex with is the man who raped all those women and murdered Sister Kate.'

She stared at me. I had a sudden presentiment that I was risking everything by telling June all this. Abruptly, I stood up.

'Does Harry have a Polaroid camera?'

She nodded, looking bewildered. 'He keeps it in his workshop.'

I dragged her to her feet. 'Where is it? Show me.'

Looking confused and frightened, she took me through to the kitchen. Then she opened a door in the corner of the room and stood back, looking at me uncertainly. Stepping forward, I could see wooden stairs leading down into what appeared to be a cellar. The mouldy smell of decay came up to meet me. For a moment I recoiled.

Then I nudged June towards the steps.

'Go on. Show me where it is.'

Awkwardly, she descended the wooden stairs, going sideways because they were narrow and very steep. I could hear her fumbling around in the dark when she reached the bottom, then a light was switched on.

We were in a cellar just over six feet in height. A tall man or woman would have had to duck between the rafters overhead. I had a sense of a vast underground cavern, disappearing into recesses of blackness around us. What light there was came from a single bulb hanging over a long wooden trestle table, scarred from use, which stood against the far wall. It had been swept clean. Various small implements hung from nails and hooks stuck into pegboard above the bench and some shelves along the wall at right angles held a selection of power tools. To the right side of the bench, there was an old wooden filing cabinet. June picked her way across the uneven cement floor towards it. She tried to open the top drawer.

'Locked,' she said in a tone of finality, and with a shrug began to move past me towards the staircase, clearly anxious to get away from here.

But there was no turning back now. I caught her shoulder. 'That's where it is?'

She frowned. 'Yes, but it's—'

'And you don't have a key?' My grip had tightened on her arm. She looked frightened, shaking her head uncertainly. I closed my eyes for a split second. Opening them, I scanned the tools above the workbench, letting go of June to grab something that looked like a long chisel. The honed edge slid easily into the gap between the top drawer and the case.

'What are you doing?' June's voice had a note of panic in it. For answer I pushed up on the other end of the chisel with all my might. The wood creaked. I relaxed, took a deep breath and tried again. Nothing happened for a couple of seconds then with a splintering of wood, the drawer sprang open.

'Look what you've done!' June looked aghast. 'Harry'll go berserk when he sees this. Bel!' She put a restraining hand on my arm, but I shook it off as I yanked out one of the lower drawers. It held a series of manilla folders. Deciding that there was no time to go through those now, I hauled open the drawer above. It too held nothing but files.

I was becoming more and more frantic. I knew Harry had a mobile phone, and wondered how far I could push my luck before June reached the end of her tether and called him. I pulled out the top one. What if I found nothing? What if I had to retreat, empty-handed, giving Harry time to destroy the evidence?

'You're mad,' June whispered. 'You've gone crazy.' The cabinet rocked forward a little, unbalanced by all the open drawers. I leant against it to stop it falling.

'I'm going to phone Harry.' She turned away. Instantly, I lunged after her, to stop her, to plead with her. My fingers closed on the tail of her sweater. Behind me there was an almighty crash. June screamed and we both spun round. The filing cabinet had toppled over, sending drawers sliding onto the cement floor and scattering the contents.

June had started to cry. 'Now look what you've done! Just look at the mess!' She shook off my hand and ran back, trying to hoist the cabinet upright.

'Hang on. I'll help.' I moved to the other side. Together we managed to heave the cabinet back onto its base. That was when I noticed the box. It must have fallen out of some cavity behind the drawers. With trembling hands, I picked it up.

It was an ordinary cardboard carton, the sort of thing you can find at the grocery store. Nestling inside on what looked like a pair of dark overalls, was a set of handcuffs, a collection of keys of all shapes and sizes, plus a large brown envelope. Beneath all that was a Polaroid camera.

I glanced inside the envelope. It contained sheaves of photographs of women, taken as they went about their daily lives, then later when they had been kidnapped, their eyes dark with shame and fear. I gazed at them, transfixed by horror.

Perhaps that was why I didn't hear the sound of footsteps overhead, of creaking floorboards, or perhaps he was just very quiet. But whatever the reason, Harry's voice came as a shock.

'June, is that you?'

I froze. From the first moment I had begun my descent into this hole, this was the nightmare that had lurked at the back of my mind.

June stepped forward eagerly.

232

'Harry? It's me. I'm here.'

His feet appeared on the upper steps and began to descend.

For one dizzy moment, I thought of trying to hide, but almost immediately I discarded that idea. June knew where I was; she would probably tell. In any case, as Harry continued his descent, all thoughts of escape flew out of my mind.

Another pair of feet and legs had appeared, swinging loosely against Harry's body – the feet and legs of a child. As Harry came into view, ducking his head under the level of the ceiling, and bracing himself against the metal bannister, I saw that one arm gripped George around the waist, holding him up, while the other hand was clamped across his mouth.

George was not struggling. His eyes looked huge. There was blood pouring from a gash on his forehead, mingling with tears on his face.

'Well, well, well. What have we here?' Harry's voice was very quiet. I couldn't see his eyes behind the blind glassiness of his spectacles. He released his grip on George, allowing the small body to slide down until his feet touched the ground. Harry removed his hand from George's mouth, still keeping him pinned tight around the neck. George gave a sobbing gasp, choking for breath. He looked at me, bewildered.

'I wanted my crisps,' he said apologetically. 'You went off with them in your car. I was on my way to your house when I saw—'

'Shut up!' Harry yanked his arm higher, so that George's chin was jerked up and he gasped with pain.

My mind was racing. Harry couldn't afford to let any of us live. Not now. Not even George. Not unless he was prepared to go to gaol for life. I glanced at June. She had stopped in her tracks, several feet away from her husband. She seemed uncertain.

'Harry . . .' she began tentatively.

'Who said you could talk?' Harry gave her a vicious look. June's face went limp. Harry was speaking again, this time to me. 'Don't try anything funny or the boy gets it.' He grinned unpleasantly, before switching his attention back to his wife again.

'June, there's handcuffs in that box over there.' He directed her to the carton which had fallen from the filing cabinet. June lumbered clumsily over to the bench. 'No, you stupid piece of shit! Not there. Over *there*!' June stared at him, fearful, hurt by his words.

'Harry, I didn't . . . I wasn't . . .' she stammered weakly. She turned to find the box, which lay on the floor, then lifted it onto the bench and began fumbling around inside it. She brought out the handcuffs. They gleamed hard in the dim light.

'Now put one of them round that cow's wrist,' ordered Harry, jerking his head in my direction.

'Harry . . .' June started to demur, her voice shaking.

'Do it!' There was a manic note in Harry's scream. Her hands trembling, June obeyed as quickly as she could, fitting one handcuff round my left wrist.

'I'm sorry,' she murmured brokenly under her breath. She glanced behind her quickly, so fast it was like a nervous tic. Harry had disappeared into a dark corner, dragging George, his trainers catching on the cement. Before I realised what was happening, there was a dull thudding sound and a muffled cry, which broke off in the middle.

'Don't touch that kid or—' I yelled at the top of my voice.

Harry had reappeared, moving menacingly back out of the gloom. 'Or what? What will you do then?' he sneered. He had some rope in his hands.

'Now put the other one round that pipe up there,' he instructed June, indicating a narrow pipe which ran up one

234

of the metal girders supporting the floor overhead, then ran alongside the rafter above the bench. He turned back into the darkness, disappearing into the recesses of the cellar. There was no sign of life from there. No sound.

I could try to make a run for it. June wouldn't stop me. But Harry was between me and the stairs. And I couldn't leave George.

'June,' I breathed. 'Get out. Call the police.' She would not meet my eye. Instead she gave a sharp little shake of her head.

'Don't make him angry. It'll be all right if we just humour him.'

I stared at her in disbelief. Was this how she had kept her marriage going? Was this how she had managed to live for so many years with a monster – by trying not to rock the boat at all costs, by denying the severity of the situation?

Harry loomed out of the darkness and stood by her side.

'Give me that!' He snatched the other end of the set of handcuffs. I felt a stab of pain as the metal cut into my wrist. Harry had hauled my left arm up and clipped the other cuff round the pipe. I was now immobilised, unable to help myself or George. I felt a rush of bitter anger at my own feebleness. Why hadn't I made a run for it when I had the chance? Nothing could be worse than the situation I was in now.

Harry had grasped hold of June's arm, pulling her away from the light into the centre of the cavern.

'Right, June. You first.' He slid one foot in front of hers and pulled back hard so that she fell heavily with a dull crack onto the cement. She gave a shriek of pain. Harry had produced a length of rope. He looped it round June's neck. I felt as if I were in some nightmare. He adjusted it almost tenderly, so that it nestled against her skin. June was looking up at him, pleading.

'Harry, what are you doing? What did I do wrong?'

At that, something seemed to snap in him. He jerked the rope savagely so that his wife whimpered in pain.

'Oh, you've done plenty wrong, Junie, plenty.' I could see his teeth bared as he tugged on the rope again, increasing her agony. 'It would all have been fine if you hadn't had to put up your hand and say you'd been raped.' His voice was gravelly. 'Even then it might have been all right if only you'd been smart enough to carry it off. But, oh no,' he jerked the rope again and June gasped with pain, 'not you. You're so stupid. So when this bitch,' he nodded his head in my direction, 'put two and two together about the pictures, it was only a matter of time before you were caught out and landed me right in it. So I knew I had to get rid of you smartish. That's what I came back for. Only,' he chuckled mirthlessly, 'I didn't expect to find the brat outside as well and the bitch inside. So I get to kill three birds with one stone.'

Harry's laughter died away. He looked down at June, shivering on the floor at his feet, her head pulled at an awkward angle. 'You're a loose cannon, Junie. You could blow me all to hell. I'm forty-seven. I'd be an old man before they let me out again.'

He hunkered down on his heels. 'I'm going back to Tracy – she'll give me my alibi. They'll think it was the rapist come back to finish the job. I might even start a fire to make sure nothing,' he jerked the rope again, but this time June's body flopped limply and she made no sound 'nothing survives.' He stood for a moment, looking at his wife, pulling on the rope a few times as if amused by the weak way her body moved.

I had been mesmerised by the horror of this scene. Now I looked around me frantically. With the urgency of desperation, I memorised the layout – the chisel lying on top of the filing cabinet, the single naked light bulb. I looked back at Harry. He had taken hold of both ends

236

of the rope. His lips were pulled back from his teeth in a grimace. He had moved his legs slightly apart and bent his knees. He was a man preparing for a tremendous effort, a man getting ready to strangle his wife. After that he would kill me. And then he would kill George.

I looked at the light again, tensed my muscles for one second, then moved. With one stride I had positioned myself, pulling the handcuff so that it scraped along the metal pipe as it slid after me. Harry heard the noise. Out of the corner of my eye, I saw him stagger to his feet, dropping the ends of the rope, turning to look. I was reaching up, flinching against the searing pain, grasping the light bulb and twisting it out.

The darkness slammed against my eyeballs, stunning me with its suddenness. I tossed the bulb into the centre of the cellar and heard the multiple tinkling and skittering of thin glass as it scattered across the concrete.

Then I reached behind me and grabbed the chisel. My ears were straining for sounds, to know where danger was coming from. I had no escape. I could only let Harry come to me.

There was a slight noise to my left, like a rubber sole turning on concrete. Then I felt the rough, surprisingly powerful hands scrabbling at my throat and I could smell his oniony breath. He squeezed hard, pressing on my windpipe. If I passed out, there would be no second chances. Not for any of us.

With the combined force of fear and desperation, I brought the chisel down where I sensed his head to be. I heard a dull sound and felt his body lurch with the impact, making him tighten his grip convulsively round my throat. Things had started to swim. My sense of myself was fading, my legs going limp. Suddenly his grip shifted. But before I could move, he had caught hold of my arm. Moments later, the chisel had been wrestled from my grasp and I heard the metallic clatter as it hit the

237

concrete floor, skidding away, far beyond my reach. I had nothing left to fight with now.

But in that moment, as Harry twisted away slightly to fling the chisel aside, some instinct made me bring my right knee up. As Harry's hands curled round my throat again, I pulled my head back, trying to get away from him, bracing myself against the bench and manoeuvring until my toes and then my whole foot was against his solar plexus. My breath was coming in gasps and there was a distant rushing in my ears. I put the whole of my dying effort into one last push.

It seemed to take Harry by surprise. He made an odd, snorting sound and fell back. I could hear the thump of his body hitting the ground and a grinding noise as he rolled on the splinters of glass. I heard him swear. He was moving. He had started to get up. I was swaying in and out of consciousness. I knew I had made my last effort. I was done for. I could do nothing more to save myself, or George.

Glass grated on the concrete as Harry shifted his weight – a funny, distorted sound, mixing with the ringing in my ears. He was breathing heavily. The darkness was spinning towards me, swooping down. At its centre was a sudden stillness, a sense of inevitability, that everything, this whole sordid mess, had come to this. I wondered if our bodies would ever be found; if anyone would ever discover how we had died or who was responsible.

From somewhere far away, a strange noise pierced my consciousness, a sort of choking gasp, a liquid sound that ebbed and flowed and went on and on for ever, it seemed. Then the noise stopped abruptly. The darkness pressed in against me. With sudden clarity, I understood that I was standing alone in this dark hole and that all around me, life was ebbing away.

Chapter Sixteen

I looked up. Far above me I could see a deep blue sky encircled by green leafy branches. A scene of perfect tranquillity. Voices drifted from somewhere behind me – Lucinda and Mags talking in the house. I leaned back into my deckchair. Almost without noticing, my eyelids drooped. I jerked them open sharply to get away from the images of blood and death that swarmed at me.

It seemed to take me hours that night to find the keys for the handcuffs even though the box was within easy reach. If they hadn't been such an unusual shape, I might never have been able to identify them in the dark and get free. And all the while, I had this awful sense of foreboding.

When the handcuffs finally snapped apart, I had stumbled to the stairs, tripping over someone lying immobile on the floor. It took all my willpower to talk coherently to the 999 operator.

Then, my limbs shaking spasmodically with fear, I got the torch from my car and as the sirens sounded in the distance, coming ever nearer, raced back to the cellar. I wanted to find George, to find him alive.

The sight which confronted me, captured in the beam of my torch, struck me almost like a physical assault. Blood was spreading silently over the cement, finding new channels, flowing towards me across the floor.

It was only much later, after the autopsy, that Henderson told me Harry had rolled over onto the socket of the shattered light bulb, stabbing himself in the throat on the single shard of glass still embedded in its core. But even then, standing in the cellar, I knew he was dead. As the full impact of what had happened hit me, I shrank back, sinking down in a huddle on the stairs, paralysed with shock. That was where the police found me.

It had helped to have Lucinda back. In the initial turmoil, after I had been taken home, I had debated whether to phone her and interrupt her holiday. I was still undecided when she had called me just to check on things and, with her ex-detective's nose for something being not quite right, had got the whole story out of me. So she was back home in under eight hours.

She had been as devastated as I was. We had sat up two nights in a row, going over and over everything, asking ourselves if it could have been different, trying to come to terms with what had happened. The paramedics had managed to revive June after strenuous efforts. But apart from that piece of good news, it all seemed such a waste, such a loss of life.

Paradoxically, it was Mags who broke this obsessive cycle of remorse, when she heard the news and telephoned to find out how I was. It seemed as if, having reached rock bottom herself, she had discovered a strength and purpose she did not have before. While she had been as shaken by events as we were, she had insisted that we must hold on tight to what remained, the life that was still there to be lived. Fifteen minutes ago, she had arrived with a bottle of champagne – to celebrate our survival she told us firmly.

'Here we are!' At that moment, Lucinda and Mags appeared, carrying the bottle of champagne plus three flutes. With great ceremony, they popped the cork and poured the bubbling wine into our glasses.

Mags raised hers, sparkling in the sun. 'To us!' Her words seemed to be an act of blind faith in the midst of chaos and tragedy. Lucinda and I echoed her toast. As sipped the wine I wondered if, after all, this pain could heal and my life be free of the dark undertow which had haunted me the past few days. It was ironic that, having finally recovered from Jamie's death, I should have been plunged into such turmoil again. Perhaps with these, my best friends, I might recover a sense of peace and tranquillity.

Mags and Lucinda were chatting.

'How's June?' I interrupted them. I knew Lucinda had visited her cousin-in-law earlier in the day. Even though we had survived such a terrible ordeal together, June had refused to see me.

'Not too good, I'm afraid.' Lucinda held her glass up to the sunlight, apparently engrossed in its twinkling reflections. 'She refuses to believe that Harry was the murderer, in spite of everything. She's convinced there's been a mistake – that you set him up, actually.' Lucinda turned her head languidly towards me and grimaced.

'I suppose,' suggested Mags sympathetically, 'if she accepts his guilt, then it must throw their relationship in doubt and she has to face problems such as whether he really loved her, whether he really meant to kill her – God, it's a minefield!'

There was one question which had been twisting and turning in my mind since the night Harry died. 'Do you think June had any inkling, ever, that her husband was a rapist and murderer?'

'Oh, surely not,' broke in Mags quickly.

Lucinda pursed her lips. 'I think the evidence is always there if you want to see it. He must have been coming and going at odd times of night. He couldn't have been raping women or committing a violent murder and then arriving home and behaving normally. But people only see what they want to see. I've known that happen time and time again. God save us from weak and passive women. Sometimes they can perpetuate more damage than any vicious criminal because it's easier for them to let it go on than to stop it.'

'But wouldn't the police have worked out it was Harry Evans eventually anyway – because of the DNA tests?' I asked.

Lucinda shook her head. 'He wasn't a suspect. June said he'd been away for two weeks and they hadn't had sex during that whole time. Even if the police had decided to ask him for a sample, he'd have been perfectly within his rights to refuse. Unless they had other evidence against him, there was no reason to suspect him and no way they could force him to cooperate.'

There was silence for a moment. 'By the way,' she added in a changed tone of voice, 'I saw Alan last night. He wouldn't admit to anything but I know he's been spying on me. I can always tell when he's fibbing. He knew all about Ian. My guess is he was staking this place out, trying to discover what I was up to. Anyway,' she drained her glass, 'we had a huge row, so I think he's got the message.'

She looked across at Mags, who had been sitting lost in thought. 'What about you? Have you managed to get things sorted out?'

'What? Oh, after a fashion.' Mags was startled out of her reverie. 'Everyone accepts now that I *was* raped and that I was right about the car.' She gave an ironic laugh. 'Barry is so overcome with remorse for having harassed me when I was in trouble that he's backed down on the custody issue – for the time being, at any rate.' She paused. 'I wrote a letter to Trevor to apologise. Much as I loathe him, I owed him that.'

'I went to see him yesterday.' At this announcement, the other two stared at me in surprise. 'I couldn't rest till I'd got it over with,' I explained. 'I said I was sorry for hounding him the way I did.'

'What did he say?' Mags was intensely curious.

I gestured dismissively with one hand. 'Nothing much. He just muttered something about putting all this behind us and making a fresh start. Then he said he had a meeting and left.'

Mags nodded thoughtfully. 'Well at least he's willing to give it a go. Martin has told me unofficially that I'll be reinstated, by the way. He's persuaded Trevor to drop the lawsuit – told him I'd end up getting more sympathy than him. So I start again on Monday. For what it's worth,' she added with a wry smile.

I sighed. 'It would have been nice to have got rid of old Heavy Trevy, but I suppose you can't have everything.'

Mags tilted her face towards me. 'It doesn't really bother me any more. All this has given me time to think. Trevor's not a big bad wolf. He's just a pathetic, lonely, middle-aged man who's not very good at his job and probably knows it. I, on the other hand, have my children and my friends and love my work. I can afford to ignore his taunts. We all can.'

'You know, I forgot to ask,' Lucinda broke in. 'How *did* Harry get hold of Trevor's car? I thought those posh ones were supposed to be virtually burglar-proof.' Both of them looked at me.

I shrugged. 'He had a contract with Corders' to provide a valet service. When cars were put in for repair, a lot of times the owners would ask for them to be cleaned up too. Harry would get the paperwork with the owner's name and address and telephone number on it and be given the keys.'

Mags looked serious. 'So that's how he found out where I lived – and Paula, too, I presume.'

'But what about Sister Kate?' Lucinda had already seen the one hole in this explanation.

'I can answer that one.' We all started at the masculine voice. I squirmed round in my deckchair to see who was behind me. Commander Henderson stood there, dressed

243

like he always was, in a greenish checked shirt with a navy tie and a crumpled grey suit. He clutched yet another bottle of champagne, a really big one this time, and standing next to him was a diminutive young woman in a neat cream-coloured dress with a long flowing skirt. She had Henderson's deep blue eyes, but her features were small and pert.

'I'd like you to meet my daughter, Mandy. She's home from college for the holidays,' he said, with more than a hint of pride in his voice. There was a round of introductions and helloes and more deckchairs were unearthed from the tumble of things in the garden shed. Henderson popped the cork with a flourish and filled everyone's glasses except his daughter's.

'I'm driving,' she explained, then frowned at her father.

He caught her look. 'Just one,' he pleaded. He turned to the rest of us and added jovially: 'She got in the door from college, took one look and put me on a diet before she even got her coat off. Takes after her mum. Well, cheers.' He raised his glass, oblivious to his daughter's exasperated sighs.

'So what were you going to tell us about Harry and Sister Kate?' Lucinda prompted as soon as he'd had a few sips.

'Ah yes. Nice stuff, this, isn't it?' Henderson smiled happily. 'Well, apparently she used to teach old Harry at St Xavier's. So we've put two and two together. Cloud Nine is only a couple of streets away from his office. We think he either bumped into her one day, or perhaps spotted her without her seeing him – at any rate, he found out where she worked.'

'So why did he kill her and not us?' Mags' voice was quiet, but there was an underlying intensity to her question.

Henderson pursed his lips. 'Well, between you and me

we're working on a couple of theories. He may have had a grudge against her from way back. We don't know. Or she may have recognised him, perhaps tried to appeal to him as a former pupil and then he felt he had to finish her off.' Henderson shrugged and looked off into the distance. 'We may never know.'

'What about the so-called burglary? That filing cabinet belonged to Andrew Marmot and he had the only keys.'

An ironic smile had spread across Henderson's face as I spoke. 'How did you know that?' he grinned at me.

'So was he involved?'

'Not in Sister Kate's death, no, but we've had our eye on him for a while. We know exactly what little game he's up to.'

'Dealing?' Lucinda hazarded a guess.

Henderson nodded. 'But you didn't hear that from me. He's been in a right state since Sister Kate died because he thought it was all his fault. He owed some heavies a lot of dosh, apparently, and he assumed they'd come looking for him and got her instead. He panicked when he found her body, threw some stuff around to make it look like a burglary that went wrong, and hid anything he thought would be incriminating.'

'Dad.' Mandy had been sitting quietly listening. Now she tapped her wristwatch. 'We'll miss the shops.'

Henderson grimaced. 'I'm being frogmarched down to the High Street to get some new clothes.' He looked down at what he was wearing and flicked at a piece of fluff on his chest. 'Milady seems to think these are not good enough.'

'You've had that suit since I was little,' scolded Mandy, but she was smiling as she said it.

Henderson lumbered to his feet, standing huge next to his tiny daughter. He put a hand on her shoulder. 'You know what it's like. She who must be obeyed is back home.' He waved cheerfully and his daughter smiled shyly. We watched them crossing the grass to the back gate. As they disappeared into the lane, we could hear his daughter's voice, speaking low but carrying clearly on the still summer air.

'Dad, I wish you wouldn't refer to me as she who must be obeyed because it just makes people think I . . .' Her light voice faded into the distance but Henderson's throaty chuckle floated back.

Lucinda stretched luxuriously and stood up. 'I'm off to have a shower. Hot date tonight.'

Mags got to her feet also. 'I must be going too. My sister's bringing the kids back at five.' She shook the stiffness out of her limbs. 'I don't know if I can face work on Monday after all that's happened.'

I accompanied her as far as the gate. 'I wouldn't worry. It won't be as bad as you imagine. Martin and Ron and the others will give you a big welcome, I know. Trevor will just have to fall into line.'

She leaned forward and kissed me on the cheek. 'Thanks for everything. I won't forget.' She closed the gate, heading off down the lane, intent on walking home.

'Bel!' I looked up. Lucinda's naked head and shoulders were poking out of her bedroom window. She gestured wildly. 'There's someone at the front door – can you get it? I'm starkers.'

I hurried indoors, feeling the champagne warming my nerve-endings nicely. The doorbell was ringing insistently. I yanked the front door open, prepared to do battle. George was standing on the doorstep, one arm reaching up to the doorbell, the other clutching Chipper's box. He was wearing a pair of khaki shorts and a blue and orange Hawaiian shirt and someone must have bought him new glasses because the sticky tape was gone. Beyond him on the street, a taxi stood with its motor running. I could see Caroline in the back seat peering out anxiously.

This was the first time I had seen George since the night of Harry's death, although I had spoken to him several times on the phone. George hadn't been in very good shape. He had regained consciousness just as the ambulance team had arrived. Opening his eyes to a scene of mayhem he had started sobbing uncontrollably. When the paramedics were satisfied he was suffering from nothing more than mild concussion, I had put my arms round him and pulled him against me. We sat together on the steps in a state of shock waiting for someone to tell us what to do.

Sykes was surprisingly considerate.

'It's okay, lad. You're safe now,' he had said, patting George on the head. Then, more awkwardly, to me: 'How are you feeling?'

'A bit shaken,' I answered quietly.

He nodded sympathetically. 'Well done. I should have paid more attention to what you were saying.' I could only stare at him in amazement.

After a brief consultation, it was decided that I should accompany George home to his mother at once, not least because she might have discovered he had slipped out of the house without her knowing and be in a panic. A woman police officer would drive us there and would stay with Caroline and her son overnight.

Something about being in the police car seemed to help George calm down. The heaving sobs stopped and he took off his glasses to wipe away the tears with the heel of one hand.

'You know,' he said, with a catch in his breath still from the crying, 'if you hadn't forgotten to give me my crisps even though I was yelling and waving to you to come back, this wouldn't have happened. This is all your fault,' he ended severely.

Now he was standing on my doorstep looking indignant.

'Where have you been?' he asked accusingly. Then,

without waiting for my answer, he held out Chipper's cage to me. 'Mum and me are going on holiday. The newspaper's paying so they can get an exclusive on how I saved everybody from that murderer. We're going to Majorca and I'm going to scuba dive and study fish and the photographer said he'd smuggle an octopus back in his bag for me.'

'George!' Caroline had wound down the window of the taxi.

That had the effect of making George talk even faster. 'Look after Chipper for me. I'll be gone two weeks.' He started to run down the path, then stopped and turned back. For a moment, he wavered, seemingly undecided.

'I've been thinking,' he finally got out. His brow was furrowed. 'It probably wasn't *all* your fault. He thought for a moment longer. 'Probably only about half.' Before he could move, I had taken one bound down the path, picked him up in my arms and given him a big kiss.

'Aagh!' he yelled, squirming free. He raced down the path and jumped into the cab. The driver let in the clutch immediately. George hung out the window. 'Remember to feed him his cheese.' The taxi was gathering speed so he was having to yell now. 'He missed the last episode of—'

The taxi careened round the corner, George still hanging out the window gesticulating and mouthing instructions while his mother vainly tried to pull him back in and I waved wildly until he was out of sight.